PETER MILES HAS TO DIE

PETER MILES HAS TO DIE

A NOVEL

KATIE COLLOM

BANTAM
New York

Bantam Books
An imprint of Random House
A division of Penguin Random House LLC
1745 Broadway, New York, NY 10019
randomhousebooks.com
penguinrandomhouse.com

BANTAM & B colophon is a registered trademark of
Penguin Random House LLC.

Hardback ISBN 978-0-593-97461-2
Ebook ISBN 978-0-593-97462-9

Printed in the United States of America on acid-free paper

2 4 6 8 9 7 5 3 1

First Edition

BOOK TEAM: Production editor: Ted Allen •
Managing editor: Saige Francis • Production manager: Maggie Hart •
Copy editor: Madeline Hopkins • Proofreaders: Muriel Jorgensen,
Barbara Greenberg, Deborah Bader

Title-page photo: Valmedia/Adobe Stock

Book design by Alexis Flynn

The authorized representative in the EU for product safety and compliance is Penguin Random House Ireland, Morrison Chambers, 32 Nassau Street, Dublin D02 YH68, Ireland.
https://eu-contact.penguin.ie

To G

PART ONE

THE FRIENDS

CHAPTER
ONE

DYLAN

There are events in life that mark you and events in life that make you.

Beck's death had marked Dylan. She'd carried it like a burden the past several months, a ghost taking up a permanent lease in her mind. She thought about Beck more now than when she'd been alive. At home, at the grocery store, even during her busiest shifts at the bar, it was impossible for Dylan to exorcize the memories of her dead friend.

She'd been coping. Furious, but coming to terms with it.

Until *he* slid onto the barstool across from her that Thursday night.

"Hi there, gorgeous," he said.

For a moment Dylan froze, her eyes locked on him. Then the pint glass she was holding slipped from her fingers and shattered around the toes of her Doc Martens 1461s.

"Fuck," Dylan said, but not because of the broken glass.

"Oh, shit!" He pressed his fist to his mouth. His eyes were round in mock shock. "Didn't mean to make you nervous."

Lowering his hand to the bar, he grinned. A swarm of goosebumps crawled up Dylan's back.

If he knew who she was, he didn't show it. Was she not worth remembering? Of course, the first and last time they'd met had been at Beck's New Year's party. That was nearly a year ago. It'd been dark, he'd been drunk, and they'd spent less than two minutes together. Since then, Dylan had also let her hair grow longer and dyed it from blond to black.

He didn't remember who she was. And now, here he was, sitting on a stool at the bar where she worked, looking at Dylan like she owed him something.

"I'll be right back," she said.

Carefully stepping around the broken glass, she left the bar and pushed her way through the swinging door that led to the back. The smell of cooking oil spilled from the kitchen at the end of the hall. She stepped into her manager's tiny office. Jason rarely used it, preferring instead his regular booth out front where the beer taps were within arm's reach, and he could make sure she wasn't skimming from the till or drinking on the job herself.

Hand trembling, she brought the phone to her ear. Her fingers hovered over the keypad. Who should she call? Isabel? Priya? Both?

She shifted her gaze to the clock over the filing cabinet. It was just after seven. Isabel would be home by now, her classes done for the day. Closing her eyes, Dylan tried to remember if Priya worked evening shifts at the hospital on Thursdays.

But what would she say? That their best friend's killer had just walked into Aces of Spades?

Her mind raced, Beck's ghost elbowing out every other thought, screaming at her: *Do something*. Beck had always said the three of them—Dylan, Priya, and Isabel—were like her sisters. They were supposed to have one another's backs. But they'd failed Beck. Dylan most of all.

Slowly, she lowered the receiver back into place. It wouldn't do any good to call either of them. Not now. She glanced at the calendar tacked to the wall over the desk. Above SEPTEMBER 1993, two impossibly small kittens were asleep inside a pair of coffee mugs. Dylan grabbed a red pen from the pencil cup and drew three angry circles around that day's date: September 2.

A small, hard walnut of rage formed in her as she left the office, grabbed a broom and dustpan from the storage closet, and headed back to the front bar.

He hadn't moved.

"Be with you in a sec," she said, keeping her tone neutral and eyes on the shattered glass as she swept it up.

"That's fine, gorgeous. You take your time."

Dylan's fist tightened around the broom handle at the indulgence in his tone. As if he were doing her a favor.

She dumped the glass in the trash and returned the broom and dustpan to the closet. As she stepped out into the front again, Dylan pulled her damp gray shirt away from her lower back. Despite the ancient AC unit's best efforts, the heat had snuck in to wrap its fleshy arms around the room. That was September in the Texas Panhandle: eager for fall, reluctant to let summer go.

For once, she welcomed it. The heat stoked her mood like embering coals, helped raise her anger to a fever pitch.

Now she didn't hesitate. Dylan walked right up to the counter and, to stop herself from settling her knuckles in his face, gripped the edge with both hands as she asked, "What can I get you?"

"Thought you'd never ask." Another grin, partnered with a wink. "I'll have a Bud."

This time, she didn't care. Let him think he was in the clear. That he was too clever, too well-connected, too untouchable.

By the time she'd filled the beer glass and set it down on the counter, Dylan had made up her mind. She knew it as certainly as she knew her eyes were blue.

And that she'd never talk to Beck ever again.

An image became clear in her mind, a telescope twisting into focus. Beck's death had marked her, but this day would make her. It might even redeem her. She understood what she had to do next.

Dylan didn't know when. She didn't know how. But she did know one thing for sure.

The thought flared bright, a neon sign at the back of her mind:

Peter Miles has to die.

CHAPTER TWO

TEXAS STATE PENITENTIARY
Fall 1999

Time is cheap in prison. So, they tell me there's no point counting it.

    On the outside, I used to complain about wasting time.

Five years.

About it slipping through my fingers.

Sixty months.

About how there was never enough to go around.

One thousand eight hundred twenty-six days.

In here, it's a depreciated currency. There's too much.

Forty-three thousand eight hundred and twenty-four hours.

We're fat with abundance. Rich with it.

Two million six hundred twenty-nine thousand four hundred and forty minutes.

    Locked in a bank vault with all this wealth, and it's worth absolutely nothing.

One hundred fifty-seven million seven hundred sixty-six thousand four hundred seconds.

    Give or take, that's what I've spent so far. They say there's no point counting, but I can't help it.

    Sometimes, I lie awake at night calculating how much I need to waste for this to finally be over. But how do you estimate the seconds, minutes, hours, days, months, years, of a life sentence? I have a surplus of time, and nowhere to spend it.

So, when the CO approaches me in the prison yard to say I have a visitor's request, I consider saying yes.

I know who it is before he even gives me a name.

Years ago, I told her to stay away. He's dead. I'm in here. What was there left to say?

But as I sit on my bunk turning the request over in my mind like a smooth pebble, I think: Why not?

The last half decade has changed me. I'm stronger than I used to be. Different. Maybe I'm finally ready.

After all, I have the time. Could it hurt to spend a little on her?

CHAPTER
THREE

PRIYA

There was blood on her hands.

For a moment Priya didn't move. Then she slowly stripped the gloves off and dropped them in the bin.

The woman had arrived on the tail end of Priya's shift, a blood-soaked kitchen towel pressed to her forehead. Priya—who'd been on her feet for twelve hours already—could have pushed her on to the next nurse. But there was something about the woman's entrance, like she was a mouse tiptoeing into a cattery, that caught Priya's attention.

So did the man who dropped her off. He wore a trucker hat and jeans, his beer gut straining against the fabric of a blue T-shirt that looked like it had been washed one too many times and yet not at all. He'd come as far as the doors and stood glowering as his wife approached reception. Two little boys flanked him, their faces coated with a mixture of snot and tears.

The woman's name was Kelly, and as Priya cleaned the wound, she tried to coax the truth out of her. But, whether from fear or a need to protect him, Kelly refused to admit her husband had hurt her. She kept insisting she'd tripped and smacked her head against the edge of her kitchen table.

Out in the hall, Priya stopped the doctor before he went in.

"I still think we should notify the police of a domestic violence situation," she said.

He sighed, his expression telling her that she was the latest in a long list of inconveniences today.

"We've been over this. You can't force the patient to speak with the police if she doesn't want to." His next words felt like a verbal kick to Priya's gut. "For all we know, she could be telling the truth. Maybe she really did hit her head on a table."

The doctor paused, his liver-spotted hand resting on the door handle. "Go home, Shah. You've done enough for today."

A shroud of defeat settled on Priya as she entered the changing room. She sat staring down at the smatter of blood decorating her blue scrub shirt like a gruesome Jackson Pollock painting. Should she have done more? *Could* she have done more?

Two nurses walked into the room, and their presence jerked Priya into action. As she stood, she checked the clock by the door. It was nearly six. She was going to be late. Exhaustion burrowed into her bones. She still needed to buy snacks and pick Echo up from the pet sitter before heading to Dylan's for the night.

Tears pressed to the backs of her eyes, threatening to spill over. Leaning her forehead against the locker door, Priya forced herself to take a few deep breaths.

You're tired.

It was more than that. Just once, Priya wanted to save someone. But no matter how hard she tried, she couldn't.

• • •

Isabel's powder-blue Honda was already parked in the driveway behind Dylan's dark Toyota when Priya pulled up to the curb. Echo whined and shifted his eighty-pound heft in the small passenger seat, his eyes trained on the wasteland of Dylan's front yard.

Clutching the Fritos and bottle of wine in one hand, Priya got out and crossed around to the other side of the car. She barely managed to grab Echo's leash before he was off.

"Hold on," she grunted, struggling to close and lock the door.

The dog dragged her across to the oak tree occupying Dylan's front yard like a drunk man sprawled on a sofa. Echo paused long enough to lift a leg and mark it. Nose to the smooth earth, he wove his way back to the concrete walk.

They climbed the porch steps, Priya carefully avoiding the second one. It sagged in the middle, and Dylan was always promising to repair it but hadn't yet. A pile of gardening tools—shovel, rake, and an enormous set of shears, amongst other things—lay in a pile at one end of the porch. The yard must be the latest work in progress. Priya could picture Dylan stripping it of the hard brown tufts of moss and weeds, working out her anger with a hoe.

Her gaze settled on the off-white front door. It looked new. Or newish. At least it was in better shape than the previous swollen monstrosity, which had shed scales of wood like a molting snake. Priya knocked and Echo barked helpfully, announcing her. A moment later Dylan opened, dressed in paint-splattered jeans, a plain gray shirt under a black-and-green-plaid button-up, and black socks. Her long, dark hair hung in a messy braid over one shoulder.

As he always did when he saw Dylan, Echo whined and rose on his back legs to try to lick her face. His tail whipped back and forth in an excited frenzy.

"Hey, Maneater," Dylan said, ruffling his ears.

Echo barked and attempted to dart past her, his leash winding around her shins.

"Echo, no!" Priya tugged at the lead. "I pay for obedience training every week so you learn to behave."

A smile pulled at the corners of Dylan's mouth. "How the fuck are you, Pri?" She leaned forward to hug her.

"Fine. Is your door new?" she asked as she stepped inside.

"No." This seems evident from the "No" on its own.

"Are you doing work on the front yard?"

"Yeah." This, apparently, she had more to say about. "Stripping it, then reseeding it. It'll look great next summer."

"You're way more motivated than I am. I'd pay someone to do it for me."

Dylan half turned to look at her. "Why?"

Because I'd rather have a tooth pulled sans anesthetic than do months of yard maintenance.

Priya shrugged. "It's easier."

"Well, I like the challenge," she answered, continuing down the hall.

The living room was at the back of the house in what had originally been intended as a main bedroom. When she'd bought the ranch-style fixer-upper two years before, Dylan had immediately swapped the rooms. She spent more of her free time in the living room than any other part of the house, she once explained. She preferred that it face the quieter backyard rather than the street.

It was strange to Priya how Dylan didn't appear concerned with quiet when it came to sleep. Her bedroom sat at the other end of the house, looking out over the front yard. It infuriated Priya who, in the aftermath of Beck's death, started experiencing nightly battles with insomnia. Real insomnia. Not the I-don't-sleep-as-much-as-I'd-like insomnia she and her perpetually fatigued colleagues complained about at the hospital. The knowledge that Dylan never slept more than five hours at night, and was perfectly fine and functioning the next day, was maddening.

Of course, Dylan was only a bartender. It's not as if the job required a high level of brainpower. Once you learned how to mix all the basic cocktails and pour a proper beer, that was it. It was a one-rung ladder. Not like her job, where Priya had to study the latest medical innovations to stay on top of her field. If Dylan put too much liquor in a drink, the worst result was a drunk client. If Priya miscalculated a dosage of medicine, she wagered someone's life.

"Hi!" Isabel greeted her brightly from her spot on Dylan's huge secondhand chesterfield sofa.

"Off the sofa, Echo," Priya said before leaning over to hug her. In spite of her thick yellow cardigan and the muggy temperature of the room, Isabel had wrapped herself in one of Dylan's couch throws like she was bracing for an arctic blast.

With a prick of irritation, Priya noticed she was already holding a glass of white wine. This was the cherry on top, and just like Isabel too; tell her friends to bring wine and still show up with her own. The bowls of chips and salsa on the coffee table sent another wave of annoyance through Priya.

"Whoa, not for you, boy." Dylan snatched the bowls up out of Echo's reach just in time. "C'mere. I've got something better."

"Looks like you don't need these." Priya held up the Fritos.

"What? Don't be silly," Dylan said. "Can't have enough snacks. What do you think about pizza? Maybe in an hour?"

"Fine." Priya set the wine and chips on the table, then lowered herself into the love seat opposite Isabel and rested her head back. Eyes closed, she pulled her lighter from her pocket and began passing it between the fingers of her right hand. She willed herself to relax and to not think about Kelly. About the next time. Or the time after that. Until the final time when, inevitably, her husband took things too far and killed her.

"Priya?" Isabel's soft voice broke through her thoughts. "I've been thinking, it'd be good if you tried to celebrate Diwali with the Grants again this year. It was so nice when you talked about your first in your eulogy. I think everyone loved hearing the story of how you and Beck met."

Priya had chosen the anecdote because it seemed to capture best who Beck was. They were both ten when Priya's family moved in next door and a curious Beck wandered over to investigate her new neighbors. Within an hour of setting foot in the Shah household, she'd somehow garnered an invite to the Shahs' Diwali party, then showed up with her entire family too. It'd been the start of a yearly tradition where the Shahs and Grants celebrated the Festival of Lights together.

"I tried," Priya said, keeping her eyes closed. Eighteen years. She and Beck had been friends for nearly two decades. How was it possible to know someone for so long and still feel it wasn't nearly long enough?

"You should keep up the tradition, it might be a healthy way to collectively grieve."

Collectively grieve. The sheer impossibility of it bothered Priya. How could they collectively grieve when they were all experiencing such different levels and types of grief? She tried to focus her exhausted brain long enough to think of an adequate response, but it was like trying to signal to a distant space station using a transistor radio.

Instead, she pivoted away from the topic. Sitting up, Priya pocketed her lighter and began to comb her fingers through her shoulder-length waves, disentangling them.

"So, what's the plan?" she asked as Dylan came back into the room, a bag of bones in her hands and an eager Echo at her side. "Are we watching a movie?" She pulled her hair back into a low ponytail. "I haven't looked at this week's *TV Guide*. Anything good on tonight?"

"Here ya go, Maneater," Dylan said. The dog grabbed the bone from her hand and retreated to his bed in the corner. "I thought we could talk first." She lifted the wine bottle from the table and unscrewed the cap.

Dread layered itself along the bottom of Priya's stomach like thick, bitter frosting. They were going to talk about Beck. She debated saying those words: *I'm sick of talking about Beck. About what happened to her.* Was it so wrong to not want to think about it anymore? Was she a bad person for feeling tired of the topic? There were only so many ways to rehash your friend's murder.

She especially didn't want to hear another rant from Dylan about how the police were protecting one of their own. After Beck went missing, they'd all been interviewed by the detectives on the case. It was standard. When asked if they could think of any likely suspects, the three of them pointed the finger at the same person. It angered Dylan that none of them were immediately believed. Afterward, she demanded Priya and Isabel recount exactly what they'd told the detectives, then picked apart their statements—pointing out all the ways she believed they'd failed to get their point across. She didn't want to explain to Dylan the difference between not being believed because you're a woman, and not being believed because you're a woman and *also* brown.

"Oh? About anything in particular?" Isabel sounded blithely innocent. Their eyes met from opposite sides of the living room and Priya spotted a hint of apprehension in her expression too.

"I saw him," Dylan said.

"Who?" Priya said at the same time as Isabel exclaimed, "What?"

Dylan's gaze shifted between her and Isabel. There was a knowing glint in her eyes and, beneath the surface, something else. Suddenly, Priya felt terribly old. Aged far beyond her twenty-nine years.

"You know who," Dylan said after a long pause. "And I think it's time we decide what to do about it."

CHAPTER FOUR

ISABEL

Isabel felt as if she were frozen on a tightrope, the world receding far below. Dylan settled into her seat with a glass of red wine.

"He's been into Aces five times in the last week," she said.

"Oh my god," Isabel said.

"Who? Peter Miles?"

A gasp slipped out before Isabel could stop it. Dylan stared at Priya as if she'd conjured the devil by saying his name.

"Peter Miles has been to your bar?" Priya asked again. She seemed determined to say it, as if that would take away its power. Perhaps it would. A name was a name. It didn't influence the man's actions. Those were all his own.

"Yes," Dylan said after a short pause. "Six other bars in this damn town and he stumbles into mine."

Maybe it wasn't far-fetched that *he* would choose Aces of Spades. People liked dive bars, if only because of the cheap beer and liquor. If Isabel went out for a drink, she'd prefer the Tipsy Cow where she might find a decent sauvignon blanc (for her) and real Scotch whisky (for Paul). Not that she or her fiancé could afford to treat themselves to either very often. Especially not on her graduate student's stipend and his junior associate's salary.

"Do you think—" Isabel stopped and cleared her throat. "Do you think he went there on purpose?"

"No. No way. He doesn't act like he recognizes me at all. It's just a sick coincidence. The universe fucking with me. With us."

"God. I'm so sorry, Dylan."

"He's out there, walking around." Dylan took a drink of her wine. "Living his life. And she—Beck, she's six feet under. Or what's left of her is anyway."

"So, you're serving Peter Miles drinks now?" Priya's question was like the twang of a taut wire.

What's wrong with her? Was she aiming to set a record for saying his name as many times as possible tonight?

"Yeah, I am," Dylan said, a note of challenge in her voice. "Look, he comes in and orders a Budweiser like it's nothing, like it's just another night at the bar. He dumped her body like a bag of trash just months ago, and he walks into Aces and orders a fucking Budweiser. Fuck."

"So . . . you talk to him?" Isabel asked.

"I take his order. So I can spit in his beer."

The laugh burst out like a gunshot. Isabel clapped both hands over her mouth. None of it was funny. Not even remotely. A second giggle pushed to escape. Suddenly Dylan was laughing too.

"I take his order so I can spit in his fucking beer," Dylan repeated.

"He murdered our best friend and you're spitting in his beer." Priya's laugh was wary. As if this were a trap.

Their laughter expanded like a hot air balloon. Then Isabel felt a stab of pain, a sharp needle piercing her heart. She couldn't tell at what point the laughter transformed, but suddenly she couldn't breathe. A sob swelled in her throat, and she pressed a hand to her face.

"He murdered her." Isabel wiped her eyes. "And he's out there buying beer."

Dylan moved over to the sofa and enveloped her shoulders with one arm. Her jaw moved against the top of Isabel's head as she said softly, "I know."

For a long while they stayed like that; Dylan holding her while she cried, her nose buried in Dylan's hair. When the tears slowed and she was able to breathe more easily, Dylan pulled away. They sat shoulder to shoulder.

"He murdered our best friend and you're spitting in his beer," Priya repeated softly. The futility of it felt immense.

"I'm sorry," Isabel said. "I didn't mean to cry."

"Jesus. Don't apologize. There's nothing wrong with crying, Isabel," Dylan said.

Says the woman who never cries.

Beck had always teased Isabel about being emotional—a conduit, an amplifier of everyone else's feelings. Sometimes it was exhausting to haul around so much. Like peeling back her skin, exposing all her nerves. The slightest touch setting off bursts of pain.

"Can't you talk to your manager about it?" Isabel asked.

"And say what? 'I don't feel like serving the man who murdered my best friend'?"

"Well, yes."

Dylan shook her head. "The fact that he's out walking around means somebody thinks he's innocent."

"Or can't prove he's guilty," Priya said.

"Or no one cares. Either way, I don't think my manager would like me making 'assumptions.'" Dylan made air quotes with her fingers. "He'd tell me to take a Midol and probably find ways to make me deal with—" She stopped.

"Peter Miles," Priya prompted.

"Yeah, that asshole." There was a pause while the three of them sipped their drinks.

"I actually don't want my manager to do anything though," Dylan said after a few more beats of silence. "I think it could work to our advantage. He seems to like the bar and I've been . . . not flirting." She wrinkled her nose as if she smelled something foul. "But I've been nice."

Isabel wondered if her own expression mirrored Priya's look of horror.

"*What?*" Priya asked.

"Why?" Isabel said, so low it was nearly a whisper.

She took a drink of wine, but it only made the sour feeling in her stomach grow worse. An ache gripped her throat.

Don't start crying, Isabel ordered herself.

"Just one night," Priya said, throwing up her hands. "One night I'd like to not talk about this. To not think about it. Is this all our friendship is about anymore? What happened to Beck? About *him*? Can't we just have a normal conversation about something stupid for once? My god, I'll even watch *Baywatch* reruns if it means we don't have to keep rehashing how angry we are. Or talk about what happened to her."

"Priya," Dylan said quietly.

"We can't change it, Dylan." She twisted in her seat, her eyes scanning the room.

"What're you looking for?"

"The remote control so I can leave this conversation!" Priya slammed a palm down on the cushion next to her.

"Pri."

She stilled, the tension in her jaw visibly loosening. "What's your point, Dylan?"

Dylan gazed at Priya intently, as if mentally picking her apart and assessing all her pieces.

"I'm not bringing this up just for the hell of it, okay? If you could hold off for a second, I'm going to explain."

Priya's hazel eyes seemed to darken as she glared back. Isabel's gaze shifted between them. Maybe Priya was right. Did they want to walk down this road again? What more could possibly be said?

Dylan believed in action like it was a religion. It was overwhelming at times how sure she could be of herself. How she always had a plan. How she innately understood what was necessary to reach any solution.

Like when she showed up to that party in high school, cornered the star quarterback, and told him to stop jerking Isabel around or he'd pay. Like when she pushed Priya to report a colleague for his racist comment about needing a nursing staff that looked more "American" and got him suspended. Like when she helped Beck move out of her college apartment because her roommate was holding boozy parties and getting high every night. Dylan hadn't just helped Beck move, she went back after and poured her roommate's coke stash all over the carpet.

Her friend's need for confrontation made Isabel squirm. But sometimes she wished she were more like Dylan: tough, decisive, immovable. Though she suspected Dylan's upbringing had a lot to do with that. An abusive father and absent mother were too steep a price to pay.

"Well?" Dylan asked when Priya didn't say anything.

"Fine." She took a drink of wine. "But if I don't like it, then I'm leaving. And I'm not coming here again. Not unless we agree beforehand that all we're going to do is stupid stuff like watch TV and paint each other's nails."

"Okay."

Isabel nodded, though she suspected they'd all show up to the next girls' night either way. Beck was the best at standing up to Dylan and calling her out. Without her, the balance was off.

"Do either of you think Peter Miles is going to be arrested for Beck's murder?" Dylan said.

This silenced them for a moment.

"Well, they took him in for questioning a few times," Isabel said. "They suspect something."

"I don't think he's even a person of interest anymore," Dylan said.

"How do you know?" Priya asked.

"I talked to Beck's mom. Apparently, the police are following another lead. There's not enough evidence for a case against him."

"But people saw them together that day! And there was the hair in his car. . . ."

"He's still got the girlfriend's alibi."

"She's lying though," Isabel said quickly, then looked from Dylan to Priya. "Right?"

Dylan nodded. "Oh, for sure. But even without the alibi, there's still not enough evidence to charge him. Him and Beck were dating all of January, remember? The hair could have gotten in his car then."

"She was afraid of him!" Priya's tone was jagged with accusation. As if this were all Dylan's fault. "Remember those creepy phone calls she kept getting? He was stalking her!"

Dylan shrugged. "Again, no actual evidence. You're the only one of us who witnessed any calls, and Beck never told you it was him."

"So, the three of us hearing the same story from her counts for nothing."

"I don't know, Pri. Did the cops seem to believe you when you told them about the stalking?"

Priya bit her thumbnail, her eyes luminous in the lamplight. Isabel couldn't move, couldn't think of anything to add. She wished she could detach from her body and shake herself to life.

"I think it's time we accept that either he was too good at covering his tracks, or the police are protecting one of their own." Dylan sat forward, resting her elbows on her knees. "Either way, we're not going to get justice unless we go and demand it."

"So what, stage a protest at the police station?" Isabel asked. She was coming up for air, emerging from her stupor.

Leveling Isabel with a look that brought the blood rushing to her cheeks, Dylan answered, "No. I mean take care of him ourselves. Get him off the streets before he does it again to someone else."

The room went quiet as a crypt. Another emotion began to work its way into Isabel's gut, pushing the unease aside. Then her heart collapsed in on itself like a folding fan and she realized what it was: fear.

Dylan's gaze was steady. "Do you understand what I'm saying?"

"I'm not completely sure," Priya said slowly.

Isabel was glad she'd spoken first; she couldn't bring herself to voice what it really meant. No, Isabel needed her to lay it out, without any prompting.

Dylan's blue eyes were bright.

Then she said, "We are going to kill Peter Miles."

CHAPTER
FIVE

ISABEL

Before

"*I've met someone new,*" Beck said.

"*You want a standing ovation?*" Dylan lifted her coffee cup in a salute.

Gripping her mug tighter, Isabel offered what she hoped was a supportive "*Oh?*"

"*Aren't you meeting someone new like every five minutes?*" Priya asked with a roll of her eyes. "*And why didn't you tell us about this last night?*"

"*Uh, hello, Miss I-Get-Way-Too-Invested-in-Monopoly,*" Beck said. "*This is the first time I've had everyone's undivided attention.*"

"*Which you clearly needed for this groundbreaking announcement.*" Priya tapped her spoon against the rim of her mug, making Isabel wince. Twin spots of pain flared behind her eyes. Why did no one else seem hungover? They'd all had plenty to drink last night.

"*What happened to the last guy?*" Isabel asked. "*Andy?*"

"*Andy and I parted ways three months ago.*"

"*Oh. He seemed nice.*"

"*Well, what can I say?*" Beck shrugged. "*I like that new relationship smell.*"

"*Gross,*" Dylan said, and they all laughed.

Coming here after girls' night was one of Isabel's favorite traditions. She felt a surge of pleasure as the sounds of a typical Sunday morning at the Coffee Pot enveloped them. The hum of conversation, the clatter of silverware, the grill sizzling as the cook cracked an egg onto its hot surface. It relaxed her, like white noise, and helped ease her headache.

"I like this guy." A flush of pink rose to Beck's cheeks. "He's a cop."

Dylan stared at Beck as if she'd lit herself on fire. "Why would you date a cop? Most of them are wife-beaters."

"Seriously, Dylan? Not every cop's like that. I wouldn't go out with him if he were."

"He sounds useful," Priya said. "I do have some parking tickets I need help with."

Isabel thought she could make out a hint of tension in Priya's smile. Love came hard to her. Meanwhile, Beck seemed to move from one romantic encounter to another, like a migrating bird briefly touching down on an island before heading off to explore the next.

"When do we meet him?" Dylan asked, gathering her blond hair into a ponytail.

"Haven't decided yet, maybe New Year's," Beck said.

"You're worried we won't like him." Her tone was dry.

"You just implied he's a wife-beater. Of course I'm worried you won't like him."

The waitress arrived with their orders, and they dug into their food. The opening stanzas of "Jingle Bells" began to play on the diner speakers—festive music to match the artificial snow spritzed across the windows and the Christmas lights strung along the length of one wall. Someone had even draped the iron Texas star by the door in a web of comically large green, red, and blue lights.

"So, what's his name, Beck?" Dylan was dousing her hash browns with Tabasco.

Beck held up her butter knife. "First, you have to promise not to be judgmental."

"Oh god, it's fucking Archibald or something, isn't it," Dylan said.

"Bartholomew Babington the Third," Priya added with a laugh.

"Clarence Chesterton the Seventh," Dylan guessed again.

Isabel choked on a bite of oatmeal.

"No." Beck was straight-faced, her focus back on her food. "It's Peter Miles."

"Peter Miles," Priya repeated. "That's actually ridiculously normal."

"Peter Miles." Isabel tested the name out, like rolling a marble around on her tongue.

"Okay, can you stop saying it like a bunch of weirdos?" Beck looked from one to the other with raised eyebrows. "Now you'll never forget it. And when we break up, you—"

"Why would you say that?" Isabel asked, pressing her thumb against the cool curve of her engagement ring.

"What?"

" 'When we break up,' like it's a given." Why did she feel so defensive? Beck's nonchalance was not a criticism of her own more traditional relationship with Paul, Isabel knew that. But sometimes she felt like the odd one out. Priya rarely dated, Beck got bored easily, and Dylan was so secretive Isabel knew almost nothing about her romantic life.

"Because I don't think this is it for me, Isa." Beck's gray eyes were fixed on her.

"How do you know?"

"Just a hunch. I really doubt Peter Miles will be the last guy I ever date." She popped a bite of pancake into her mouth, chewed, and swallowed. "That would be way too depressing."

CHAPTER
SIX

ISABEL

The first thing Isabel saw when she opened her eyes were the three wineglasses. Two were stained purple, a clear residue coated the third. Hers. The bottles came into focus next, sitting on the floor next to the wooden chest Dylan used as a coffee table.

I should ask Priya if she'll go halves on a real coffee table for Dylan for Christmas.

Isabel had been checking garage sales and secondhand shops for months now; Dylan's stubbornness about not buying anything new unless she absolutely had to was a common joke among the group of friends. It suited Isabel's tight academia budget just fine. Especially because she could set aside a little extra for Priya's gift, whose taste was diametrically opposed to Dylan's.

Odd, considering part of Priya's childhood had been spent in hand-me-down clothes from her cousins. Or maybe it was *because* of that secondhand childhood, Isabel often thought. She could some-what understand. Until her teenage years, Isabel had been relegated to clothes her older sister, Lourdes, had outgrown.

Feeling like she'd aged half a century overnight, Isabel pushed her-self into a seated position and lifted the bottle of sauvignon blanc. It was empty.

Did all that really happen?

She was in too fragile a state to know for sure if it'd been a bad dream—perhaps the effect of too much wine. The back of her head was like a cracked window. She probed it tenderly, as if it would shatter into a hundred tiny glass shards, but to her surprise it wasn't sore. Her brain ached. Not her head, her *brain*.

Curled up like a cat on the love seat, Priya sighed in her sleep then continued to snore lightly. Isabel had a hazy memory of Dylan covering Priya with the cotton blanket before heading to bed herself. Another blanket lay crumpled on the floor by Isabel's feet, probably where she'd kicked it in the night. Isabel flailed. Lourdes had complained about it frequently when they were growing up. The bed they'd shared had seemed like a battleground. It was as if Isabel was always trying to escape something while she slept.

It got better as she got older—or at least Paul hadn't mentioned it after they moved in together—but ever since Beck died, she'd experienced a relapse. Isabel would wake every morning to find her bedsheets tangled on the floor, or her bedside table swept clean by a somnambulant swoop of her arm. When was the last time she'd slept peacefully through the night?

The smell of fresh coffee arrested these thoughts, and she turned to peek over the sofa toward the hall. Just as she was debating whether she could hold the nausea and headache at bay long enough to make it to the kitchen, Dylan appeared in the doorway, a cup of coffee in each hand. A jangle of collar tags announced Echo's arrival as he followed on her heels.

"I thought you'd be awake," Dylan said, holding out one of the mugs.

Isabel accepted the offering and cupped it between her hands. Lowering her face to the rim, she lingered there a moment, letting the steam warm her before taking a sip. It was delicious. Ridiculously delicious. And not just because she had a hangover. Dylan's drink-making skills extended way beyond cocktails. Her coffee was as close to perfection as it could get.

"Mmmm, good," Isabel murmured.

"Yeah?"

"I didn't think I'd drink so much last night," she said by way of apology.

"I would've let you have the bed, but you conked out before I could offer."

The coffee was beginning to work its magic, easing her hangover just a little and clearing her thoughts. Piece by piece, like slotting matching squares into place on a Rubik's Cube, the events of the night before started to fall into place.

Something poked against the base of Isabel's spine. She reached between the couch cushions and pulled the paperback free.

"*Carrie*," she read the title aloud. "Stephen King. Is it any good?"

"Oh, that's where that went." Tilting her head, Dylan added, "You wouldn't like it."

Isabel stared at the image of the wide-eyed girl on the cover. Rivulets of blood ran through her shoulder-length brown hair and over her face. *Trust her and she will lead you into a nightmare,* the caption below the title warned.

"No, I probably wouldn't," Isabel said. "It looks . . . gory."

No wonder she's talking about murder.

She laid the novel face down on the table. They sipped their coffee in silence. Echo sighed softly from where he'd stretched out on the floor by the love seat.

"Wish I could sleep like that." Dylan jerked her head in Priya's direction. "It's like she flips a switch."

"I know. It's her talent." They shared a smile.

"About last night," Dylan said.

Isabel's stomach clenched into a tight ball. She waited, hoping for an apology.

"I know you have your reservations," she continued. "But I want you to know I'm serious about it. And I'm going to do it with or without your help."

The coffee cup was suddenly like a blazing hot coal in her hands. Folding her legs up to a lotus position, Isabel balanced the mug on the pillow, her fingers lightly holding the ceramic handle so it wouldn't tip and spill.

Half-turning to Dylan, she instinctively dropped her voice to a whisper. "You're talking about killing someone, Dylan."

"Not someone. Him."

"Still, that's . . ."

"Wrong?"

They'd fought about this last night, she remembered, going around and around in circles. *An eye for an eye,* Dylan had said. *An eye for an eye makes the whole world blind,* Isabel had shot back. Eventually, too tired and drunk to argue anymore, the three of them had fallen asleep with no resolution.

"Yes. Murder in any context, for any reason, is morally wrong," Isabel said. She usually loved their sleepovers but now wished she'd had a single glass of wine last night and driven home after. Living with Paul could be suffocating at times—her fiancé loved to over-share, no matter how mundane the details might be, and often expected her to do the same. But this was worse. "Two wrongs don't make a right, Dylan."

"What about a wrong and a right?"

"You think . . . you think killing him is the *right* thing to do?" Isabel asked.

Dylan stared into the contents of her mug, as if her coffee held all the answers and was simply choosing to withhold them. "I actually do, yeah." She lifted her eyes to meet Isabel's. "Will you turn me in if he shows up dead?"

"What?"

"I want to know if you'll turn me in, Isa."

She tensed at Dylan's diminutive use of her name. Her parents called her that as a term of endearment. To hear Dylan reverse it—use her diminutive to drive home a point—felt deceitful.

"Are you asking me to be complicit?"

With a shake of her head, Dylan folded one leg over the other and pursed her lips. "No. I just want to know beforehand what you plan to do, so I can be prepared."

It was like a cleaver had sliced into her chest. Would she—could she stay silent? It wasn't as if she'd know anything. Suspect, yes, but genuinely know for a fact Dylan had done it? She wouldn't be sure unless she was there.

By that logic, you don't really know if he murdered Beck. You weren't there. He could be innocent.

The thought made her sick. She blew on the coffee before taking another long drink, her gaze trained on the far wall. She could feel Dylan's eyes on her, waiting. Expectant.

Saying yes would mean admitting to wanting it to happen. Wanting him to die, to pay for his crime.

"You can leave the hard part up to me." Dylan seemed to read her mind. "Don't worry, I can handle it."

"No."

The two of them jerked in surprise and looked toward the love seat. Priya lay on her side watching them. Two black smudges rimmed the bottoms of her eyes where her mascara had smeared.

"No what?" Dylan sat up straight, visibly steeling herself. Echo lifted his head from the floor as if sensing an oncoming storm.

"The only way you're going to pull it off is if we all help," she said. "So no, you're not going to do the hard part. Not by yourself."

Dylan returned her gaze to Isabel. She'd expected to see triumph in Dylan's face. A two-against-one expression. To her surprise, Dylan looked almost sad. As if she were really saying, *I'm sorry it's come to this. But it's absolutely necessary.*

CHAPTER
SEVEN

DYLAN

Every time he came into Aces of Spades, Dylan made sure to turn on the charm, even though acting friendly toward him made her want to douse her body in bleach.

It was a means to an end, she reminded herself as she sidled up opposite him. Dylan put a coaster between where his hands rested on the bar (*hands that wrapped around her throat, pressing until she died*) and asked with a smile, "The usual?"

He smiled back, a splay of wrinkles crinkling the corners of his sharp blue eyes. The kind of eyes that charmed a woman. Lured her into his car. Kept her under a spell—until it was too late. Dylan wanted to gouge those eyes out with an ice pick while he screamed in agony and begged for mercy.

"Budweiser, gorgeous," he said.

"Sure thing." While pouring his beer, she mentally replayed the images of all the horrors she wanted to afflict on him. Glancing over her shoulder, she made sure he was looking elsewhere. A woman in jeans and a baby-doll tee held his attention. Taking a quick look around to make sure no one else was watching, Dylan lobbed a giant ball of spit into the pint glass. It mixed nicely with the foam.

"Want to start a tab?" she asked, placing the drink in front of him.

"You know it." He made the three words sound suggestive some-how, like he was complying with her demand that he strip.

Dylan did as he said, then turned away. There were other drink orders waiting. She moved down the right arm of the counter to grab a fresh bottle of Johnnie Walker from the back shelf and realized with a start that there was a new customer seated nearby, as if she'd sprouted from the stool like a mushroom. For a moment, Dylan froze. Had the woman seen her spit in Peter's drink? But the cus-tomer was on the second-to-last stool—far enough from him and the taps that it didn't seem likely. She smiled at Dylan and shrugged, then made a motion with her hand that said, *No rush.*

She wouldn't still be here if she'd seen.

Methodically, Dylan began to work her way through the backed-up orders; refilling someone's whiskey, mixing a couple tequila sun-rises, and serving up a round of beers. Finally, she walked over to the new customer and rested her palms on the countertop across from her.

She was attractive. One of those lucky women who aged into good looks instead of out of them. Short, curly brunette hair flipped over to one side so a few strands fell suggestively over her right eye. Wide brown eyes framed by dark lashes. A fine nose. Time had chis-eled her face, laying the core of it bare like a beautiful statue. Firm curves filled out her jeans and UMass sweatshirt nicely. She probably looked better now closer to forty, Dylan guessed, than she did at twenty. Experience and confidence played a part in that.

"What can I get you?" Dylan asked.

"You stock Kozel. That's unusual."

Dylan followed her gaze to the clear-door fridge behind the coun-ter. For a second, she wasn't sure what the customer meant. Then her eyes locked on the row of brown bottles with the beer-clutching ram on the labels.

"Oh. Yeah," Dylan said. "I forget we have those. Not many peo-ple order 'em."

"No. They don't. It's hard to find. I haven't seen it since I was in Europe." The woman smiled. "I'll have one of those, please."

A ball of heat found its way to the center of Dylan's rib cage. Did she deal with so many assholes every night that a simple *please* felt like a special treat? It wasn't just that, she realized a moment later. She could feel the woman's eyes on her as she took out a bottle. It wasn't an abrasive gaze, or one that made her feel uncomfortable. It was a look of appreciation—for the beer and for the attractive bartender serving it to her.

Dylan set a pair of coasters in front of the customer, then placed a clean glass down too. She retrieved the bottle opener from the hook next to the register.

"Do you mind?" The woman made a motion with her hands.

It took a second for it to dawn on Dylan that she was indicating to the opener and the Kozel.

"Oh. Sure."

Aces clientele weren't the types to offer to open their own drinks. Dylan didn't think there existed a barfly anywhere that was, but she handed the beer and the opener over anyway.

The woman popped the cap and returned the bottle opener with a smile. "Thanks. I just find that really satisfying."

"Wanna start a tab?" Dylan asked, hanging the opener back in its spot. Rolling with the punches was a built-in part of the bartender profession.

"No, thank you. I'll pay now. I'm driving home, so about half this will be my limit." She held out a five-dollar bill.

The woman occupied that corner, there was no other way to put it, Dylan thought. She counted out the change and laid it next to her drink.

"I've never been in here before," she said.

"Oh, yeah?" Dylan set a bowl of peanuts in front of her and leaned on the bar.

"I drive by all the time though." She looked around. "I don't know why I've never come in."

"Tonight a special night?"

She tilted her glass and poured some beer into it. "I'm just off a long, boring workday. I guess it had me in the mood to try something new. Now that I know I can get Kozel here, I'll be back." She smiled and extended a hand. "By the way, I'm Bree. Like the cheese."

Dylan couldn't help but laugh. "Dylan," she said, shaking her hand.

"After Bob or Thomas?"

"Pardon?"

"Are you named after the singer Bob Dylan or the poet Dylan Thomas?"

Again, she laughed. "Neither. My mom was never into poetry, musical or otherwise. Least not that I know of."

"Ah. Well, you never know. Anyway, they're sort of one and the same."

"How do you mean?"

Bree took a sip of her beer before answering. "Bob Dylan was originally Bob Zimmerman. Rumor has it, he changed his last name because he was a fan of Dylan Thomas. But your mom couldn't have gone wrong with either namesake."

"Oh yeah?"

"Yeah, they're both excellent poets."

"Huh. Good to know." Dylan's smile widened.

"Anyway, Dylan." Bree popped a few peanuts in her mouth, chewed and swallowed, then nodded. "You have a great name."

She's flirting with me. This was not a surprise but a confirmation. A lot of people who came into the bar flirted with her. Though this was the first time it was a woman.

"Thanks, Bree-Like-the-Cheese," she said, still grinning.

She wanted to linger, but her manager, Jason, was glaring at her from his booth.

"Wave me down if you need anything," Dylan told Bree. She patted the bar top once and moved off.

The minute her eyes landed on *him,* Dylan's good mood took flight, an errant balloon caught in the wind. Peter Miles had already drunk half his beer and, with the focus of a pool player taking aim to sink the last shot, was trying to work a peanut out of its shell. Finally, he cracked it open and the peanut broke free. His eyes met hers and he winked. In quick succession he popped it into his mouth, tossed the shell on the floor, and drained the rest of his beer.

While she filled a bowl with more peanuts, Dylan imagined cramming his mouth full of them until his eyes bulged and his face turned blue.

Be patient. Take your time. There's no rush.

She placed the fresh bowl in front of him along with another pint.

"Thanks, gorgeous," he said with a smile that sent an army of spiders scurrying down her spine.

Dylan nodded and turned to other tasks. It wouldn't do any good to give him more or less attention than normal. If she was too friendly, he might suspect she was up to something. Too standoffish, and she might piss him off.

When she passed by fifteen minutes later, he'd emptied his glass again.

"Another one," he said. His eyes had taken on the glaze of a man who was drinking too fast.

Forcing her face into a pleasant expression, she poured another pint.

"I think I know you from somewhere," he said as she set it in front of him. His words were slightly slurred, and she wondered if he'd already been drinking before coming into Aces. He seemed too tight after only two beers.

"Oh, yeah?" Dylan said tonelessly.

"Yeah. Where do I know you from?" His nose was red, like he'd been sitting close to a fire. He ran a hand through his thick brown hair, and she imagined pulling his fingernails out one by one.

"From here," she said, not bothering to smile this time.

"No. I mean . . . I'm serious, okay? You look familiar."

"Sorry, man. We've only met here."

He squinted into his beer like he was working out a difficult formula. Taking it as her cue to go, Dylan began to turn away. Suddenly, his fingers wrapped around her wrist, holding her palm against the bar top.

"Did we screw and I forgot to call you back the next day? Is that it?" A fleck of spit flew from his lips and hit her squarely on the cheek. Probably her own spit coming back to her. "You pissy about that? 'Cause I know you from somewhere."

Dylan's heart sprinted in her chest. "I'd remember that," she said, forcing her voice to stay level. "Sorry, man. Can I get you a shot of anything? On the house."

His fingers loosened and he slid his hand back across the counter to clutch his beer. "You remind me of somebody, I guess." There was a greedy glint in his eyes when he added, "Get me a shot of tequila. The good stuff."

No one seemed to have noticed what had gone on between them. The other customers at the bar were either squinting aimlessly into space or talking to one another. But then Dylan caught Bree's gaze. She was staring at her, eyes wide.

Her eyebrows rose in an unspoken question: *Are you okay?*

Dylan smiled and rolled her eyes as if to answer: *Drunks, right?*

Bree nodded once but didn't smile back. Turning her focus to the liquor shelf, Dylan tried to calm her agitated thoughts. For a second, the red streaking across her vision like a comet made it impossible to read the labels on the bottles. She could sense his eyes on her as she took down the Jose Cuervo Especial. He didn't comment on it when she set the full shot glass in front of him. It confirmed her suspicions that he didn't know shit about tequila and didn't care. He just wanted it because it was free.

"How about you take one with me?" he asked and grinned.

It was a leer, wet and predatory. Dylan wondered how much of it was hindsight, or if he really was that much of a creep. If she didn't know what she knew about him, would she have found him charming? Beck saw *something* in Peter Miles, or else why would she have dated him in the first place? He'd hidden it well enough to make it through nearly two months with her before she caught on—and Beck, she was sharp.

"Can't drink on the job, thanks though," she said, forcing a smile. "Enjoy."

She raised her hand to catch her manager's eye before signaling she was going to the bathroom. Her heart seemed to be trying to squeeze its way up her throat as she walked down the short hallway. The employee toilet was next to the kitchen where two cooks served up greasy bar food from four to eight every evening. Inside, she slid the wobbly latch across and faced the mirror, her hands gripping each side of the sink. Kohl-lined blue eyes stared back, her skin sickly in the dim bathroom light. She inhaled and exhaled.

Get ahold of yourself.

If only she could stop imagining what he'd done to Beck, just for a second, it'd make it all easier. The thoughts of what she'd like to do to him weren't helping either. They raced around her mind, intersecting and tangling together like kites caught in a storm.

Eyes on the prize, Dylan.

She needed to remember the end goal, where this was all going. She'd play nice until she didn't have to. He was in for a rude surprise if she handled it right.

Dylan washed her hands and splashed her face with a little water, rubbing a wet palm across the back of her neck too. She patted her face dry and took one final deep breath before walking back to the front bar. He was still there, the empty shot glass toppled on its side in front of him.

To her surprise, he was talking to someone.

"—drink somewhere else," he said, as she sidled behind the counter. "It's a free country."

She followed his gaze and clocked Bree shrugging, her jaw clenched. Unwilling to deal with him for the moment, Dylan walked over.

"Everything okay?" she asked, trying to keep the tension out of her voice. "He giving you trouble?"

Bree's hand trembled slightly as she pushed a strand of hair behind her ear. "It's fine. Just drunk talk."

"Okay." Dylan glanced over her shoulder. Luckily, Peter was already looking elsewhere. "You sure?"

Getting to her feet, she leveled Dylan with a tight-lipped smile. "Yes, don't worry. I better head out though." She looked at her half-full beer glass and shook her head. "Such a shame to waste, but I'm driving."

"Well, now you know where to find it."

"I guess that means"—she lowered her tone to a near-growl—"I'll be back." When Dylan didn't react, Bree added, "You know, from *Terminator*?"

She couldn't help but laugh. "Okay, Bree-Like-the-Cheese. I'll see you around."

"Hey, gorgeous, think you can help me?" The voice came from behind and they both stiffened.

"Take care, Dylan," Bree said, laying a few bills on the counter. "I'll see you around."

Pocketing the tip, Dylan pushed back her shoulders and swiveled to face him.

"Yeah?" she said.

His hand shook as he pulled the nearly empty pint glass closer. "Think you can call me a cab?"

"Sure."

At the door, Bree turned to meet Dylan's eyes. She lifted her hand in a wave. Dylan waved back and watched her step through the swinging door and disappear into the night.

Regret tugged at the corner of her mind as she lifted the receiver from its place on the wall. What if Bree didn't come back? She stared at the list of numbers for taxi services they kept taped next to the phone.

I should have asked for her number.

Half-turning in his direction, Dylan said, "What's your address?"

He was silent, as if unsure.

"Where you going?" Dylan said, unable to keep the barb out of her voice this time.

"Thirteen-thirteen Larimar Street," he said finally.

Thirteen-thirteen Larimar Street.

Thirteen-thirteen Larimar Street.

Thirteen-thirteen Larimar Street.

She repeated it to herself, cementing it at the back of her mind as she dialed the first number on the list.

"They'll be here in fifteen," Dylan told him after she'd hung up.

"What'd you put in those drinks? My fucking brain is turned to mush." He wavered back and forth on the stool, unable to focus on her for more than a few seconds at a time.

You don't want to know. She pictured her spit sloshing around in his stomach with the beer and tequila.

Disgust heaved itself up in her own gut as she leaned on the bar. A sour smell poured off him.

"Did you hear me?" she asked. "It's coming in fifteen minutes."

Dylan caught him staring down the top of her shirt and straightened up quickly, heat filling her cheeks.

"Thanks, gorgeous." He downed the rest of his beer and got to his feet. "See ya next time."

It sounded like a threat.

CHAPTER
EIGHT

TEXAS STATE PENITENTIARY
Fall 1998

I stop sleeping.

It's that time of year again, and by now I ought to know I can't force it. I should let the insomnia run its course. Wait it out.

But sleep is the only way to battle the incessant boredom. To temporarily forget the overwhelming despair that lies over this place like a heavy cloud.

My sleepless state amplifies everything I hate about life inside. As if all my senses are dialed up to eleven, my nerves bared to the elements. Prison is like riding a public bus on an endless loop through the twilight zone. It's hot and loud and never quite clean. No one explains the rules. Not that it matters because they're always changing anyway. Time feels meaningless, and yet like it's the only thing that matters.

You'd think after four years I'd be acclimated. That the constant noise and chaos would bother me just a little less. Sometimes they do, but sometimes, like now, it feels like I'm going insane.

Lying on my bunk between meals, head counts, and work duty, I stare at my stack of worse-for-wear paperbacks—gifts that arrived in the mail my first months here.

Gerald's Game
Under Milk Wood
To the Lighthouse

The Secret History

At least I have something to look at when I can't sleep.

Something other than her.

This is the anniversary of his death, so why doesn't he come to my bedside at night? Instead, it's her. Not as I knew her. Not with her bright smile, colorful nail polish, and dark blond hair that was somehow both mussed and styled at the same time.

The version I get is soaking wet, covered in bruises and lesions, her lip split open and dripping blood all over my cell floor.

She's not a ghost—I don't believe in those.

She's a reminder. She's my regret, come back to haunt me.

CHAPTER
NINE

PRIYA

Dylan made Priya memorize the address. There would be no writing information down. No *evidence*. They had to be careful. The simple rationale of it felt comforting to Priya. The mundane logistics of Dylan's instructions lent a certain casualness to plotting a murder.

She had the simple task—at least that's how Dylan put it—of finding out if Peter Miles lived alone and, if not, with whom. To see what kind of neighbors he had, to see how vulnerable his house was to break-ins.

After driving by once to pinpoint which house was number 1313, she parked beneath the shade of a large tree at the end of the block. His neighborhood was more upscale than Priya had expected. She'd pictured a dilapidated house slowly crumbling into the ground, surrounded by crack shacks and sinister characters on street corners. But no, it was a wide, well-paved street flanked by sidewalks on each side. Trees stood at even intervals along the edges of the road, and all the yards were neatly groomed.

Normally, this orderliness would have appealed to Priya. She might have imagined herself living here alongside a trim, handsome husband. Maybe someone like Dr. Richard Schmidt from the hospital. Although he was a colleague and nearly two decades her senior, he seemed to sense her secret crush and sometimes even encourage it. He'd tease her about her taste in books or tell her to call him Rick when they weren't around patients. Each time, Priya would feel herself fall in love just a little more.

Not that it mattered. She'd never have the courage to tell Dr. Schmidt how she felt. Even if she did, she wasn't sure she could stomach the demands of a relationship. And she'd never be able to introduce him to her parents. The age difference would be the least of her problems. Priya wasn't sure if they'd go so far as to disown her, but she'd underestimated her parents' willpower before. Just last month, they'd ambushed her with an acquaintance's son—appropriately aged, careered, and Indian, of course—who they thought would make a good match.

She glanced to the white house on her left. The black lanterns hanging from each side of the royal blue door screamed *nouveau colonial,* while the pair of rocking chairs occupying the front porch whispered *Southern comfort.* A yellow blanket trailed over the arm of one of the chairs, as if someone had vacated it just moments ago. Call-Me-Rick *would* look nice sitting across from her on that porch. They could drink whiskey in the evenings after dinner and watch their kids play on the front lawn.

The fantasy soured when she returned her gaze to number 1313. Peter's house wasn't as nice as the one to her left, but still pretty. It had gray siding and red shutters. Little purple flowers waved from the flower boxes beneath each of the windows. If that house could hide a monster, what other dark secrets lurked beneath this neighborhood's shiny veneer?

Did his neighbors know what he was accused of, she wondered. Had they seen the police escort him away, watched as his house was searched? What did they think when he returned as if nothing had happened? Maybe they didn't care. Maybe they all thought he was innocent.

Shifting in her seat, she checked the time. Six twenty-seven. Only twelve minutes had gone by, though it felt like an hour. Priya's instincts were already telling her to leave. But thoughts of Beck kept her anchored in place, staring at the red sedan dozing in Peter Miles's driveway. She owed it to her to stick it out. To try.

A flash of movement caught her attention. Resting her forearms across the steering wheel, Priya watched as a woman emerged from the front door of number 1313, climbed into the Ford, and started it up. She backed down the drive slowly, as if afraid a small child might materialize out of thin air and dart behind her vehicle. Carefully, she angled her car around to point in Priya's direction. The woman lingered there for a few seconds, looking for something in the passenger's seat or glove box, then put the car in drive.

Priya's pulse thrummed.

Look inconspicuous. Like you're just waiting for someone.

Her breathing accelerated and she almost lost her nerve and ducked. As the woman drove by, they locked eyes. Priya froze, her breath trapped in her throat. A moment later, she remembered to jerk her hand up in what she hoped was a friendly wave. But it was too late. The red Ford had already passed.

Priya counted to ten then kept counting until her breathing slowed. Finally, her pulse followed suit and eased down to a reasonable rhythm too. Pressing a palm to her hot cheek, she forced herself to pull up a mental image of the woman in the red car. She'd looked to be in her sixties, with bottle-blond permed hair, sunken cheeks, and a pair of thin lips. Was there a resemblance between her and Peter Miles? Priya couldn't be certain. If Dylan had gotten his address right, then the logical conclusion was that he lived with an older family member. Perhaps his mother, or an aunt.

The dashboard clock showed six-forty. How had it only been twenty-five minutes since she'd parked?

Just ten more.

Book club was at seven-thirty. She needed enough time to pick up Echo from the pet sitter, take him home, and grab the snacks and drinks she'd bought yesterday to contribute. Like Dylan said, they had to carry on acting normal.

"Don't change any of your routines. That's the first thing cops'll notice after," Dylan had lectured her and Isabel a few days before.

Priya glanced to the passenger seat where her copy of *The Secret History* by Donna Tartt sat—that evening's focal point. She hadn't had time to finish it, though Priya suspected she knew where the story was headed. Usually, an unfinished novel would have been the perfect excuse to flake on book club. But now she had to go, even though she hadn't finished the book and wasn't in the mood to dissect the overly privileged lives of a group of white college students. They were studying classics at a liberal arts college, for Christ's sake. This impracticality infuriated Priya.

Dusk stretched its languid paws along the street. Lights began to blink on in some homes, transforming blank windows into luminous, warm squares. Number 1313 remained dark and still, even as the houses around it flared to life.

Priya's knee jiggled as she counted down the seconds. Dylan would be unhappy. Another kink in the plan. The unoccupied house was an inauspicious sign—that's what Priya's father would say. It was proof they needed to abandon the endeavor. If not for another time, perhaps altogether. It just wasn't meant to be.

What would her parents think if they knew? The thought stilled Priya. Despite their struggles after immigrating, they always trusted in the American Dream. They believed the law was the backbone of society, and hard work and ethics would get you far in life. Even if they somehow saw the justice in it, the love in it, her parents would still be horribly, horribly ashamed of her.

But wasn't divine justice a superstitious act in and of itself?

She wondered if Beck would have agreed with them. She'd always respected the lucky dates and times that ruled the Shah household. Maybe because Beck seemed to carry her luck with her. For a long time, it'd made Priya jealous. Life's challenges came naturally to Beck, and good kismet seemed to just alight in her lap. Perhaps that's why she'd been so fearless. How she could do things like take solo trips to climb Mount Toubkal in Morocco or camp out in the Atacama Desert in Chile. Beck was a woman of fortune. Until her luck ran out.

A shadow shifted in the corner of her eye, and Priya jumped. Someone in the house to her left was turning on lights as they moved from room to room. Returning her gaze to number 1313, she tried to swallow back her apprehension. In the twilight it had transformed, as if warning her away. The dark windows seemed to stare back, and the red door gaped like a bloody mouth.

The dashboard clock showed a few minutes to seven. All the houses on the street except for *his* were lit up, the people inside going about their evening routines. The hard part was over. Priya could go now.

Resting her hand on the clutch, she quickly checked the rearview mirror. Her heart shot into her throat. A silhouette stood behind her car, outlined against the deep blue, orange, and pink of the darkening sky. The figure didn't move. Eyes trained on the mirror, she fumbled blindly with the ignition key.

Finally, she managed to turn it, and the car rumbled to life. This seemed to break the silhouette out of its frozen reverie, because it began to move around and alongside the car.

No. No. No.

She found the clutch and put it into first gear. But the figure was already at the driver's side window, blocking her from pulling away from the curb. At the last second, it occurred to her to slam on the lever to lock the door. But it was already locked. She'd made sure to do that when she'd arrived.

Priya's pulse thundered in her ears as she watched the figure lean over. Peter Miles's eyes narrowed, and he tapped on the window.

She lowered it a few inches, her foot ready to quickly move from the brake to the gas pedal.

"Do you need help, miss?" he asked.

A friendly question from the lips of a killer.

"Uh, no. I just pulled over to get my bearings." To her relief, the lie came quickly.

"Where you headed? I can probably give you some directions." He smiled.

"Oh." She swallowed. *Stay calm. Stay calm.* "That's all right. I think I know where I am now."

One hand came to rest on top of the car, the other found the gun holstered to his right hip. Priya's fingers tightened around the steering wheel.

"Well," she said. "I better get going."

He didn't move. Dread was building in her chest, clawing up her throat. In another second she was either going to puke or have a panic attack. Or both.

"Sure you don't need directions?" He squinted in the low light.

"No. No, thank you." She placed her hand on the gearshift, hoping he'd take the hint.

A few long seconds ticked by.

"Well," he said finally, patting the roof of her car. "I live just down the road there." He pointed. "If you need anything, just knock on 1313." He winked. "You have a nice evening, miss."

"Uh, thanks." Her voice was nearly a whisper.

He moved off and she slowly eased out into the street. When she passed him, he waved. As if they were friends. As if he knew her.

Black curled against the edges of her vision. *One. Two. Three.* She counted, trying to slow her breathing while glancing in the rearview mirror. He walked up the front steps to number 1313. He did live there.

Five minutes later, she pulled into a gas station. Priya sat staring through the windshield at the neon ICE sign in the store window and willed her heart to slow. For the first time, she realized what a delicate thing it was, this plan of Dylan's, to hold a life in their hands. The slightest wrong move, and it would explode and rain its jagged pieces around them.

CHAPTER
TEN

ISABEL

Cradling the casserole dish in the crook of her left arm, Isabel took a deep breath and rang the bell. The sound ricocheted around inside the Grant house, then slowly died. She reversed a few steps and craned her head to look at the second floor. There was no movement in the windows. The house seemed emptier than before. Haunted.

Beck hadn't lived there in at least a decade—not since going off to Berkeley at eighteen—but her death had gutted the house. It was full of ghosts.

She rang the doorbell again. Another long silence followed, and Isabel was debating whether to leave the lasagna on the stoop with a note when the door swung open. Mrs. Grant stood in the entryway gripping the edge of the door, her expression like a blank sheet of paper. She looked put together in high-waisted navy slacks, a white blouse, and pale pink leather loafers—Isabel hadn't expected that.

"Hello?" Mrs. Grant said, as if blindly answering the phone. The fingers of her free hand rested lightly on the string of pearls at her neck.

"Hi, Mrs. Grant. It's Isabel."

The older woman's eyes seemed to focus on her for the first time. "Isabel? Oh. Hello, sweetheart."

There was a pause, the two of them suspended, frozen alive.

"My mom sent over some food." Isabel held up the casserole dish. "I hope that's okay? She sends her love. It's lasagna." She wanted to pull Mrs. Grant into a hug and absorb her pain.

"Come in, sweetheart." Without waiting for an answer, Mrs. Grant turned and disappeared into the shadowed interior of the house, leaving the front door gaping open.

Isabel stepped into the foyer and paused, the dish clutched to her chest like an awkward baby.

"Mrs. Grant?" she called.

Silence layered the house. Then, from a distance, "In the kitchen."

That was her cue. She shut the door and her eyes immediately locked on the coatrack just inside. Beck's blue hiking jacket hung from a hook, squeezed between her parents' more practical tan ones, as if nestled in for a hug.

In that moment, Isabel wanted so desperately to leave again. But she forced herself to continue down the hall, past the framed photographs and other knickknacks that spoke to a well-lived-in family home. The house seemed to communicate its grief to her, pumping her full of sadness like an invasive needle plunged directly into her artery. Tears welled up in her eyes. She knew every inch of it, had walked this same hall thousands of times in the last nearly thirty years.

In a way, this was her childhood home too. They'd known each other since birth—their mothers were friends before Isabel and Beck were conceived. The Grant home had been an unmoving core at the center of her own less-reliable life and the dictums of the year-to-year leases that ruled her parents' existence. By the time Isabel turned fifteen, the Guerrero family had moved nearly as many times. Meanwhile, Beck was one of those lucky kids whose family stayed put for the entirety of her life.

It was infused with memories. Isabel remembered going trick-or-treating around the Grants' neighborhood every year. Building blanket tents in their living room. Watching *Mister Rogers' Neighborhood, Scooby-Doo,* and later, when they were older, *Charlie's Angels.* Sleepovers with Priya and Dylan. Painting one another's nails and conferring in the bathroom when Dylan, the first to do everything, got her period.

These memories were soaked into the foundation of the house, sewn into the furniture, pressed into the windows, walls, and doors.

From cradle to grave.

That's what she and Beck always jokingly told each other. It was what friends were supposed to do: grow old together. Sometimes, when she woke in the night disoriented from a dream, Isabel thought for a moment they still would. Then she'd remember Beck was dead. They'd never get to be spunky, purple-haired octogenarians. Never get to complain about the aches and pains of age. It seemed like the hardest part of all to accept: that she would spend more of her life without Beck than she had with her.

She took another deep breath and stepped into the kitchen.

"Could you put it in the fridge for me, sweetheart? Thank you," Mrs. Grant said, her back to her.

"Sure." Isabel pulled open the large fridge door and paused.

It'd been months since the funeral, but casserole dishes, Tupperware containers, and cling-wrapped food items still occupied every shelf. There were at least a dozen meals already there. Suddenly she felt foolish for showing up with yet more food the Grants probably wouldn't eat. She glanced over at Mrs. Grant. She'd changed since the funeral. The tendons seemed to protrude from her stalk-like neck and her wrists looked as delicate as wineglass stems.

"Have you eaten lunch yet?" Isabel asked, stacking a container of what looked like some sort of crumble on top of a neon green casserole dish. "I'd be happy to put the lasagna in the oven. It just needs a few minutes to warm up."

The kitchen was silent. She turned to find Mrs. Grant standing still as a stone sculpture, staring out the French doors that led to the back garden.

Isabel set the lasagna on the island counter and rounded it to switch on the oven. Then she placed her hand on Mrs. Grant's shoulder.

"Mrs. Grant?"

The woman started, then shivered lightly beneath the pressure of Isabel's palm.

"I'm sorry, sweetheart. What was I saying?" she asked.

"Why don't I finish fixing you that cup of tea," she offered, guiding Mrs. Grant by the elbow to take a seat at the table.

In silence, she moved about the room, setting the silver kettle on the stove to boil, taking down two mugs, getting out the box of tea. She flipped up the lid and scanned the compartments, each one housing a different type. Her gaze moved from there to the clock on the wall to Mrs. Grant. She sat where Isabel had left her, the fingers of her right hand once again grazing the necklace at her throat.

Isabel couldn't understand why she was wearing the necklace at all. Was it something Beck had given her? She couldn't think of another reason why a grieving mother would sit in an empty house dressed in pearls. And then there was the constant touching, as if the necklace were a talisman. As though a person's soul could live on in an object.

The kettle started to sing, guiding Isabel's thoughts back. She pushed the sleeves of her cardigan up to her elbows and flicked off the stove, then in a fluid movement opened the oven and slid the lasagna inside.

Isabel had just finished mixing honey into the second mug of chamomile tea when the front door opened.

"Hello? Honey?" Mr. Grant's voice, raspy and mottled as a smoker's, called down the hall.

Before she could decide if she should say something back, or what to say, he appeared in the kitchen doorway dressed in a wrinkled tan shirt tucked into dark pants. The sleeves were rolled up to his elbows, revealing the black hair on his forearms, and he'd loosened the maroon tie's grip around his neck. Mr. Grant's face was drawn, the circles under his eyes an alarming purple. But his expression lit up when he saw her.

"Isabel! How nice of you to come by! How are you?" he asked.

"Hello, Mr. Grant. I'm fine, thank you." She squeezed the fingers of her left hand, nerves fluttering in her stomach like lost butterflies. "I was just heating up some lasagna."

"Oh, that's perfect. Just perfect. I actually came home to see what you were having for lunch." This was directed at Mrs. Grant, who hadn't moved or acknowledged his arrival. "Sorry I'm late, there was a problem at one of the sites and . . ." he trailed off. "Anyway, enough boring contractor stuff. Good to see Isabel has taken charge of things around here."

His smile was alien—as if he were trying to mime how he thought a human being should behave. Isabel shivered. She'd jumped into the deep end here and wasn't sure she could even swim.

Mr. Grant nodded, as if responding to an unspoken question. "Well, I'll go wash up then." He crossed the room and kissed Mrs. Grant on the forehead. His hand lingered on the back of her skull. Then Mr. Grant nodded once more before turning and leaving.

He climbed the stairs like he was battling quicksand with each step. His slow, heavy footfall grew softer when he reached the carpeted second floor and walked down the hallway. A moment later, the pipes groaned to life. She placed both mugs of tea on the dining table and took a seat across from Mrs. Grant. There were a pair of muddy prints in the kitchen doorway, as if a ghost had tracked them there. In a way that's exactly what had happened.

The silence was excruciating, but Isabel couldn't think of what to say to break it. She focused on her mug, watching the steam rise and dissipate. By the time Mr. Grant reappeared in the doorway, Isabel's tea was cold, and the room had taken on the hazy texture of a noiseless nightmare. His presence brought only a marginal sense of relief.

"How are you, Isabel?" Mr. Grant asked, pulling out a chair next to his wife's. "How's school?"

"Fine. A lot of work." She tried to infuse her voice with some brightness.

"You were always a very studious girl. Beck too. Always studying. Smart as a whip. I knew she'd turn out to be a doctor or a lawyer." She had to rest her elbows on the table and lean forward to catch his next words. "You know, you were like a sister to Beck. All three of you were."

"Yes," she answered, not knowing what else to say.

"They have a suspect in custody," Mrs. Grant announced suddenly.

Mr. Grant winced, and Isabel froze in place, her grip tightening around her mug.

"They do?" She directed the question at Mr. Grant, who nodded. Did they have Peter Miles in custody finally? That would mean Dylan didn't need her plan. They could let the police take care of it.

"Not a suspect," Mr. Grant gently corrected his wife. "Just a woman who worked with Beck. At the center. Melanie something-or-other. She threatened her once, apparently. She's had a few run-ins with the law too. I don't know why they'd hire a crazy person at a place that's meant to help crazies. Seems counterintuitive."

It was an oversimplified way of talking about Beck's psychiatry residency, but that wasn't what clinched Isabel's focus.

A woman? Her mind raced. Could a woman have done it?

Mrs. Grant seemed to read her thoughts. "I don't know how they think a woman could have done—done that to her." Her voice broke and she fell silent.

Her husband reached across and placed his hand over hers. "There's a possible motive. Apparently, she was very jealous of our Beck. Maybe even stalking her. The police are doing their due diligence, my love. I'm sure of it."

It happened so fast Isabel didn't have time to react. The tea splashed in Mr. Grant's face and he jumped, an animal-like yelp escaping his lips. Mrs. Grant placed her empty mug back on the table. Tea dripped through Mr. Grant's grayed hair and off his beard.

"Coward," Mrs. Grant said.

The smoke alarm let out a piercing wail and they all started. Isabel hurried over to turn off the oven. More smoke billowed out when she opened the door, bringing with it a sense of defeat. How could she have been so careless?

By the time she'd climbed up on a kitchen stool to silence the alarm and returned to the dining table, Mrs. Grant had left the room. Mr. Grant's mouth jerked as if he were trying, and failing, to paste on a smile.

"Are you okay?" Isabel took a towel from a nearby drawer and handed it to him.

"Thank you. It's hard sometimes, waiting on the police." Removing his glasses, he dried his face. "We don't know all the details of the investigation, so sometimes it looks like it's not going anywhere. Sometimes . . ." He paused, twisting the towel between his hands. "Sometimes I want to go find the man who did this and hurt him like he hurt Beck."

The tick of the clock filled the silence.

"But you have to trust the system, don't you. That's what they tell us anyway." Again, his mouth jerked, as if malfunctioning. "Don't feel obligated to stick around," Mr. Grant added. "I'm sure you're a busy girl."

• • •

Fifteen minutes later, she let herself out and crossed the street to her car. She sat in the driver's seat, her hands gripping the steering wheel, the tears coming hot and fast.

The police had a new suspect. A woman. Isabel knew she ought to be relieved by this, but she wasn't. Somehow, it still didn't feel right.

Could a woman have done that? Her death had been so violent. So angry. It seemed impossible a woman would, *could* inflict that sort of damage.

I want to go find the man who did this and hurt him like he hurt Beck. That's what Mr. Grant had said.

After what she'd witnessed in that mausoleum of a house, Isabel was beginning to feel the same. Maybe it was the only way to set Beck free.

CHAPTER ELEVEN

DYLAN

Isabel and Priya were already sitting inside Chen's Kitchen when Dylan pulled into the parking lot. They were near the window, Priya nursing a cup of tea while Isabel talked. As Dylan crossed the lot to the restaurant, Priya locked eyes with her through the glass. Her nod seemed suggestive.

"Hi," Dylan greeted the two of them at the table.

"Hey," Priya answered.

As she took a seat, Dylan tried to get a read on Isabel's expression, but she was staring at her hands in silence.

A long-haired, lanky waiter with a narrow strip of beard on his chin appeared at their table. He was dressed in faded jeans, scuffed Converse sneakers, and a light green smock. The smock, Dylan knew from past visits to the restaurant, was part of the uniform. All the waiters wore different-colored versions of the same style.

"Hiya, ladies, what can I getcha by the way of beverages?" he asked in a voice gooey as cough syrup.

"I'll take one of those." Dylan pointed at the teapot on the table in front of Priya.

"One green tea for the lady, far out. You, miss?" He looked at Isabel.

For a second it seemed like she wasn't going to answer, then she said softly, "Water, please."

"Far out."

Dylan almost rolled her eyes. There was nothing worse than someone trying way too hard to seem casual and laid-back. It was an annoying contradiction.

"Make that a pitcher for the whole table," Priya added.

"Yes, ma'am." He grinned.

"Well, I think we found the last washed-up hippie in Texas," Dylan said once the waiter was out of earshot.

"Probably stepped into a time portal at Woodstock and showed up here twenty years later," Priya quipped, but her voice was listless.

Normally, the two of them would have kept the joke going while Isabel tried to be the voice of reason ("Maybe he grew up on a commune!" she'd protest). Now, no one laughed, and the banter fizzled out as quickly as it'd started.

"How you doing, Isabel?" Dylan asked.

"Terrible." She was fiddling with her napkin, unfolding and refolding it.

"You look it." Priya kicked her shin under the table, but Dylan ignored her and added, "You been sleeping much?"

Shaking her head, Isabel ran a hand through her hair. "I visited Mr. and Mrs. Grant yesterday."

Dylan coughed into her fist. She needed to pay them a visit too but had been putting it off. Sitting with Beck's grieving parents sounded about as appealing as suffering through Sunday service at her local Presbyterian church.

"How are they?" she asked.

"How do you think?" Priya leveled her with a look.

"They have a new suspect. The police do," Isabel said.

The waiter appeared at her side and the three of them fell silent as he filled their water glasses.

"What can I getcha ladies by the way of victuals?" he asked, setting the pitcher in the center of the table.

Dylan and Priya placed their orders, the waiter interjecting with "Far out" as he scribbled each item down on his notepad.

"Isabel?" Dylan nudged her with her elbow.

"Um." Isabel was staring at the menu as if it were written in a foreign language. "I guess I'll try the chicken fried rice?"

"Far out. I'll get your tea, and your food will be right out." He held Dylan's gaze and his grin widened. "Catch you ladies in a hot minute."

Wrong audience, dude.

He walked away toward the kitchen and Dylan turned her focus back to Isabel.

"The Grants told you the police have a new suspect?"

Isabel nodded. "Someone named Melanie."

"A woman?"

"I know," Priya said softly. "It's crazy."

"They think a woman did all that to her?" Mindful of the couple seated a few tables away from them, Dylan kept her voice low.

"I-I don't know," Isabel said. "I guess she didn't get along with Beck. Did you know about her?" Her eyes shifted from Priya to Dylan. "Did Beck ever mention a Melanie?"

Priya and Dylan shook their heads in unison.

"Sounds like bullshit to me," Dylan said.

"She has a record with the police," Isabel said. "She hurt someone before. Attacked a woman in a bar fight or something."

Struggling to keep her voice level, Dylan said, "It's bullshit, Isabel. What about—" She stopped, then added, "What about the rest of it? A woman couldn't do that. Not alone."

Priya's expression was pained as she shifted in her seat. "Maybe the police know something we don't?"

"Fuck off, Priya. I'm not doing this with you again. You know as well as I do what's going on here."

"I know, Dylan. I get it! I'm just trying to be optimistic!" Her hazel eyes seemed to spark, the volume of her voice barely contained.

"They're trying to pin it on someone else," Isabel said in a small voice.

With a sharp intake of breath, Dylan nodded. "Yeah. Yeah, they are."

A hand lowered a teapot and a cup to the table, and she glanced up, startled.

"Thanks," she told the waiter.

"No problemo," he said. Bobbing to some internal beat, he made his way over to a table where four customers had just taken seats.

"I saw him," Priya said.

For a second, Dylan was confused. *Who? The waiter?*

"I was watching his house, like you asked," she continued. "And he showed up. Right next to my car."

Isabel's eyes widened.

"Fuck," Dylan said. "Did he see you?"

"Of course he saw me!" She glanced to the other diners and took a deep breath before lowering her voice. "He knocked on my window. He had a gun!"

"Oh my god, are you okay?" Isabel asked.

"Fuck," Dylan repeated.

"He asked me . . ." She paused and took a drink of water. "He asked me if I needed help, if I needed directions. I told him I'd pulled over to get my bearings. I can't go back there, Dylan."

"Hey, hey, it's all right," Dylan said, even though it wasn't. How could Priya have let him see her face?

"He lives with an older woman, his mom, I think," Priya said. "It didn't look like anyone else lives there. She left and the lights stayed off. That's when he walked by." She crossed her arms over her chest. "I'm sorry."

"Why do you think he stopped by your car?" Isabel asked.

"I probably looked suspicious. A brown woman in a white neighborhood, sitting in a bright yellow car. I mean, what did you expect?" She lobbed the question at Dylan like a grenade. As if she'd forced Priya into it against her will. Or as if she knew this would happen and sent Priya anyway.

Fucking great, Dylan thought as she filled her cup with green tea. She'd forgotten about Priya's car. It was looking more and more like she'd have to do everything herself anyway. She should have left Isabel and Priya out of it. Kept things simple.

Swallowing her irritation along with a sip of the tea, she asked, "Did he act like he recognized you? Like he knew who you were?"

"Why would he? It was almost dark and it's not like we've ever spoken before."

Dylan sat back, surprised. "Didn't you two meet at Beck's New Year's party?"

"I saw him there, but we never talked. Not that I can remember anyway." Priya jerked her shoulders in a shrug. "But . . ." She grimaced. "It did seem like he was trying to flirt with me. Like maybe he wanted to get a good look, so he knocked on my car window."

The muscles in Dylan's neck and shoulders compacted like mattress springs.

"Then he . . ." Priya shook her head. "Well, like I said, he was flirting."

Dylan wasn't sure how to take this. It tracked with Peter Miles's usual behavior; he just couldn't stand to leave women alone. But Priya had never been good at picking up on cues. Was she even capable of reading the signs? Or did she interpret it that way because she knew what he'd done; how he'd charmed Beck and then killed her?

"Fried rice for the lady!" The waiter had the impeccable timing of an awkward party clown. Isabel winced. "Vegetable chow mien!" he added, as enthusiastic as if he were about to eat it all himself. "The far-out Beijing beef and a side of rice for you!" The waiter presented Dylan with both a grin and the dish. "And"—with a magician-like flourish he lowered the final two dishes from the tray to the table. "Egg rolls and fried pork wontons to share. Anything else I can get you ladies?"

Dylan reached for a wonton and took a bite.

"Everything looks good," Priya told him after a beat of silence. "Thank you."

"Just wave me down if you need anything. Enjoy." Dylan didn't look up to see his face, but some of the energy had drained from his voice.

"You didn't have to be rude," Priya said after he'd gone.

"Was he flirting with me?"

"What?"

"Was the waiter flirting with me?" Dylan repeated.

The inside corners of Priya's eyebrows dipped. "That's a weird question, Dylan."

"Yes or no?"

"I don't know. Yes, probably."

"Hm."

There was another silence. Isabel poked at her rice, then set her fork down with a sigh. "I guess I'm not hungry," she said, like it was a surprise.

"You don't believe me," Priya said, staring at Dylan.

Taking a bite, Dylan chewed and swallowed before answering, "It's not that I don't believe you. I just know you have a hard time seeing the signs."

"You think I'm too stupid to know when someone's flirting?"

She set down the wonton. "It's got nothing to do with that, Pri. I'm just speaking based on experience. Remember that guy at work who spent months trying to ask you out?"

"Did it ever occur to you maybe I *pretend* not to see the signs because it's easier than having to explain why I'm not interested in dating?"

"We're getting off topic," Isabel interjected. The tension between them slackened slightly. "Why does any of that matter?"

"Because." Getting the words out was like trying to suction wet cement up into a syringe. "Because if he was flirting with Priya, that means she could be bait."

Silence fell like a hammer. Dylan forced herself to look back without flinching at the horrified expressions on their faces.

"You're insane," Priya said finally. "I'm not going anywhere near him. I'm definitely not talking to him again."

"I won't let anything happen to you."

"You have absolutely no way of guaranteeing that," she answered flatly.

Throwing up her hands, Dylan sat back and crossed her arms. "Okay, what do you suggest then?"

"Oh, I don't know, Dylan. Something else. Maybe we should wait for the police to conclude their investigation. They could arrest him any day now."

Dylan rolled her eyes.

"Maybe they're taking time to build a solid case!"

"That's bullshit and you know it." She leaned forward. "And at this point, I don't care. I don't care if they plan to arrest him later. I don't care if he eventually gets prosecuted for the crime. I. Don't. Care. Because he killed her and there's no"—she did air quotes—"'justice' enough to make up for that. I want him to fucking pay. Really pay. Not get some bullshit life sentence with other violent dirtbags. Or worse, not go to jail at all. Is that what you want, Priya? Him wandering around? 'Cause he'll do it to someone else. They always do. Men like that don't stop."

"Don't you dare try to manipulate me," Priya said. The rage in her face pushed Dylan off-kilter for a second. "Quit acting like you're the only one who—"

"Stop fighting." Isabel's head was in her hands. "Just please stop fighting. You two are always arguing!" She looked up. "How are we going to pull any of this off if all you can do is fight about it?"

This silenced them.

"I'll do it." Isabel's gaze found Dylan's. "I'll be the bait. Would that work?"

"I can't ask you to do that, Isabel."

"Why not?" A flush of pink stained her cheeks. "Why can Priya do it, but I can't?"

Dylan hesitated. She didn't want to say it aloud, not to her face, but she'd always seen Isabel as the weakest. She was a scholar, a library mouse, more comfortable hiding away with a book than out in the world. And she was too gentle. It felt okay to ask her to keep their secrets, but to be an actual participant? That seemed wrong. Like offering vodka to a child.

"I thought you didn't want to be a part of it," she said, buying time.

"Have you seen Beck's parents since the funeral?"

It made it only slightly better that Priya shook her head too.

Isabel picked up her fork and started toying with her food again. "They're like . . . like two zombies. It's like they've been scooped out. Emptied. Especially Mrs. Grant. There's nothing left. It's awful."

"How you ladies doing over here?" The server's voice brought them out of the conversation with a jolt.

Dylan forced a smile and said, "Everything's great, thanks!" She made sure to hold eye contact just a second too long. After, when they started investigating Peter Miles's death, the only thing she wanted the server to remember was the attractive woman who flirted with him. Priya, Isabel, and the whole argument needed to be a blurred afterthought.

"We need to do this for them," Isabel said, once the waiter walked away. "Otherwise, I think her death will slowly kill them. So, yes." She looked from Dylan to Priya. "I'll be the bait, if that's what you need. I can do it. But we need to stop fighting."

Dylan nodded. "Agreed. We need to get along. No matter what."

"Yeah," Priya said with a small smile. "Yeah, okay."

"Sorry, Pri."

Her eyebrows rose. "That's okay. I should have been more careful, I guess."

"Hug it out?" Isabel said cheekily.

"Shut up," Dylan told her with a laugh. Spearing a forkful of beef and rice, she said, "Well, now that we're all friends again, we better eat some of this or that waiter is going to think something weird is going on."

"I don't think he'd know what weird was if it slapped him across the face," Priya said. "He's pretty much the walking epitome of weirdness."

"What's normal anyway?" Isabel asked no one in particular. "And why are we always trying to define people by whether they are or not?"

Balance was restored, and the three of them dug into their food in companionable silence. As she chewed, Dylan stared at the empty seat opposite. For a second, just a brief second, she could picture Beck sitting there. And she was smiling.

CHAPTER
TWELVE

DYLAN

Before

"You look like you need a beer."

The man held the bottle out to Dylan as if they were friends.

She lifted her glass of Coke. "No thanks. I'm on designated driver duty."

Squinting in the low lighting, she scanned the room for her friends. Beck had draped red silk scarves over all her lamps, casting everything in a dim pink glow. Like they were all standing around inside a giant vagina.

She spotted Priya and Isabel wedged next to each other on the sofa. And Beck—

"One beer won't do you in." The man leaned closer, and she caught a whiff of his smoky cologne. "Might make you less miserable too."

"Do I know you?" Dylan asked, a slight bristle in her voice.

"Not yet." He grinned and set one of the beers on the kitchen table. "Peter."

It took a second for it to click in Dylan's brain. Ignoring his outstretched hand, she asked, "Peter. As in, Beck's boyfriend?"

He laughed and picked up the beer again. "She tell you about me?"

Her gaze found Beck by the stereo, flipping through her CD book.

So, this is Peter Miles.

• • •

"*God, can you believe it's already 1993?*" *Beck said.*

It was just the four of them now, sitting in the living room amongst the dregs of the party having one last drink.

"*I can tell you right now what your New Year's resolution should be, Beck: Date more appropriate men,*" *Dylan said, only half-joking.* "*Peter's kind of a loser.*"

Beck's first reaction was to widen her eyes. Her second was to laugh.

"*He is not. He's hot.*"

"*He's hot? Or he's not?*" *Priya asked, her words gummy as warm taffy.*

"*You're drunk.*" *Beck got to her feet.*

"*Aren't we all?*" *Priya stretched her arms overhead.*

"*And you're going to feel like crap in the morning if you don't hydrate,*" *she told Priya as she brought her a glass of water.*

"*Beck knows best,*" *Isabel quipped from where she was nestled in one corner of the sofa, a throw pulled around her shoulders. She was a quick and quiet drunk and nursing her third or fourth glass of wine now.*

"*Yeah, yeah, yeah.*" *Beck rolled her eyes and told Priya,* "*Drink up.*"

Beck's shoulders seemed to relax a little as Priya finished off the water. Even Dylan had to admit, Priya tended to go hard. But she was so buttoned up the rest of the time that when she let loose, she just really let loose.

She also suspected Beck had diverted the conversation on purpose.

Dylan stood. "*We should get going.*"

Priya rose too and looked blearily around for a place to put her empty glass.

Beck took it and came in for a hug. "*Drink more water when you get home, okay?*"

"*Mhm.*" *Priya nodded.*

"*You sure you don't need help cleaning up?*" *Isabel asked as she hugged Beck.*

"*Nah. I'll take care of it tomorrow.*"

Dylan passed the car keys to Isabel and leaned in to wrap her arms around Beck.

"*I'm serious, Beck,*" *she said, unable to let it be. Not on New Year's anyway.*

"*About?*" *She stepped back with a smile.*

"*About Peter.*" *The placid expression on her friend's face slipped away.* "*You asked me what I think, so I'm telling you. You're better than this.*"

Dylan jerked her chin toward where he slept behind the closed bedroom door. "Than him."

"Seriously? You had one conversation."

"Sometimes one is enough."

"See, this is what I was afraid of! You always judge people too quickly, Dylan."

"Maybe." She shrugged. "But I'm usually right."

Beck was quiet, as if internalizing this. Then she said, "It's not like it's serious or anything. Not yet."

"If you say—" A honk from outside cut her short, another sounded quickly after. "Jesus, I knew I shouldn't have given them my car keys. I better get going."

"Yep." Beck folded her arms tighter, her mouth set in a hard line.

By the time she got to the car, Isabel had already fallen asleep in the rear seat. Dylan backed out, then glanced toward Beck's apartment one final time. At some point in the last few minutes Peter had emerged from his drunken slumber. He stood in the doorway with Beck, an arm resting possessively on her shoulders.

Beck lifted her hand in a wave. He stayed immobile, partially trapped in the shadows.

CHAPTER
THIRTEEN

DYLAN

Aces was filling up with its usual Wednesday crowd. A few of Dylan's regulars were already perched on their stools, hats pushed back on their heads as they silently drank beer or McAfee's neat. Every now and then, someone recognized somebody else and struck up a conversation. But it always died quickly, a fire that couldn't quite catch. It was just one of those days.

Dylan wiped down the bar before placing another whiskey in front of a customer, then busied herself restocking clean glasses on the overhead shelf. It was always a little painful to watch people thinking too hard over drinks. Liquor tended to color your thoughts in a certain way if you came to it feeling morose.

When Dylan turned around again, she found a woman with her elbows propped up on the bar. She recognized her right away. Dylan had been tracking Peter Miles's movements for weeks now, jotting down the times and dates he came in on an old receipt she kept in her back pocket.

Slowly, she was gathering more and more information, learning the ins and outs of a killer. He was a man of habit. He came in on the same days, around the same time, and drank the same thing. But, the last few times something had changed: Peter hadn't been drinking alone.

"Vodka soda, right?" Dylan asked.

The woman's eyes stopped roaming the room long enough to meet Dylan's. Her penciled-on eyebrows rose a fraction of an inch.

"You remember me?"

"You were here last week with—" She stopped herself short of saying his name. "With that guy, right? Did you manage to get his puke off your shoes?"

Luckily the incident, Peter vomiting after one too many tequila shots, had happened outside the bar. Not so lucky for his companion, who was standing in the line of fire.

Twisting her turquoise necklace around, the woman wrinkled her nose. "Nope. They're suede, completely ruined."

"Shit, sorry."

She shrugged. "Probably not the last time. Pete—my boyfriend— can be an asshole when he's drunk." The woman's gaze was back to drifting about the bar.

The base of Dylan's neck prickled in anticipation. This was her. She had to be *the girlfriend*. The one who'd alibied Peter Miles and helped him get away with murder.

Take it easy, she reminded herself. *Don't want to spook her.*

"You looking for him?" Dylan asked.

The woman's glossy pink lips pulled back into a smile. "Yeah! You seen him around?"

"He hasn't been in yet today." She didn't add that Peter Miles, for reasons unknown to Dylan, rarely came in on Wednesdays.

"Oh, okay." She bit her lip. "I mean, we said we'd meet here, was all."

It was a lie, Dylan could tell by the way the woman didn't look at her.

"You want a drink while you wait?"

"Yeah, sure. I'll take that vodka soda."

"Coming right up."

As she made the drink Dylan's thoughts flared in fits and starts. She set the vodka soda down on the bar and asked, "You wanna open a tab?"

"Nah, I settle as I go. Makes it harder to drink too much." She held out a five-dollar bill with a laugh. "Thanks," she said when Dylan handed her the change.

"Sure thing. Just give me a shout if you need anything."

It was better to give her some space, to not seem too eager to talk to her. Dylan made her way down the arm of the bar and locked eyes with Bree. Immediately a weight lifted.

"How's that beer treating you?" she asked, indicating the bottle of Kozel with her chin.

"Just fine," Bree said.

Leaning against the back bar, Dylan crossed her arms. "I need to order more. Seeing as you're a regular now and our stock's getting a little low."

"Are you keeping track of my comings and goings, Dylan?" There was a spark in her warm brown eyes.

Heat flared at the back of Dylan's neck like a lit candle.

"Maybe. I like knowing who my regulars are." She grinned.

"Well, what can I say, the good beer and cute bartender keep bringing me back."

Another soft flutter of her pulse. "I'm glad. Can't say I mind seeing you around here."

What was this, Bree's fifth, sixth visit to Aces? And today, in an unexpected gesture, she'd let Dylan uncap her beer bottle for her. Someday she'd find out more about this odd quirk, Dylan was sure of it. Bars were like confessional booths for strange secrets, bartenders the liquor-serving priests.

"By the way," Bree said, reaching into her purse. "I brought you something." She laid a book on the counter.

Dylan stepped closer and swiveled it around to read the title.

Selected Poems by Dylan Thomas.

Her eyes lifted to meet Bree's.

" 'Do not go gentle into that good night, / Old age should burn and rave at close of day /' "—raising her clenched fist, Bree lowered her voice to a baritone—" 'Rage, rage against the dying of the light. . . .' " She thumped her fist onto the bar top and smiled. "And so on, and so forth. I think you and Dylan Thomas will get along."

Dylan stared at her in silence. "You are so fucking weird," she said finally.

"I'll take that as a compliment."

"You should," she said, and meant it. "Weird is good. And . . . thanks." She picked up the book and flipped through the pages. "I don't usually read poetry."

"Don't worry, there won't be a test on it." Bree laughed. "But I hope you like it."

"Thanks." Her cheeks were starting to ache from grinning. "Well, I better . . ." She jerked her head toward the opposite end of the bar.

"Of course. Duty calls." Bree tipped the glass and poured more beer.

Turning the book over in her hands, Dylan crossed to the other side. As she slid it into a storage nook beneath the counter, she clocked the empty stool and abandoned glass of vodka soda. Peter Miles's girlfriend was gone.

"Shit," she said out loud.

She was just here.

Ignoring the customer trying to wave her down, Dylan rounded the counter and hurried out the front door. She came to a stop in the center of the parking lot and looked left and right. Had she missed her chance?

"You got a light?" a voice asked.

She turned. The woman was leaning against the wall beside the door. Dylan must have walked right past her. A breeze pulled a few stray tendrils of blond hair across the woman's face as she placed a cigarette between her lips.

At that moment, like the click of a combination lock falling open, Dylan realized what it was about the woman that seemed so familiar. It'd nagged at her ever since she'd first spotted her in Aces. The woman resembled Beck. Same build, same hair color, similar eyes, same smattering of freckles across her nose and cheeks. Peter Miles had a type.

The tension in Dylan's shoulders wound tighter. "Yeah, sure." She dug a bar matchbook from her pocket. The scent of artificial straw-berries tickled Dylan's nose as the woman leaned toward the lit match and drew on her cigarette.

"Why don't you come inside?" Dylan asked, not liking the idea of her standing by herself out in the dark. "You can smoke at the bar."

"I got somebody coming to get me." She shifted from one foot to the other.

"Your boyfriend?"

She snorted. "Like I could rely on him."

It was now or never. Pushing her hands deep into the pockets of her brown corduroys, Dylan leaned against the wall, so they were shoulder to shoulder. "Can I ask you something?"

"I guess." Even in the dark, Dylan thought she could see her fin-gers tense around the cigarette.

"Why do you put up with that?" It was a risky question to ask a stranger. "I mean, it's none of my business, but you seem like a nice person. Last time he left you here after puking on you and today he's stood you—"

"You know that girl that was murdered? Rebecca something or other?" the woman interrupted. Dylan's pulse began to thrum an anxious beat. Was it really going to be this easy?

"Yeah, I heard about that."

"He was a suspect in the investigation." The woman frowned and angled her face up to exhale. "Or a person of interest. I don't know. But being a suspect? It traumatized him, I guess."

"You think your boyfriend could do something like that?" Keep-ing her voice level and disinterested was like wrestling with a furious rattlesnake.

"He had an alibi." The statement was shot through with a layer of steel. "Last I checked, you're innocent 'til proven guilty in this country."

"Yeah, sure." Dylan lifted her hands, palms out, in a show of sur-render. "Sorry if I crossed a line."

There were a few beats of silence as she smoked.

"He wasn't always this way, you know," she said finally. The defensive edge in her voice had dulled. "He owes me better, you're not wrong. 'Specially now."

"Especially now?"

The woman's eyes darted sideways to meet hers. "Well, I stuck with him through all that shit about that girl, right? Made sure they knew he couldn't have done it."

Careful to keep her face neutral, Dylan nodded.

"He should be more grateful," the woman continued. "I'm the only reason he's not in jail for murder and he treats me like . . . this." She sniffed and stubbed her cigarette against the wall. "Look, I know how pathetic it makes me look. I've just known him a long time. We've been together off and on since high school. He wasn't always like . . . Well, he wasn't always a mean drunk, I guess. That whole business with that girl really messed with his head."

"Doesn't it scare you though?" Dylan asked. "That they suspected him in the first place? I mean, what that woman went through . . . it doesn't scare you?"

"He'd never hurt me. But I guess you never really know what people are capable of, right? Anyway, I'm done coming 'round here to wait for him. No offense," she added, as if Dylan could possibly feel insulted by her staying away. As far as she was concerned, it was a win if she did.

The woman stood upright with a shrug and, indicating a car turning in to the Aces parking lot, said, "That's my friend. Gotta go."

Dylan watched her climb in and disappear into the night. As she stepped back inside the bar, she ran into Bree.

"Everything okay?" Bree asked.

"Yeah, sure," Dylan said, even though her brain felt like it was on fire. "Just taking a break."

She could sense her manager shooting her daggered looks from the booth where he'd been sitting all night, shuffling through piles of invoices. He wasn't actually doing anything, Dylan knew. Jason always left payroll and the bar accounts until the very last second. Most nights he sat there drinking beer from a coffee mug and watching her work. A few times, she'd even caught him dozing off.

Ignoring him, she asked, "You heading out already?"

"I am." Bree smiled.

Cool tendrils of disappointment curled around Dylan's heart. "Okay. See you next time."

"Dylan?" The way Bree said her name had the same effect as if she'd run her fingertips along Dylan's arm.

"Yeah?"

"I was hoping you'd find it on your own, but on the off chance you don't . . . my phone number's on the bookmark inside that Dylan Thomas book."

"Oh. Okay." She couldn't keep the grin out of her voice.

"Maybe you could call me sometime."

"Maybe I could, Bree-Like-the-Cheese."

For a moment it was just the two of them in a bubble, smiling at each other. Then the noise of the bar rushed back in. From the corner of her eye, Dylan could make out Jason motioning to her.

"Okay," Bree said. "Well, see you later, Dylan."

"See you."

Still ignoring her manager, Dylan rounded the bar and got to work. As she filled drink orders, she dissected the conversation with Peter's girlfriend, pinning each word, each expression, each mannerism to a mental corkboard to be closely studied. She'd been the one to confirm his alibi, to say he was with her the day Beck went missing. She and her word were one of the key things standing between him and a prison sentence. If Dylan read between the lines of what the woman had said, it seemed plain she'd lied to protect Peter Miles.

Dylan paused to raise a hand and hold it level. Steady as a slab of granite. It was a good sign she wasn't easily spooked.

When she went to clean the area Bree had vacated, she found three bills pinned beneath her half-full pint glass. The gesture, at least, brought a smile to Dylan's face.

CHAPTER
FOURTEEN

PRIYA

"Chair. Rope. Gag. Wire. Knife," Dylan said in a low voice, arms folded across her chest.

Priya felt a small wave of nausea crest in her stomach at the monotony of it. As if Dylan were repeating a grocery list.

"We can park the car around back," Dylan continued, turning to the window. Priya crossed to where she stood and peered through the layers of grime and dirt at the rear of the house. There was a paved driveway where the car would be out of sight from the road. "You did good, Pri. How'd you find it?"

"During one of my walks with Echo," she answered, as if it'd been a lucky coincidence. As if she hadn't been looking for a place to do *it* for weeks.

"Old Maneater helped out, huh." Hands on her waist, Dylan nodded. "You did good, Pri."

A thread of shame wove its way through her. What did it say about Priya that she'd gotten her beloved dog involved in the plot too? Each time she took him for another long walk, Priya tamped down the guilt. Echo couldn't understand his role in the murder, nor could he judge her for it.

And Echo made her feel safe. When she first saw him at the shelter,

Priya had immediately been drawn to the size of the dog. He was listed as a high-energy German shepherd–golden retriever mix and, at two years old, weighed nearly a hundred pounds and was on the larger end, even for those breeds.

He'd looked up at Priya with big brown eyes, tongue hanging out one side of his mouth as if to reassure her, *I'll always protect you.*

In the months that followed—as the investigation into Beck's death stalled and Priya grappled with her grief—she'd found comfort in the large dog. And, over the past few weeks, Echo had steadied her, helped her stay the course.

Priya had approached the search with purpose. She kept a map with the places they'd already visited marked off, and before each walk, she'd select a new area. In her pocket, she always carried an extra measure of security: the Mace she'd bought at an army surplus. She wasn't sure how useful it'd be in an attack, but like Echo, its presence made her feel better, a hypothetical *Break Glass in Case of Emergency.*

They'd gone on eleven walks together before they found the right place. When she'd seen the abandoned house standing alone near the water, Priya had the same thought as when she'd stood in the animal shelter looking down at Echo: *You're perfect.*

The house was ominous, something out of a gothic novel. Its siding had long gone gray from neglect and exposure. The roof sagged a little at one end like it wanted to give up the ghost if only the rest of the house would agree. And, strangely, the windows were all boarded over. It'd been a surprise to find it empty. Priya had expected to discover drugged-up squatters inside, but they seemed to give the house a wide berth, as if they believed it haunted. Or cursed.

Now, here she was with Dylan—Echo stayed home this time—shining her flashlight around what appeared to have been a living room in some distant past and visualizing a murder. *His* murder.

It was becoming real.

"We'll have to do it all at once," Dylan said. "Bring all the supplies and then . . ." She fell quiet.

"How do you think we should do it?" Priya asked.

Dylan turned her eyes on her. "How do you think we should do it?"

"I hate him so much," she answered after a beat of silence. "And I really want him to suffer. But it's hard to . . ."

"Think about the details?"

"Yeah, the details. I mean, are we talking torture here? I'm not sure I can stomach that."

"Wait until you have him in front of you." Dylan sounded certain. "You'll feel differently."

"Once we get him here, there's no going back."

"Nope."

"We'll have to follow through, no matter what."

"Yep."

"Do you think we're prepared for that, Dylan?"

Her friend swiveled so they were facing each other. "I know we don't always see eye to eye, Pri. Why do you think that is?" When Priya didn't answer, Dylan said, "It's because we're the same type of person."

Priya almost laughed. "That's not true. For one thing, you're tough."

"So are you." Dylan looked at her straight-faced.

"I'm not so sure about that."

"You are, Priya. I don't know if it's the pressure from your parents or growing up a brown kid in a white neighborhood. Fuck, you've been pushed to the margins your whole life because of how you look. Maybe it's that. But you're tough. Tougher than most people, and the toughest person I know. Besides me, of course," she added with a lopsided grin.

"Such modesty." Despite herself, Priya smiled too.

"Look." Dylan placed a hand on her shoulder. "My point is, I know if one of us freaks out, starts to regret it, or doesn't think she can follow through, the other one will finish the job."

"You're sure?"

"One hundred percent fucking confident."

CHAPTER FIFTEEN

TEXAS STATE PENITENTIARY
Fall 1997

Sonia starts acting out.

Always in minor ways—cursing at the officers, drawing crude pictures and taping them to the walls, lingering in the recreation courtyard after the guard has ordered us to file inside—but always with the guarantee of punishment. She starts spending an obscene amount of time in solitary.

At first, I think she's acting out to stand out. That, after eighteen months inside, she's tired of being reduced to an inmate number.

Property of the state.

A nonentity.

A nothing.

Then I realize what Sonia's doing isn't rebellion. It's self-flagellation.

When I ask Dory about it, she says, "I heard they took her kids away. That she won't get to see 'em again, even when she gets out." She shakes her head like a sage, disappointed judge. "She thinks punishing herself over it means something. It don't. But you can't convince her otherwise."

I understand what she means. I've known people like Sonia too. The ones who can't be reasoned with. No matter how hard you try, you can't force them to make better decisions. To stop hurting themselves. That's how Sonia wound up here, with nothing to lose.

But it's not like I can talk. I'm in here too, aren't I?

CHAPTER
SIXTEEN

ISABEL

Isabel entered Aces of Spades in the same way she might plunge into an ice-cold lake; eyes squinted half shut and holding her breath. She'd never understood the appeal of dive bars. The other graduate students in her program seemed to spend most of their free time at the one near the university but Isabel always turned down their invitations to join. She'd rather curl up at home with a glass of wine in her hand and a book in her lap than compete with loud music and louder conversation while drinking mediocre beer.

Inside Aces, she paused by the door and waited for her vision to adjust to the dim interior. It didn't smell nearly as bad as she'd expected. The homey scent of peanuts overlaid a hint of lemon cleaner. Maybe Dylan ran a tighter ship than she'd given her credit for.

Dylan watched her approach the bar.

"Hey, Isabel. What are you doing here?"

"I'm here to get that book, remember?" Isabel answered, a little too loudly.

The corner of Dylan's mouth twitched.

I'm a terrible liar. I'm sorry. Isabel tried to communicate a silent apology.

"Oh yeah. It's in my car. Give me a minute." She moved away to where a man was sitting in a booth near the end of the bar. Dylan rapped on the counter to get his attention. "Hey, Jason, I'm going to step out for a few seconds. Have to grab something for my friend."

Jason lifted his gaze from his magazine as if there were an invisible bowling ball balanced on his head. His focus shifted past Dylan to Isabel. He had crumbs in his mustache and a ketchup stain on the collar of his green polo shirt—probably from the half-finished plate of fries on the table in front of him. Running a hand through his thinning hair, he stifled a yawn and nodded.

Isabel smiled and his expression brightened. She had that effect on people. It was hard for them to say no when she looked so harmless.

"Sure. It's slow anyway. But don't take too long. No standing outside gossiping for hours." He snorted.

"Come on." Dylan was at her elbow, keys in hand.

Outside, daylight hit Isabel like a slap to the face. Shading her eyes with her hand, she followed Dylan across the lot.

"Sometimes I just want to smack him," Dylan said. She lowered her voice to a mock male baritone and repeated, " 'No standing outside gossiping for hours.' Like that's the only reason women ever get together."

For once in agreement with her friend's assessment of someone, Isabel nodded. They continued toward the far end where, as instructed, she had parked her car near Dylan's.

"Okay," Dylan said in a low voice after they'd walked a few steps. "Did you see the camera?"

Willing herself not to turn and look back to where the security camera maintained vigil from over the bar door, she answered, "Yes." There was a tremor in her voice.

"It doesn't reach very far, about five or six feet around the door. Which is good. You can back in here"—she indicated a spot halfway down the lot—"and watch the entrance. Don't go past that bush or you'll be in the security footage."

"Okay. What if he doesn't show up?"

"He will." Dylan slid the key into her car door and turned it. "He's got a routine, at least most nights he does. I'll fill him up with a couple extra shots to really get him tight. Around eight-thirty he always bums a smoke off somebody—the jerk's too fucking cheap to buy his own pack—and comes out here to smoke. And piss. I've caught him doing that a couple times around the side of the bar."

She lifted something from the back seat and turned, holding it out.

"What's this?" Isabel asked.

"You came by to borrow a book, remember?" She waved it. "So, I'm giving you a book."

"Oh." Heat burst in her cheeks as she took it. "I didn't know you were serious."

"This is serious, Isabel. As much as possible we have to make it look like things are how we say they are. Got it?"

"Yes. Okay." The book felt alien in her hands. How could she spend most days surrounded by books then suddenly feel like she didn't know what to do with one?

She looked up to find Dylan watching her, eyes slightly narrowed.

"You can handle this, right?" Dylan asked. "Do I need to get Priya to do it?"

For a moment, Isabel was tempted to say yes.

"I thought she couldn't because he'd recognize her."

"It wouldn't be ideal." She folded her arms across her chest and leaned against the car. "But he'll probably be too drunk to see straight anyway. Maybe he won't notice it's her."

"No, it's too risky." She paused. "But maybe it'd be better to have a different car? Just in case someone notices me and remembers mine?"

Dylan was silent, her bottom lip caught between her teeth as she thought. "It's too big a risk to rent," she said.

This is all too risky.

"Well. I—" Isabel cleared her throat. Did she really want to do this? Passively completing an assigned task was one thing, actively helping was another. "My cousin and her husband go out of town a lot. I have a key to their place. I could . . ." Suddenly embarrassed and unsure, she let her voice trail off.

There was a glint in Dylan's eyes. "You mean Miranda?"

She nodded.

"You can get the keys without them knowing about it?"

Again, Isabel nodded. "They have two cars. And they always leave the keys hanging on a hook by the door."

Just voicing it aloud made her heart pound harder.

"Isabel Guerrero, I didn't know you had it in you."

Isabel felt an immediate burst of pleasure at the admiration in her friend's tone.

"Of course, this means we'll have to plan it around Miranda and her husband," Dylan continued. "But it'll work. It's doable."

"Do you think they could get in trouble? Afterward, I mean?" She squeezed the book hard. What had she done? Now she'd dragged innocent Miranda and Gil into it too.

"I don't see why," Dylan said. "They'd both have alibis. They drive regular cars, right? Nothing that stands out? Nothing flashy?"

"No, nothing flashy."

"Then it'll be fine, Isa. Don't worry. Using a different car is a fucking great idea."

Warmed by the compliment, but also feeling traitorous for it, Isabel glanced down.

"*The Communicative Pacifist,*" she read the book's title aloud.

"I'm trying to learn how to communicate better." *And don't make me explain why,* Dylan's tone ironically seemed to imply.

"Dylan . . . always on a self-improvement journey." She looked up again.

"Okay, so like I said, you pull up just as far as that last bush." She indicated to the row of browning shrubs that ran from the door to the corner of the building. "Call Peter's name. Tell him the bartender phoned in a taxi pickup for this location. If he asks questions, say you're with a new taxi company. Unmarked cars, female drivers, it's a new concept they're trying out or something. Once he's in the back seat, back up and leave the same way so you're not in the camera footage."

"Sure."

Fear tightened into a knot in her chest. For a moment, Dylan seemed to waver.

"You can fucking do this, okay?" Dylan added. "He'll be harmless, too pissed to stand up straight. I'll give you a Taser, just in case."

"Okay."

Dylan stepped forward as if about to hug her, then half-turned and slammed her car door shut instead.

"I better get back," she said. "Any questions?"

"Can you call me at home when he comes in? So I know for sure he's here?"

Dylan was already shaking her head before she'd even finished.

"You know we can't do that. If the cops get their hands on the record of calls to and from the bar for that day, I don't want them to see your number. It's too dangerous. You'll just have to watch the door. You know what he looks like, and I'll do my best to get him out by nine. The rest is up to you."

"Okay." She riffled the pages of the book with her thumb. "God, I'm nervous."

"Me too."

"Really?" Her hands grew still. "You seem so calm."

"Obviously that's just an act."

Isabel wasn't so sure. She suspected fear had been scared out of Dylan long ago. Although she rarely spoke of her violent father, Isabel knew the story about twelve-year-old Dylan holding a kitchen knife to his throat and telling him to get out or she'd kill him. She'd grown tired of watching him beat her mother, wanted to stop it, wanted to protect her little sister. In the end, it hadn't mattered. Shortly after her father left, Dylan's mother overdosed, and the state separated the two sisters.

The story seemed to reveal something unique, something mutant in Dylan, but it wasn't until now that Isabel was finally able to put a finger on what. She didn't know what she herself would be capable of if backed into a corner—she'd never had to find out. But she suspected she knew what Dylan would do. The world had been backing her into a corner for years now, and she thought Peter Miles might be the final proof of what Dylan was capable of.

What about me? What am I capable of?

She'd find out soon enough.

"Well, one of us has to keep it together, I guess." Isabel's laugh was mirthless.

"We're all keeping it together," Dylan said. "Because it won't work if we don't."

"Of course. You're right."

"Anything else?"

"What if we can't get away with it?"

Dylan blanched, as if Isabel had said something insulting.

"We will. It's a solid plan, Isa."

"You're not worried?"

"Don't think about it. Just think about this one thing you have to do, not the rest. That's what me and Priya are for. I'll worry about after. Okay?"

"I'll try," Isabel said.

"See you Friday at my place? We'll run through the plan in detail then. But the whole thing's solid, okay?"

"Okay. Well, thanks for the book."

"See ya."

Isabel crossed to her car and climbed inside. Carefully, she backed out. Dylan was standing near the trunk of her own car, bathed in the glow of the afternoon sun. She waved.

You make one decision, then the next, and they all build on top of one another toward something big.

As she drove, she mentally replayed the conversation with Dylan. She would try not to think about the big picture. About after. Not yet. The details were what mattered.

One decision at a time.

Like planning a wedding.

The topic had come up again that morning—the third time in a week—as Paul was getting ready for work. Isabel knew he was trying to be patient, to give her space to mourn, but a year-long engagement without even the hint of a date was starting to wear on him.

Her hands tightened on the steering wheel as she remembered what Beck had said about Isabel and Paul's meandering engagement weeks before she'd died.

"Have you stopped to think maybe there's a reason you don't want to marry Paul?" Beck asked. "I mean, not yet. If ever? You shouldn't feel obligated to someone just because you've been together a long time, Isa. There's no blueprint that says you *have* to marry them."

At the time, it'd seemed like an insult to her and Paul's relationship. They loved each other. They'd been together for years, knew each other's quirks, loved each other's families. What else was there? Shouldn't it be natural to settle down, get married, have kids?

And yet, every time she tried to plan out some aspect of the wedding, Isabel hit an invisible wall.

She pulled into a spot at the university and idled for a moment, listening to her car cool down. Work awaited her: stacks of papers to grade in her office, a study group lecture to prepare for tomorrow. Yet her thoughts lingered on Beck.

She'd always been so sure of herself, of her choices. Whether she was climbing a mountain in some far-off place or dealing with a difficult patient, Beck had always taken on life with her heart wide open. She thought that the world—its people, places, possibilities—was there for her to explore in the same way it was for Beck's two older brothers.

Maybe that's where everything went horribly wrong, Isabel thought. Beck believed the world would treat her with the same respect and consideration Luke and Sam always received.

And *he* killed her for it.

It was a harsh reminder of why she had to do this. Isabel gazed out the windshield, willing herself not to cry. It was a mistake to trust the world too much. When you're young, you feel invincible. You can do anything. Nothing can harm you. That's what they claimed anyway, but Isabel knew it was only true for boys. Most girls were fully aware of their vulnerabilities and the dangers they faced in the world early on. And even though they were armed with that knowledge, even when they knew they were living in a world that, at its core, hated women, it wasn't enough to save them.

She wished Beck had understood this too.

But it didn't matter. It still wouldn't have been enough to save her.

CHAPTER
SEVENTEEN

DYLAN

Dylan sat opposite Bree, trying hard not to think about the rope and gag in her car. The taqueria, housed inside a small neon yellow building with blue trim, was bustling. It wasn't because of the sign boasting BEST TACOS NORTH OF SAN ANTONIO—though for all she knew, it could be true—but because the Lonestar Drive-In was less than a mile down the road. Everyone was filling up before the Clint Eastwood double feature.

"So, Dylan." Bree took another taco from the basket and motioned with it in her direction. "If there was one moment from your past you could relive, what would it be?"

It was the first question she'd asked that didn't seem intended to fill the silence. They'd been verbally circling for the last half hour, two wary cats trying to decide if they liked each other enough to get any closer. Now it seemed like Bree was making her approach. Dylan preferred when they were keeping the conversation superficial.

"Who'd want to relive anything in this dead-end town?" Dylan said, only half joking.

Across the road, the sun was dipping out of sight behind Jimmy's Car and Truck Repair. It was the best time of the day. When the heat made its retreat and the wide Texas sky dimmed to a softer blue, tendrils of wispy clouds sown through it. There was a nostalgia to the way the landscape mellowed in the dying light; for a moment it was calendar-spread worthy.

Sometimes it's not so bad, Dylan thought.

The last few rays glinted off the windshield of the tire-less brown Cadillac—ironically propped up on cement blocks beneath the word TIRES spray-painted in red on the side of Jimmy's—briefly transforming it into a spotlight.

Shielding her eyes, Dylan answered finally, "I don't know. I'd probably pick a time when I was a teenager and all my friends were still around. Before anyone . . . moved on."

"Moved on?"

The question was an offering, hesitantly laid between them on the picnic table. For a second, Dylan debated telling her everything. About Beck. About *him*. Then she thought of the rope in her trunk and instead said with a shrug, "People always move on. One way or another."

They fell quiet, staring out at the weed-cracked concrete bathed in gold. Off in the distance, mesquite trees bent their mangled limbs to the coming dusk. The light snagged on a nearby water tower rising on spindly legs like an immense insect keeping watch.

"It's a nice sunset," Dylan said, both to break the silence and to steer the conversation back to a lighter topic.

"It is nice. One might even say romantic." Bree nudged Dylan's foot.

The two lengths of rope pulsed at the back of her mind like lit-up mosquito coils. She should have dropped the supplies off at home beforehand. But Dylan had driven two towns over to buy them and by the time she started making her way back, she was already running late. So, she left it all in the car. It wasn't like Bree would go rooting around in her trunk anyway.

Except Dylan was so nervous about the date that she didn't remember the gag. Not until Bree opened the car door and, lifting the plastic bag with the mouthguards, bandana, and duct tape from the passenger seat, asked, "Where should I put this?"

Dylan wanted to smack herself for the slipup. She'd shoved the bag out of sight beneath the seat, but it was too late. The date felt tainted. Peter Miles hovered at the edge of it, preemptively haunting them both.

It was supposed to be a break from thinking about *him,* about what she and Priya and Isabel had to do. But she couldn't seem to stop. Not even when the distraction was a beautiful woman wearing maroon lipstick and a black, long-sleeved top that Dylan just wanted to take off.

Chair. Rope. Gag. Wire. Knife.

Well, it was two things off her list at least. She had the rope and the gag.

"Have you ever thought about moving?" Bree asked. "Starting over somewhere else?"

The question caught Dylan off guard, reeling her thoughts back to the present so fast she felt a mental whiplash. Overhead, a string of fairy lights stretching from the corner of the taqueria to a post at the end of the lot blinked on.

Picking at the label on her beer bottle, Dylan said, "I'm not really the moving type. Started over plenty as a kid, not interested so much in doing it now."

"No regrets you need to run away from?" A breeze caught Bree's curls, sending a few fluttering across her face.

Was there an unspoken question there? Dylan wasn't sure, so she laughed and answered, "No. Nothing that'll make me want to leave, anyway."

"Hm." There was a pause while Bree finished the last few bites of her taco. "That's good. Hopefully I don't end up being one such regret."

The gentle nudge of her sneaker against Dylan's boot made her smile. "I don't think that's likely, Bree-Like-the-Cheese."

Their eyes locked. The desire to lean across the table and kiss Bree was so strong it almost physically hurt. But Dylan couldn't. Not here, with so many people around.

Bree seemed to read her mind. "Do you want to get out of here? Maybe come back to my place for a nightcap? Or"—she glanced to where the sun was rapidly sinking below the horizon—"an evening-cap? That's a thing, right?"

"What about the movies?" Dylan asked before downing the last of her beer.

"There's always next time."

In the car, "Runaway Train" came on the radio and Bree's hand slipped into hers like it'd always belonged there. Dylan knew it was a mistake. There would be no next time. No shared jokes. No first or last fight. No breakups and makeups. Tonight was it.

The end of the line before they'd even begun.

The thought unearthed an ache in Dylan's chest. But it didn't stop her from driving Bree home. From following her up the steps. From tangling her fingers in her hair and kissing her just inside the door.

They went at each other like they were running out of time. Later, as they lay in bed, Dylan's mind drifted back to the supplies in her car. She pictured Peter—probably sitting in Aces of Spades right now—waiting, without knowing it, to die.

Bree shifted against her side.

"You know, Dylan, I like you. A lot." She sounded half asleep. "I really hope you stick around."

Regret enclosed Dylan like a steel cage. Without moving, she felt herself begin to withdraw, to pull away. Luckily, Bree didn't seem to expect an answer because she had already fallen asleep.

CHAPTER EIGHTEEN

PRIYA

They sat like three strangers, the only sound in the room the ticking of the grandfather clock. In his dog bed in the corner, Echo sighed and changed positions again, his brown eyes alert. Their restlessness was catching.

There wasn't anything left to say. Now it was a question of doing. You couldn't go backward, except in your mind.

Priya did, mentally rewinding to how it all began. To when Beck stopped and asked about the festive chalk designs she was drawing on her parents' driveway that Diwali, all those years ago. Soon after, Priya met Isabel. She'd seemed almost like an extension of Beck, and at first, Priya was jealous. Then, later, Dylan—sent by child services to live with an aunt—had joined their class halfway through the seventh grade. One day, after facing off during a heated dodgeball game, Beck pulled Dylan into her orbit too.

Thirteen was the formative year. Somehow, the timing was just right for four girls from very different cultures and backgrounds to come together. Now, Priya wondered if their friendship would finally disintegrate. Beck had been the thread uniting them, but the thread was fraying, their friendship straining at the seams. Revenge was postponing the inevitable.

Or maybe revenge would save them. Bond them in a different way.

"Are we ready?" Dylan said.

Silence wound its way through the room, tense as a viper watching its prey. Priya felt as if the plan were tattooed on her. An unspoken oath they couldn't back out of.

Dylan's blue eyes bored into them. "Remember why we're doing this. Who we're doing this for. He stalked her. He threatened her. He was the last person seen with her."

"He had motive," Priya added. "And his girlfriend gave a false alibi."

"He killed Beck." A fissure ran through Isabel's voice as she said her name.

I should have brought wine. Screw Dylan. Drinking while the three of them talked wouldn't make Priya incapable of remembering the plan. It wasn't as if she couldn't control herself and needed Dylan to manage her.

"The plan is solid." Dylan's tone was neutral, as if she were discussing something as simple as deciding to order Chinese takeaway instead of pizza. "We just have to trust each other. If everyone keeps their cool and does what they're supposed to, we'll be fine. We won't get caught as long as we follow the plan."

Priya's eyes met Dylan's. She seemed to be waiting for a confirmation.

"Follow the plan," Priya said finally.

Isabel nodded. "Follow the plan."

A hint of a smile tugged at the corners of Dylan's lips, but her expression was blank as she said, "Follow the plan."

Priya let out a long breath. "Now let's go get a drink."

Dylan's eyebrows lifted. "I got something just for this."

She rose and disappeared into the hall. When she returned, she held three glasses stacked inside one another in one hand, a bottle of unopened liquor in the other. After setting them all in the center of the table, she took a seat on the sofa next to Priya.

"Don Julio," Priya read off the bottle.

"Don Julio," Isabel corrected her, softening the *j* into an *h*. "Tequila?"

Dylan nodded. "Beck's preferred poison, remember?"

"I thought you didn't keep liquor in your house," Priya said.

"It's kind of a special occasion, isn't it?"

"Ah yes, no more special occasion than a man's impending murder."

Dylan grimaced. "You know what I mean. I thought it'd be good to pour one out in her memory."

She filled each glass with a finger of liquor and passed them around. For a moment they were quiet, each woman hovering at the edge of her seat as if waiting for a race to start. Dylan cleared her throat and lifted her glass, they did the same.

"For Beck," she said.

"For Beck," they repeated.

The three of them clinked their glasses together and threw back the shot.

CHAPTER
NINETEEN

PRIYA

Before

Priya rapped on the door, her heart pounding double time to each knock.

A group of crickets harmonized nearby, signaling dusk's arrival. The sky was transforming from blue to the tempting pink and yellow of melting sherbet. So rich she could have dipped a spoon in and tasted it.

But something marred it all, a fly in an ice-cream vat. Glancing over one shoulder, she clocked the man in the car and turned back to Beck's door. Priya had first noticed him sitting there when she'd pulled up. It was too far away for her to make out his features or see if he was watching her, but she felt unsettled, nonetheless.

She knocked again. A moment later the door swung open to reveal Beck dressed in shorts and a Berkeley sweatshirt. Confusion rippled across her flushed face.

"Priya?" Behind her, a Doublemint commercial played out in silence. "What are you doing here? Is something wrong?"

"I should ask you that," Priya said, stepping inside. "You haven't called me back. I've left like a hundred messages."

"I forgot to check my messages." Beck yawned as she crossed the room.

"I can see that." Priya eyed the answering machine on the side table by the pink corduroy couch. A red light—the alert for waiting messages—blinked periodically, like a beating heart. "I've paged you too."

"*Want some wine?*" *Beck asked, motioning to the open bottle on the coffee table.*

"*Can't. I have an early shift tomorrow.*"

"*Suit yourself.*" *In a move that seemed distinctly Isabellian, Beck wrapped herself in a throw so only her head and the hand holding the wineglass peeked out.*

"*If you're trying to go full hermit, I have some news for you.*" *Priya took a seat at the opposite end of the couch.* "*We're all going to keep bugging you, so you'll have to move to a remote forest or something if you really want us to leave you alone.*"

"*That's the next part of the plan, once I figure out how to make my own clothes out of fern fronds.*"

The phone rang. Beck stiffened and twisted away to lift the receiver from the side table. "*Hello?*" *There was a beat of silence, then she repeated,* "*Hello?*"

"*What was that?*" *Priya asked when she hung up.*

Beck didn't move, her back rigid as an iron pole.

"*Beck?*"

She turned, smiling. "*Nothing. I've just been getting these weird prank phone calls.*"

"*That's annoying.*"

"*Hm.*" *She took a sip of wine.*

"*So? Why are you ignoring me?*" *Priya asked, determined to keep the conversation on track.* "*No one's heard from you in over a week.*"

Something flitted across Beck's features. It came and went so quickly that Priya didn't have time to identify its meaning.

"*Honestly? The breakup is taking a lot out of me,*" *she said.*

"*Is?*" *When she didn't answer, Priya added,* "*Oh my god, you're still with Peter?*"

"*It's complicated, Pri. Breakups aren't instantaneous.*"

"*Uh, you two barely dated. How long has it been, two months?*"

"*He just . . .*" *She paused, as if searching for the right words to say. This was also unlike her. Beck used words the way a rich person spent money: effortlessly and without thought.* "*He got attached, I guess. He's having a hard time letting go.*"

"*Typical.*"

She glanced at her sharply. "*Meaning?*"

"That you're too cavalier about relationships, Beck. Do you ever think about how hurtful this is for the other person involved?"

"Like you have the right to lecture me on relationships and breakups."

Priya recoiled like she'd been slapped. "Beck—"

"You should leave, Pri. You've checked up on me. Everything's fine. The last thing I need right now is judgment from you."

"I'm not judging you," Priya said.

Beck kept her eyes trained on the television screen. Silence inserted itself between them like an unwelcome guest.

The phone rang again, making them both start. Beck quickly lifted the receiver, then hung up without bringing it to her ear. After a moment's thought, she took it off the hook.

A suspicion announced itself in Priya's brain. "Was that . . . was that Peter?"

"Just go, Pri." She pressed her hand to her throat, as if protecting it from a potential blow.

The faint, steady hum of the dial tone was an ominous soundtrack to Priya's whirring thoughts as she let herself out.

CHAPTER TWENTY

DYLAN

Relief and repulsion wound together in Dylan's stomach when Peter Miles walked into Aces on Friday. She'd been worried that tonight of all nights he might decide to go elsewhere to drink. Everything was timed down to the minute, and it would all be for nothing if he didn't show.

But here he was, meandering his way toward the bar like a minnow swimming upstream. He slid onto the stool opposite her. "Hi, gorgeous."

"The usual?" Talking to him felt like crawling into a sewage pipe.

"Yep. And pour something for yourself. I'm buying."

She didn't respond. Instead, Dylan focused on fixing his drinks and what she needed to do next. Priya had given her some pills to crush into his beer, but that would come later, after he'd had a few.

Kurt Cobain sang over the speakers.

With the lights out, it's less dangerous

Here we are now, entertain us

It was Jason's selection, his latest attempt at bringing Aces into the modern era. Her manager complained that Dylan played too many songs from the 1970s. Two decades and several lifetimes out of date, he'd said.

"Where's yours?" Peter asked when she set the beer and shot in front of him.

"I don't drink on the job."

"Aw, come on." He put his palms together in mock prayer. "Just this once. I'm celebrating today."

Down out of sight beneath the bar, her fingers curled around the rim of the sink.

"What's the special occasion?" It was a struggle to keep her tone steady.

He leaned closer as if sharing a delicate secret, and she recoiled slightly. His face glistened with sweat, his hair hung limp against his cheeks.

"I'm getting my job back." Peter Miles grinned, like he'd just told a funny joke. "Got the call today."

Her vision telescoped inward, his face in central smoky focus. The bar sounds dimmed to a distant hum. Each breath felt loud as a cannon shot as she struggled to halt the spiral.

"I'll be right back," Dylan managed to say.

Her hip hit the corner as she rounded the bar. At the door, she ran into someone coming in.

"Hey, watch it!" they snapped, but she didn't stop.

The cool air on Dylan's face calmed her almost immediately. Hugging her torso, she leaned against the wall and took a few deep breaths. She wanted to slap herself for reacting the way she did. Hopefully he was too caught up in his self-important good news to notice, but it'd been stupid of her just the same. Someone else could have seen the conversation, seen her reaction. They could remember it and later, after everything, bring it up to the cops.

The door opened outward next to her. When it swung closed again Bree was standing there. Three lines formed on her forehead as her eyes found Dylan.

"Are you okay?" she asked. "Did something happen?"

Shit. She'd forgotten about Bree drinking Kozel at the end of the bar. *Stupid. Stupid. Stupid.*

Thinking fast, Dylan forced a smile and said, "What? No. I just get a little nauseous around the first day of my . . . well, you know. Just needed some fresh air."

She couldn't read in Bree's brown eyes whether she believed her or not.

"Oh, okay. It's just that I've seen that man in there before. He . . ." She stopped and glanced at the closed bar door, as if she could look right through it. Goosebumps rose on Dylan's skin when Bree moved closer and gently took her wrist. She caught the faint whiff of lavender coming off Bree's hair. "He didn't say or do something, did he?"

It was kind of sweet, how much she seemed to care. Dylan wondered exactly what Bree would do if it were something as simple as an inappropriate comment.

"Nah. It's just being a woman fucking sucks sometimes." To further the point, she placed an arm over her stomach.

"Right." Bree nodded. "Anything I can do to help? I might have some Tylenol in here somewhere." She hoisted up her purse and hovered a hand over the opening. "Happy to excavate if necessary."

"Thanks, but I'll survive. Just need a minute."

"Okay, well." She paused. "About time I head off, I guess." Looping her arm through her purse strap, Bree lingered a moment, as if waiting for something, then started to walk away.

Dylan's mind raced. She couldn't let this be the last impression Bree took away from tonight. She needed to overlay the memory with something else.

"You like breakfast?" she called.

Bree stopped and turned. "Depends. Why?" she asked, backtracking to stand in front of Dylan.

"There's this diner. The Coffee Pot. I like having breakfast there on Sundays." She took a step closer.

Her eyebrows rose. "I think I know the place."

"Next time we go to the movies, maybe you could come to my house after. Then we could have breakfast at the Coffee Pot the next morning." Another step and she was inches from her. Bree didn't move back, as good a sign as any. "We can hold hands under the table. Play footsie. All that cute high-school bullshit."

"Hm, subtle." Her expression was serious, as if she were gazing up at a cathedral ceiling. "But you're too cool for school. Aren't you, Dylan?"

"Not always."

She tucked a strand of curly, dark hair behind Bree's ear. Then, just to be sure, Dylan kissed her.

CHAPTER
TWENTY-ONE

PRIYA

Let yourselves in.
   Change clothes.
   Leave lights and stereo on.
   Exit back.
   Pick up car.
Dylan had detailed the morbid to-do list so often—as if afraid early onset dementia might strike and cause them to forget everything—that it felt permanently branded onto Priya's brain. She thought of what came next. Isabel would drop her off two blocks from what they now called The Workshop. She'd wait in the dark house for Isabel to arrive with him. Dylan would join later, after she'd finished her shift, driven home, and followed the same trajectory down the back alley. Isabel would pick Dylan up at a halfway point between her house and The Workshop. This would give Priya time to set up the IV bag.

As they waited, Priya mentally reviewed the list again. The practicality of it calmed her. Isabel sat on the love seat opposite, dressed in a black turtleneck and matching jeans. She gave off the air of a distressed mime, her hands unable to stay still. One second, Isabel was fidgeting with her turtleneck collar, the next, she was smoothing back her hair. Looking down at her own getup—navy sweatshirt and black jeans—Priya mentally drew a line through Task Number Two: *Change clothes*.

The grandfather clock struck the hour, and like two distant ships finally making contact, Priya's and Isabel's gazes slowly collided.

"I guess it's time," Isabel said, a slight tremor in her voice. They rose, pulling on their black gloves.

From his bed in the corner, Echo lifted his head to watch them leave. In the doorway, Priya paused and waited for him to lie back down and close his eyes, then followed Isabel down the hall. She'd taken him on a long walk earlier to tire him out. Echo would sleep the night away while the three of them . . . Priya shook her head, forcing the thought back. She shouldn't get ahead of herself.

Instead, she struck off Number Three and Number Four in quick succession as they made their way outside, across Dylan's backyard, and stepped through the gate. It opened onto an unlit alley that ran between two rows of houses facing out at different streets.

As they made their way down the passageway, Priya kept looking from side to side. What if a neighbor happened to glance out their window and see the two of them lurking below? Another reason for their dark clothing, Priya reminded herself. They'd be hard to spot. And most people were eating dinner or slack-jawed in front of their TVs at this hour. Still, it wasn't until they stepped out of the alley and onto the road that Priya exhaled fully. She'd seen no one.

They hiked the mile to Isabel's cousin's house in silence. She was in Nebraska for three days with her husband, attending a college friend's wedding. They lived on three acres of land in an as-yet undeveloped neighborhood—another lucky happenstance. No one, not even the car's owners, would notice it was gone.

Isabel disappeared into the house and returned a moment later with the key. They climbed into the car and she paused, her hand resting on the ignition.

"Let's go," Priya said. Impatience gnawed at her like a ravenous dog on a bone.

Half-turning, Isabel laid a hand on her arm.

"Priya, I—" She stopped abruptly.

"What's wrong?" The question had a sharp edge.

"Could you—could you come with me?" Isabel asked. "To pick him up?"

Her eyes were wide, her pupils like bottomless black wells.

"That's not the plan," Priya said, her mind racing.

"It's just . . . I don't want to go alone."

The plea in her voice alarmed Priya. Could Isabel be trusted to follow through? Would she chicken out if forced to go on her own?

"It won't really change the plan, right?" Isabel added. "And Dylan doesn't have to know."

This deception from Isabel of all people was unsettling. But she was right. It wouldn't change the plan. Not really. It was essential to get him to The Workshop, no matter what. Even Dylan would agree. If he was as drunk as Dylan claimed he'd be, it was unlikely he'd notice Priya in the car anyway.

"Fine," Priya said finally. "We'll go together."

Isabel let out a long exhale and put the car in reverse. "Okay." Then, more softly, "Thank you."

Anticipation wound around Priya like a too-tight corset as they drove. She calmed herself by rearranging the to-do list.

Pick up car.

Go get him.

Take him to The Workshop.

Together.

By the time they pulled into Aces and Isabel backed into a spot at the end of the lot, Priya's entire body was steeled with resolve.

They sat in silence, eyes trained on the bar door.

"There he is," Isabel said after a while.

Priya leaned forward and pressed a palm to the dash. A breath caught in her throat at the sight of him. Everything seemed to acquire an aching clarity, as if someone had taken Windex and a newspaper to her vision.

"This is a bad idea," she said suddenly.

Hand on the clutch, Isabel froze. "What?"

"He won't get in with both of us here. He'll be suspicious."

Already, she had the passenger door open, one foot out.

"I'll wait here," she told Isabel. "Pull forward, and once he's in the car I'll get in the front. The child locks are on the back doors, right? If he panics, I'll—" She held up the Taser.

Eyes wide, Isabel nodded. Gently, Priya eased the door closed so it held but didn't quite click shut. Then she patted the roof of the car twice and Isabel pulled away.

Pressed back in the shadows, she watched her inch forward and come to a stop a ways from the bar door.

At first, it seemed like he wouldn't notice Isabel, and might not get in the car. Then Isabel called something to him that Priya couldn't make out. Whatever it was, it got his attention. She felt relief inch in as he approached and leaned down to look in the window. After a few moments of back-and-forth, he climbed into the back seat.

The car lingered for a moment, the smoke from the exhaust painting a white swirl in the autumn night. Then, slowly, carefully, it began to reverse. When the car was nearly opposite, Priya stepped forward to peek in the passenger window. At the motion of Isabel's hand, she climbed inside.

A small snore floated forward, and Priya risked a glance back. Peter Miles was on his side, fast asleep.

"He passed out right away," Isabel whispered.

Geez, Dylan filled him up good.

He stank of liquor and cigarette smoke, but they didn't dare roll down the windows to air out the car. She could have scraped the tension away with her fingernails, like a thick layer of ice on glass. There were a thousand different ways this might go wrong, any one of which could unravel their whole plan with a simple tug of a stray thread.

She had a Taser, Priya reminded herself. And so did Isabel. This was the riskiest part of the plan and Dylan had gone over the possible scenarios again and again. Make sure the child locks are on. If he gets rowdy, play nice, pull over, and tase him. She'd even made Isabel act out various potential situations. Sitting in two dining chairs, lined up one behind the other, they'd practiced what Isabel would do if he lunged forward. If he grabbed her arm. If he got angry.

But the drive was uneventful, almost anticlimactic. Still, Priya didn't loosen her grip on the Taser, not even when Isabel clicked off the headlights to turn down the street toward The Workshop. She drove slowly, trying to keep the noise to a minimum, then pulled around out of sight behind the house and parked.

Priya twisted to get another look at the back seat. He was barely visible in the dark, his mouth slightly ajar.

They climbed out and stood on each side, eyes locked for a few moments over the car's roof. Then Priya nodded and moved around to the trunk while Isabel opened the door.

"Sir?" she said. "Sir? We're here."

"Huh?" He bolted upright so suddenly that Priya jumped.

To her credit, Isabel barely flinched.

"We're here," she repeated.

"Oh, yeah. Okay." Scooting sideways, he put one unsteady foot out, then the other. "I'm not usually like this," he said, the words melting into one another like warm candle wax. A pained, snuffling sound spilled from his mouth.

Is he . . . crying?

She and Isabel exchanged shocked looks.

"I'm not a bad guy." He rose unsteadily and propped himself against the open car door. "I'm not—" He spotted Priya and stopped with a gulp. "Who the hell are you?"

"That's just my friend. Um, Alice," Isabel said.

If the situation weren't so serious, Priya would have rolled her eyes.

"She's just helping me out," Isabel reassured him.

His gaze landed back on her and the hairs at the nape of her neck stood upright. How did he go from sobbing to leering so quickly?

We should have tied his hands.

He stared, and Priya felt a moment of triumph. What he thought was going to happen was so different from the reality. But then his gaze moved past her to the house looming beyond like a dozing monster.

His eyes widened. "This isn't— Wait. This isn't."

It happened fast. He shoved Isabel and stumbled away. The blood pounding in Priya's ears drowned out the sound Isabel made when she tumbled to the ground. He ran, fell on his knees, then managed to get to his feet again. Priya's body sprang into action before her brain had time to catch up. She sprinted after him toward the water's edge. It seemed unlikely he'd try to swim away, but the longer he was out of their grasp, the higher his chances of escape.

Get him to The Workshop.

Get him to The Workshop.

Get him to The Workshop.

She homed in on him like a cocked rifle.

His drunken movements were too sporadic for him to move fast, and she caught up to him quickly. Only then did she realize her hand was empty; she'd lost the Taser. Priya hesitated and looked around, then picked up a rock and held it tight in her fist. He was still stumbling toward where the reeds marked the hem of gray water and didn't seem to notice Priya come up behind him. She hit him across the back of his head as hard as she could. He jolted forward onto his hands and knees, then tipped onto his side.

Please be unconscious. It was the first clear thought she'd had in the last fifteen seconds.

"Is he dead?" Isabel panted behind her.

"Help me," she whispered. "Quick, before he wakes up."

If he wakes up. She wasn't certain how to answer Isabel's question.

Priya threw the rock as far as she could, and it landed in the pond with a soft plunk. Isabel looped her arms through his armpit and Priya did the same on the other side. They dragged him back toward the house, grunting with the effort. It seemed to take an eternity to get there, though it was probably only a few minutes. He hadn't made it far.

Inside was trickier. His clothes kept snagging on the splintering floorboards, and at one point he groaned as if he were coming to, and they both froze. But then his head sank back into his chest, and they relaxed. He was alive and they were almost done with the hard part. Together, they hoisted him into the chair and began to tie him down.

Their to-do list had dwindled. They were so close.

Insert the IV.

Wait for Dylan.

And, most important of all:

Kill Peter Miles.

CHAPTER TWENTY-TWO

TEXAS STATE PENITENTIARY
Fall 1996

My cellmate, Sonia, and I pass the time by making lists of things we miss.

"Chocolate chip ice cream," she says.

"Diner coffee," I say.

"Bluebells."

"Bathtubs."

She laughs at my last one.

"A halfway decent library," Sonia says, thumbing the worn copy of The Count of Monte Cristo *she borrowed from the prison library. "With more than crappy self-help and old books."*

"Sunsets," I say.

"That's a good one." Then something catches in her voice when she adds, "My kids."

"I'm sorry." There's a long pause. Then I say, "Trees."

I avoid speaking aloud the ones that matter. The ones that cause a physical ache—as if someone is turning my heart on a spit.

"You know what I really miss?" Sonia asks. "Chilaquiles. And Chap-Stick." She waves her makeshift paper fan harder. "And AC."

"Me too." We share a laugh.

But memory is cruel. It doesn't care how much you want to forget. I'll be digging through my breakfast checking for roaches, or lying on my bunk trying to sleep, or waiting to use the stationary cycle in the gym, and suddenly, the spit turns. The pain is so real, I want to drop to the floor and curl up into a ball.

The feel of fur beneath my palm.

The spit turns.

A good kiss.

The spit turns.

Her.

The spit turns.

It feels like a heart attack, but somehow worse. Because I know it won't kill me.

CHAPTER
TWENTY-THREE

ISABEL

They could hear him in the next room. He was grunting with the effort, the chair groaning with every movement he made. For a second, Isabel was afraid maybe the restraints weren't tight enough. That he'd get away a second time.

"How—how do you feel?" she asked Dylan.

"Fucking great." Dylan's voice was layered with excitement. "Fucking amazing. This is it."

Maybe she'd be a little less excited if she had been here the last hour with her and Priya. Dylan had gotten the easiest part of the plan, Isabel realized now. She finished up her shift, went home, and Isabel picked her up at the agreed upon time and place. Meanwhile, she and Priya had to tie *him* down, jerking every few seconds when it seemed like he'd wake up, ready for a fight.

It wasn't resentment Isabel was feeling. Not really. She just wanted Dylan to seem less thrilled. Less like a kid set loose in a candy shop. Regardless of what he'd done, they were about to take a life.

"Should we get started?" Priya asked softly.

They each pulled on one of the black ski masks Dylan had brought. The wool was tight around Isabel's nose, and she felt a flutter of tiny threads against her nostrils when she breathed in and out. She rubbed her nose with the back of her hand, but a few seconds later it was itching again.

Isabel's pulse skipped, tripped, and ran.

Squaring her shoulders, she took a deep breath. It was all surreal, as if it were a performance and she was waiting in the wings for her cue to enter the stage. Dylan set the flashlight on the ground and grabbed her hand. After a beat, Priya grasped the other. They stood in a circle holding hands and for a long moment said nothing, just looked at one another. Isabel sought reassurance in Dylan's and Priya's eyes. What did the others see as they looked back?

"Ready?" Dylan asked, squeezing her hand. Isabel nodded. Dylan's eyes turned to Priya. "Pri?"

"Yeah."

"For Beck," Dylan whispered.

"For Beck," they both whispered back.

They lined up in front of the dilapidated wooden door, first Dylan, then Priya, and last of all Isabel. In front of her, Priya's fingers were tapping out a nervous symphony against her leg. Isabel reached forward, grasped her wrist, and stilled it.

Eyes on Dylan's back, she waited. But Dylan seemed frozen, one gloved hand resting on the door latch. Had she changed her mind? Gotten cold feet?

Inside the room, the chair scraping the floor coupled with his grunts grew more desperate. Dylan's shoulders lifted a few inches and dropped, as if she was bracing herself. Then she pressed down on the latch and pushed the door inward. The bottom ground against the floor like nails on a chalkboard, and the hairs on the back of Isabel's neck stood up.

The noise silenced him for the several seconds it took them to file inside. After Isabel stepped through, Dylan scraped the door shut again. His eyes were wide, traveling between each of them, trying to decipher from their masked faces the answer to a difficult equation.

Dylan stepped forward and said, "Hi, gorgeous. So happy you could join us."

PART TWO

THE DETECTIVE

CHAPTER
TWENTY-FOUR

An electric tension was in the air when Detective Righetti walked into the precinct on Monday morning. Something was going on. She noticed the glances between her coworkers like a football lobbed back and forth across the room. Detective Taylor caught her eye and glared.

Always a pleasure to see you too, Taylor.

She continued to her desk. It was best to ignore the looks from the male detectives. If they weren't sexualizing her, they were dismissing her. Dismissing her because of her appearance, her gender, her rank. It never stopped bothering Righetti, but she'd gotten acclimatized to it. She'd learned how to behave to survive.

But this stare from Taylor felt different. Like he was angry about more than just breathing the same air as a, oh horror of horrors, *lady detective.* Placing her travel mug on her desk, Righetti made the mistake of looking again. His eyes were still aimed in her direction.

Just ignore the baboons. Do not engage with the baboons.

It was too hard to resist. She forced herself to meet his eye, adding in a wave for good measure.

That's right, I've got your number, you incompetent jerk.

She was too far away to see clearly, but Taylor's nostrils seemed to flare. His face reddened. It did the trick, though; he looked away.

A small, utterly pointless victory, she thought wearily. A cinnamon roll sat on a paper plate in the center of her desk, a sign her partner was already here. She'd lost enough weight in the past few months for it to be noticeable. At least to Mike O'Malley. He hadn't said anything, just started bringing her food every day like she was an abandoned stray dog.

But she couldn't see her well-meaning partner anywhere in the bullpen and her pulse quickened. Was this a trick? Maybe one of the other detectives had done something to the roll and left it here, hoping she'd assume it was from Mike.

The phone trilled, jerking her attention away.

"Righetti," she said into the receiver, still eyeing the pastry.

"Good morning, Detective." It was the secretary. "The chief would like to see you in his office right away, please."

Her shoulders relaxed a little. That probably explained where Mike was.

"Sure. Thanks, Laura."

Back on her feet, she left the roll where it was but took her mug. It was safer to keep it with her and from the way Laura sounded, this meeting would probably require coffee to power through. She wove her way among the desks to the chief's office. The entrance was in the hall, but one of his windows overlooked the open space where the detectives had their workstations. This morning, the blinds were down. At the exit to the hallway, she took a sharp right, then another, and knocked on the door.

"Come in," the chief called from the other side.

She pushed the door open. There was Mike, seated across from the chief, a cup of coffee clutched in his hammy fist. The back of her neck warmed. She knew it probably wasn't the case, but it felt like the two of them had been talking about her before she came in.

"Have a seat," Chief Hunter said.

"Mike." She nodded, and he nodded back.

"We've been waiting for you," the chief said, as if she were hours late.

She glanced at her watch. It was six minutes past eight o'clock.

"Well," Righetti said, "what's going on?"

"Have you heard anything since getting in this morning?"

"I just made it to my desk when you called me in here." She looked at Mike. "What time did you get in?"

"Seven-thirty."

This was alarming news. Mike never voluntarily arrived early to anything. Like he always said, he wasn't paid enough for that.

"Officer Morales called me," he added, as if that ought to explain everything.

She quickly cycled through her mental storage of the people working at the station. Ricky Morales. A police officer. Aiming to make detective next year. She'd done bereavement duty with him at Rebecca Grant's funeral.

"I tried calling you. Didn't get an answer," Mike said.

You could have paged me. She didn't voice the thought aloud. Her partner's aversion to new technology was like a cat's hate for water. She wasn't sure he even knew how to use his own pager. What would happen when cell phones became standard at the precinct—an event that surely wasn't too far off—she couldn't imagine. By the time she finally got him on board with cell phones the world would probably have moved on to holograms.

"Why would Officer Morales call you?" she asked.

Chief Hunter sighed and sat back in his chair, placing his elbows on the armrests and interlocking his fingers. "Peter Miles was found dead early this morning."

A burst of excitement, quickly followed by the cold twist of disappointment.

"I see," she said, taking care to keep her voice level. "What happened?"

A drunk-driving accident would be her first guess. It'd be in character for him to get away with murder, only to wrap his car around a pole.

"It's questionable."

Her eyebrows rose.

The chief sighed again. "That's an understatement. It's a homicide."

"Peter Miles was murdered?"

Both men nodded.

Now Righetti's heart was sprinting. On instinct, she flashed back to the night before, trying to remember where she was and what she'd been doing. Alibiing herself.

"Listen, I just had Santos and Taylor in here and they told me they were about to make an official arrest," the chief said.

"Of Peter Miles?"

"Of Peter Miles."

I'd believe it when I see it.

Objectively, Righetti knew she should have wanted him to go to prison. Make his way through the system—a pinball lobbed back and forth in the game called "American Justice"—until he was chipping his days away on a life sentence. Or the big jackpot in the game: death row, Peter's final years spent putting in appeals and trying to eke out just a little more time.

Although she was against the death penalty on moral grounds, for him she would have made an exception.

But over the past several months Righetti had come to realize that even prison time was long odds. It'd been an open secret that Peter Miles should have been more than just a person of interest. She'd watched in silent frustration as the two senior detectives on the case—Santos and Taylor—pursued every other possible lead. It was as if the two of them couldn't accept that a fellow cop would do something so horrific. Or, more likely, they didn't want to.

To make things worse, the chief had sidelined her in the investigation of Rebecca Grant's death. He'd claimed that the case was too high profile for a junior detective like her, even though she was the only female detective on the force. She didn't know why this surprised her. The Boys-in-Blue environment was as difficult to break into as an A-list country club.

And now Peter Miles was dead.

Murdered.

She couldn't say he didn't deserve it.

"You can imagine how pissed the two of 'em are that he was murdered before an official arrest could happen," Chief Hunter continued.

"How did he die?" she asked.

"Looks planned. Premeditated."

Righetti felt clearheaded, even as her pulse fluttered like a panicked bird. She was ready for this.

"A revenge killing?" she asked.

"We should talk to the family first." Mike, who'd been silent and serene as a Buddha statue, spoke up.

"We?" She looked from one to the other.

Chief Hunter nodded. "It's your case. It'd be a conflict of interest to give it to Santos and Taylor, and most of the guys around here are . . . angry about it."

A conflict of interest. If Righetti was going to say something, now was the time. But this was a rare opportunity. Too lucky a happenstance for her to pass up.

"Yep," Mike said. "Lots of chatter making the rounds."

"Murdering a police officer is nasty business." He held up a hand. "Regardless of whether he killed that girl."

It wasn't often that she heard the men in the precinct refer to what had happened to Rebecca Grant in that way. The focus was always on her *getting killed.* Not someone *killing her.* As if the errant action were on her end. *She got herself murdered. My wife, my sister, my girlfriend, my daughter, wouldn't be stupid enough to do that.* No one said it out loud, but Righetti knew they all thought it.

"Look, Detectives, you lucked out, okay?" The chief leaned forward to fold his arms across the desk. There was a quarter-sized coffee stain on the collar of his uniform. "The only reason you're landing this one is because I'm worried about how the others will handle it. I don't need emotion clouding anybody's judgment, got it?"

The chief had deemed her too emotional to work Rebecca Grant's case and now here he was slapping the label on her male colleagues. The irony was not lost on Righetti. She nodded, trying her best to maintain an aura of calm professionalism.

"I need the two of you out at the crime scene yesterday."

"Yes, sir," she said.

"And listen. I understand Peter Miles had motive and opportunity—they found that girl's hair in his truck, not to mention his finger-prints were all over the can of lighter fluid, for Christ's sake—but there's still the problem of his girlfriend's . . ." Chief Hunter coughed. "I don't know. What do you call the girlfriend of a dead guy? Ex-girlfriend, I guess. Her alibi made Peter Miles's conviction far from a slam dunk. Stay objective, is what I'm telling you."

"Yes, sir."

The two detectives rose from their seats.

"Oh, and, Detectives?" They both turned at the door. "Do not screw this up."

"No, sir," she said, and was surprised at how confident she sounded.

"You got it, Chief," Mike said.

Outside in the hall, her shock had the space and time to multiply. Righetti followed her partner back to their desks, her brain going over every single word they'd exchanged with the chief.

"I can't believe someone murdered him," she said.

"I can."

She glanced sharply at him over the cubicle partition, but her part-ner's expression was as blank as his tone. He busied himself arranging the pens in his cup, a pre-work ritual she'd at first found odd but now thought of as endearing.

"It was only a matter of time," Mike added, lowering himself into his chair.

Was it? Sure, she could imagine there were people out there who would have *liked* to kill Peter Miles. But to actually *do* it? That was different. That took guts, and a plan.

That took a frightening level of rage.

Bree would know. She'd wanted to kill Peter Miles too.

CHAPTER TWENTY-FIVE

Before

"There's someone waiting at your desk to speak to you," Laura said when Bree came in from her lunch break. "Says she needs to talk to a female officer. There aren't any others in right now, sorry," she added, as if the precinct had dozens of female law enforcement to choose from, instead of just three. "She's at your desk."

Dread and anticipation circled Bree's mind. She could think of only a handful of reasons for why a woman would want to speak to a female officer of the law—and none of them were good. It's what she herself wished she'd done all those years ago, wasn't it?

The woman sat as if her spine were pressed up against an invisible fence post. Bree rounded the chair and, hand extended, said, "Hello. I'm Detective Righetti."

The woman flinched. "Sorry," she said, though Bree didn't know for what. "Rebecca Grant." She half rose to shake hands.

Taking a seat, Bree moved the stack of manila folders out of the way and asked, "What can I do for you, Rebecca?"

Rebecca's gray eyes met hers. She had thin lips perched like a cupid's bow on her face and a narrow nose with a little bump in the center. The smattering of freckles on each suntanned cheek and dark blond hair piled in a loose bun imparted her with a breezy, outdoorsy quality. Even in her navy pantsuit, cream blouse, and black courtroom pumps, she still seemed ready for a hike at a moment's notice.

"I was hoping to get some advice." She twisted a slim gold ring around her middle finger. "But I'm not sure how to explain it to you."

"Is there a crime involved?"

"No." Two parallel lines appeared between her eyebrows. "I'm just worried."

"About what?" Watching Rebecca's expression closely, Bree suspected she knew.

"Well." Again, her eyes scanned the room. "There's this guy. We dated for a while and now that things are fizzling out, he's been getting really intense."

"Intense how?"

"He shows up at random places to see me. Like the coffee shop I go to every morning. Comes around to my apartment without asking me first. Stuff like that."

"Do you feel you're in danger?" It was a stupid question. When did women not feel endangered by a man's desperation?

"No, I don't think he's dangerous. God." She pressed a hand to her forehead and closed her eyes. Her nails were painted light pink. "I sound insane. I'm wasting your time."

"Rebecca." Bree waited until she lowered her hand before continuing. "You don't and you're not. I'm here to listen. So, he keeps showing up unannounced?"

"I tell him to stop, but he won't listen. Should I be worried?"

Bree sighed. Feeling like a traitor, she said, "I hate to say it, but there's not really anything we can do yet because he technically hasn't committed a crime."

"Right." She nodded. "That makes sense."

Did it? Ten years of experience in law enforcement had convinced Bree otherwise, but she didn't want to get into it now.

"You could file for a restraining order. That way there's a record of his behavior. A trail." Bree didn't want to explain that there was no such thing as prevention of crimes against women, only reactions after the fact. That the onus was on women to leave a trail and preempt possible violence, to expect nothing of law enforcement until it was too late, frustrated Bree. Still, she tried to sound reassuring. "It might seem pointless, but a lot of times threat of police action can scare off a potential stalker." This, at least, was true.

Rebecca's nodding slowed. "Okay. But what if he"—Bree leaned in to catch her last few words—"works in law enforcement?"

"The restraining order is against the individual. His job doesn't matter." A fist closed around Bree's heart. "Do you want to tell me who it is? Does he work here?"

Shaking her head, Rebecca let her gaze float aimlessly to the rest of the room. Suddenly, she jerked and glanced at her watch. "God, I need to go. I've used up most of my lunch break."

Already, she was on her feet. Panic surged through Bree as she rose too.

"Miss Grant," she said, and Rebecca swiveled to face her, smiling as if she'd just popped in for a friendly chat.

"Yeah?" The brightness in her voice made Bree wince.

"Trust your gut, okay? If you're worried, consider getting a gun. It's good to be prepared. I can recommend someone for self-defense classes." She flipped through her address book and jotted the name and number down. On a whim, she added her own information, then held the slip of paper out. "He's a former marine. My number's there too. If you ever need anything, promise you'll call me. Okay?"

"Okay. Thank you, Detective Righetti."

"Of course."

Bree sank into her chair and looked around the room. Her gaze stuttered and came to a stop on Peter Miles at the far corner, by Detective Taylor's desk. His eyes were locked to Rebecca's retreating back.

It couldn't be, could it? Could he be the one Rebecca was talking about?

But the moment Rebecca disappeared out into the hall, his interest fractured. He perched on the edge of Detective Taylor's desk and laughed at something he said. Maybe it was just the superficial novelty of an attractive woman at the precinct.

Flipping open a folder, she got to work. But she'd only filled in a few lines of the report before, unable to stop herself, Bree glanced up again.

Their eyes met and her hand tightened around the pen like it was a weapon. For the first time in the three years he'd worked here, Peter Miles seemed to genuinely notice her, to acknowledge her existence.

Her immediate instinct was to look away, but she forced her gaze to stay. She would not break eye contact first.

Bree's pulse was in her ears. She felt as if she were sitting in a sauna.

His eyes never leaving her face, Peter Miles lifted his hand to the brim of his cop hat and smiled.

CHAPTER
TWENTY-SIX

Bree stood outside the run-down house, taking deep breaths. Spots speckled the corners of her vision. Nothing had prepared her for this. Despite the barrier of Vicks beneath her nose, she could still smell the stench of his two-day-old corpse. It clung to her clothes, burrowed into her hair and skin.

The image that came with it—Peter Miles tied to the chair, his features brutalized by death like plywood warped by rain—that, she'd never be able to wash away. She shuddered as she recalled the blackened tongue protruding from his gaping mouth. The fingers splayed painfully against the chair arms. The way his head was angled sharply to one side. How his wide eyes stared up at the ceiling, as if begging for mercy from a higher power; his final, eternal expression one of terror.

As she looked around at her bleak surroundings, Bree let herself picture how she would have done it. They wouldn't know the full extent of his injuries until the autopsy was complete, but Bree wasn't sure she could inflict any of that—even on someone as vile as Peter Miles. But the dignity of a quick death seemed like an insult too, a slap in the face to his victims.

She was mulling over the mold-spotted cardboard they'd found resting against Peter Miles's chest, the word MONSTER on it in black marker, when Mike emerged from the house.

"Not much more to do in there," he said.

"Did Ray get any fingerprints?"

Mike shook his head. "He says the body and the chair are clean. The rest of the house is too dirty. He's not optimistic."

"Not even on the cardboard?"

"Not even on the cardboard." Her partner jotted something down in his notepad, then looked up past her right shoulder. "Going to check out the backyard," he said, and disappeared around the side of the house without further explanation.

A headache splayed its grip along the back of Bree's skull, and she wished she had some chewing gum to quell the nausea coating her stomach like thick grease on a diner griddle. She wondered how much of the queasiness was because of what she'd seen inside, and how much of it was nerves.

She'd gotten into law enforcement because there weren't nearly enough women in the field. And men historically didn't believe female victims. Now here she was, tasked with solving the murder of a man who was exactly what that piece of cardboard said. Somehow, even after witnessing the grisly display inside, it felt morally ambiguous.

It doesn't matter how you feel.

The justice system was supposed to be black-and-white, Bree reminded herself. She was supposed to stay objective.

Chief Hunter's *Do not screw this up* flared in her mind again.

Burrowing her hands deeper into her pockets, she willed both Mike to hurry up and the ache behind her eyes to go away.

Something fluttered in the corner of her vision and Bree turned her head. A person stood where the end of the driveway met the road. They looked so spectral that Bree's first wild thought was of poor Rebecca Grant, back from the grave to see the place of her murderer's demise. Like some macabre, phantasmal tourist.

It was a ridiculous idea and Bree forced herself to laugh softly. No, whoever it was, they were flesh and bone. Crossing her arms, she felt the reassuring hard outline of her gun beneath her jacket.

Carefully, as if signaling to a feral dog, Bree lifted her hand in a wave. The person seemed to hesitate before jerking their hand up and quickly back down to grasp the hem of their shirt.

Anticipation raced through her, but Bree walked slowly as she made her way down the drive. *As if I have all the time in the world. As if I just want to have a friendly, neighborly chat.*

The person's features became clearer as she got closer. She looked like a teenage girl, though her unnatural thinness probably made her appear smaller and younger than she really was. Light, almost transparent blond hair lay in unwashed tendrils over her shoulders and protruding collarbones. A dark half-moon hung beneath each eye, and just below, the girl's cheekbones jutted out sharply before sloping into shallow craters. She looked hungry. In more ways than one.

"Hi there," Bree said, hoping the girl wouldn't notice the yellow police tape stretched across the porch, or the white forensics van parked around the bend. "I'm just taking a look at that old house."

"Oh. I'm visiting my friend. I-I can't talk." Her brown eyes shifted to the left then back. Bree wondered which of the battered houses she meant.

"Okay. I was looking at this place." She jerked her thumb back toward the crime scene. "And wondering why it's empty. It's big." She tried to think of something else complimentary to say about the house but came up short.

The girl shook her head. "You shouldn't go in there." She jittered like an old-fashioned alarm clock, constantly moving her weight from one leg to the next, uncrossing and recrossing her arms, pushing hair behind her ear even though she'd just done that a second ago. Again, she glanced down the street and back.

"Why not?" Bree asked.

Lifting one bony shoulder, she shrugged.

"You shouldn't go in there," the girl repeated. "It's not safe."

Bree looked back at the house. "Structural issues, you think?"

"It's haunted."

The two words had the effect of a bucket of water tossed on a fire. There wasn't anything to learn. Just some poor girl who thought ghosts kept house there.

"Okay. I'll be careful," Bree said with a nod. Already, her mind was moving ahead to what came next: visiting Rebecca Grant's parents.

"People've been killed there."

Bree's attention swung back to her like a scope narrowing in on a target.

"They have?"

The girl nodded. "That's why we don't go in there. You go in, you die."

"Do you know people who have died here?"

"I dunno." She was shifting her gaze again, not making eye contact. "I've seen things . . . I heard. You can't go in there."

There was a pause as Bree tried to think of what to say.

She settled on introducing herself. "I'm Bree, like the cheese." The pun did nothing to help the girl relax. "What's your name?"

She shrugged. "I gotta go."

Desperation made Bree brazen. "Have you seen anything weird going on in that house lately?"

The girl half-turned, her arms hugging her body. "It's dangerous, that's all I know."

This is pointless.

"I saw lights one time," she added. "That's how I know it's haunted. It was glowing. Like, blue."

"When was this?"

Shifting from leg to leg the girl repeated, "I saw lights. They always told me it was haunted, but I didn't believe them."

Who was *they*? Bree wanted to know, but feared asking would derail the conversation.

"I saw it glowing blue and I thought . . ." For a moment, she looked stricken. "I thought I'd see, y'know?"

Somewhere down by the water a bullfrog let out a sonorous croak.

"Did you?" Bree asked, trying to steer the girl's attention back.

"Huh?" Her eyes were focused on a point down the road, as if she thought someone might be watching them.

"Did you see if it was really haunted?"

"It is." She twisted the hem of her T-shirt in her hands. "I *saw* them."

Bree's heartbeat started doing double time.

"Who'd you see?" She kept her tone casual, as if she only had a passing interest.

"Witches. Like in the movies. All in black. Summoning them . . ." The girl was rambling. "There were three. I saw . . ." Her voice trailed off.

"Did you see their faces?"

"No." The toe of her tennis shoe tapped out a quick staccato against the ground. "They were all black. Like shadows. Evil shadows."

"How do you know they were witches?" Against her will, she felt herself drawn in. It sounded like a terrifying drug-induced hallucination, but she was fascinated by the logic the girl was using to explain it.

"They had a man as sacrifice."

Bree inhaled sharply. Three wrinkles appeared on the girl's forehead, transforming her face into a haggard grimace.

"Witches do that. Kill and eat men, right?"

"How do you know they were . . . women? Witches?"

The girl dug her fingers into the fabric of her shirt. "Just know. They looked like witches."

Mind darting in a hundred different directions at the possible new clue, Bree asked, "When was this?"

Her eyes shifted to the right and she chewed on her thumbnail as she thought. "Um, I don't know. Yesterday, I think."

It didn't match up exactly with Peter's timeline, but then this girl probably didn't even know what day of the week it was. Something told Bree time wasn't a rigid concept to her.

"How did you see them?" Bree said.

"With my eyes." She was immediately defensive, and probably with good reason. Society rarely took girls who looked like that seriously.

"I meant, did you look through a window? Go inside?" She motioned to the house.

"I snuck up. I was really quiet. I saw a light. A blue light."

"Through where?" Bree glanced over her shoulder.

"There's a hole in the boards on that side."

"Can you show me?" She tried to be gentle.

"I gotta go." The girl was already shuffling away, her arms wrapped tight around her frail body. "My friend's waiting. I gotta go."

"I'd like to talk to you again sometime. About the ghosts. Which house does your friend live in so I can find you?"

Ignoring her, she continued down to the paved road. She glanced back and immediately Bree shifted her gaze away. It was better not to make her feel like she was watching. Bree didn't want to spook her.

When she looked again, the girl had disappeared out of sight around the bend. Bree jogged to the end, then moved off into the trees clustered next to the foot of the drive. She stood behind a tree and watched the girl continue down the street. A few times she paused to peer over her shoulder but didn't seem to notice Bree. Finally, she disappeared into a brown house with gaping black holes for windows.

Making a mental note that it was the third house on the left, Bree trudged back up the drive. Female killers. Three of them. The idea vibrated in her brain like an agitated hummingbird.

Mike came walking up from the direction of the water.

"What's going on?" he asked when he saw her expression.

"Nothing." She glanced toward the foot of the driveway. "Find anything?"

"Nope. Ready to move on?"

"I'll just take a round myself and meet you at the car."

"Sure thing."

Bree waited until Mike was opening the passenger-side door before circling around the side of the house. The windows were all boarded up, but something had chewed a hole through one of the planks.

Pulse skipping, Bree bent and pressed an eye to the jagged hole. It took a second for her vision to adjust, but when it did, she knew this was it. The window looked directly into the living room. Ray, the crime scene tech, moved across her field of vision. And there it was.

If Peter Miles were sitting in the chair right now, he would have been in center stage.

CHAPTER
TWENTY-SEVEN

Bree knew they were at the right place because she'd seen 125 Pillory Lane before. The red front door and blue-shuttered windows, abundant azaleas clambering around them like colorful centipedes, had been on the nightly news for weeks. A beautiful backdrop to the Grant family's worst nightmare. The lawn still sported the same military-precise trim she'd seen on TV, but the flowers and shrubs were showing signs of neglect. Some were browning and wilted—as if they hadn't been watered in quite some time.

Putting the car in park, Bree let the engine idle for a moment. Mike didn't say anything, but his eyes were trained on the house too, as if gearing himself up for what was to come. That was a promising sign; she wasn't the only one dreading this.

The street was quiet. Bree turned to look through the car's rear window anyway. There'd been a dozen or so reporters camped outside the house in the days after Rebecca Grant disappeared and her body was discovered. Now, even the cub reporters, tenacious as hungry piranhas on the prowl for their big break, were long gone.

The quiet wouldn't last. The press would get wind of that morning's gruesome discovery soon enough. Then they'd be swarming the Grant house again, harassing the occupants with questions like

Did you murder Peter Miles? and *Did you get revenge for your daughter's death?*

"Well," Bree said. "Nowhere to go but in."

Wordlessly, Mike climbed out of the car, and she followed him up the narrow stone pathway to the front door. Bree rang the bell. It echoed inside for what seemed like a long time, then dwindled to silence. Odd. She'd phoned Mr. Grant's office earlier and learned that he always went home around mid-morning to check in on his wife. One, if not both, of the Grants should be here.

She was just about to ring again when she heard footsteps on the other side. A second later, a bolt released, and the door swung open. A man stood in the doorway, the look of a hunted rabbit on his face.

Early to mid-sixties.

About five eleven.

One hundred sixty pounds.

By the way his clothes hung loose on his frame, Bree guessed he'd probably weighed closer to one eighty before this whole terrible business started.

"Can I help you?" he said. His grip on the door was so tight his fingers were turning white.

"Mr. Grant?" Bree asked, and when he nodded, she continued. "I'm Detective Righetti and this is Detective O'Malley." They showed their badges. "Could we talk to you for a moment?"

There it was on his face, plain as a lighthouse signal: hope. Bree felt her heart curl in on itself. It was one of the reasons she'd been dreading this.

"Has there been a break in the case?" he asked.

"Could we come inside, Mr. Grant?" She kept her tone calm and professional, even though she desperately wanted to take his hands and tell him how deeply sorry she was. More than he knew.

"Yes, of course. Yes," Mr. Grant said.

They stepped into the foyer, and he swung the door closed. "I'll just call my wife." His gaze drifted to the top of the hallway stairs. "She's resting."

"That's not necessary quite yet," Bree said. "Is there anywhere we can sit and talk?"

"Yes, of course. This way, Detectives."

Everything spoke to earned comforts. There'd been a remodel sometime in the last few years, Bree guessed. They'd probably bought the house cheap thirty or so years ago and improved it over time. She looked at the framed photographs hanging on the hallway walls as she followed Mr. Grant. Evidence of a full, well-lived life. Family trips to beach locations, and Christmas photographs in front of a large tree, Rebecca Grant grinning toothily between her two brothers. A slightly blurred photo brought Bree to a halt. It was suddenly hard to swallow. In it, Rebecca stood dressed in a heavy jacket, pants, and boots, one gloved hand lifted in a wave.

"That's Beck when she climbed Kilimanjaro."

Bree turned to find that a woman had appeared, silent as a ghost, on the staircase behind her.

"She looks happy," she said, glancing back to the photograph.

I'm so sorry, Rebecca.

Guilt twisted like a knife in Bree's gut. *What a damn tragedy,* she thought. Beck wasn't the first to be killed for nothing, nor would she be the last. Sometimes to be a woman felt like the worst luck in the world.

"She was. Such a happy girl. All she wanted was to be happy, to make the people around her happy." Mrs. Grant's voice was dull, as if all her emotions were dried up. "That's why she went into psychiatric care. She wanted to help people."

Another sharp pang, the knife twisting even further.

"A very noble cause, Mrs. Grant," Bree managed to say.

Clutching the banister, she slowly descended the rest of the way. The slump of her shoulders and the haggard look on her face hinted at a very old woman, though she was probably a few years younger than her husband.

"What are you here for?" Mrs. Grant asked, her thin fingers playing a nervous, silent staccato on her creased peach slacks. "We've told you everything we know." It sounded like a plea.

"What are you doing up, sweetheart?" Mr. Grant's head poked out of a doorway farther down the hall.

"I heard the doorbell." She brushed past Bree and walked slowly toward him. Bree followed and stepped through the door into an expansive kitchen.

Mike was already settled at the dining table like an alert garden gnome. The white porcelain mug looked small in his hands.

He half rose and said, eyes trained on the contents of his cup, "Good morning, Mrs. Grant. Very sorry to bother you."

She regarded him in silence for a second. "What are you here for?" she asked.

"Why don't you sit down, Mr. and Mrs. Grant?" Bree said.

"Would you like coffee as well, Detective . . ."

"Righetti."

"Righetti," Mr. Grant repeated.

"No, I'm fine, thank you, sir."

Mrs. Grant found her way to the chair opposite Mike. Her hands rested on the tabletop, the fingers of her left hand squeezing the fingers of her right, one at a time. She'd begin with the thumb, then forefinger, then middle finger, and work her way to the pinky. Then start all over again. It was almost hypnotic. Bree wondered if it was a new coping mechanism or if the woman had always been this nervous.

At the kitchen counter, Mr. Grant was busy prepping a tray with a coffeepot, three mugs, and jugs of milk and sugar. He seemed so eager to show them hospitality, as if it might somehow alter what she and Mike were here to say. Finally, he carried the full tray over and set it on the table. Only then did she allow herself to take a seat.

Before she could protest, he'd filled a cup with coffee and, looking up at her, asked, "Cream or sugar?"

"Black is fine," Bree said, wondering if this concession would change the power dynamic between them and cost her later.

"Yes, of course," he answered, as if this should have been obvious.

He filled another cup, added cream and sugar, and placed it in front of Mrs. Grant. Finally, he filled one for himself, added a splash of cream, and took a seat next to his wife.

"So, has there been an update on our daughter's case?" His hand moved to rest on top of Mrs. Grant's, and she stopped fidgeting. The tension in the room seemed to slacken slightly.

"In a way," Bree said. "I'm sure you know who Peter Miles is?" She watched Mr. Grant's expression closely.

Unless her frailty was a good act, Mrs. Grant didn't seem physically capable of inflicting that quantity of damage on another human being. But Mr. Grant . . . even whittled down by grief he was still a large man. And he was a contractor. He would have access to the tools needed to carry out the crime.

"You mean the man who was a person of interest in our daughter's murder? Have you finally charged him?"

"He's dead, Mr. Grant."

His hand tightened around his wife's. The two of them stared at Bree.

"What do you mean *dead*?" His voice was hoarse.

"He was murdered."

Mr. Grant slumped back in his seat, but Mrs. Grant remained rigid, leaning forward as if she wanted to launch herself across the table at Bree.

"The reason we're here, Mr. and Mrs. Grant, is because it looked . . . personal."

An understatement if there ever was one, she thought.

"Did he suffer?"

"Pardon?"

"Did that man . . . that monster suffer?" Mrs. Grant asked.

At her use of the word *monster,* Bree glanced at her partner.

"We're still working out the details, ma'am," Mike said.

A smile tugged at the corners of her mouth, and she swayed back and forth. "I hope he suffered. A lot. He deserved worse."

The grieving woman's thin face was ghoulish. She grinned at the two of them, a corpse returned to life.

"Mrs. Grant, can you tell us where you were from ten P.M. Friday night up until two the next morning?" Bree asked the question the way she'd ease a car into a tight parking space.

This made her laugh outright. "Why? Because you think I did it? I didn't. But." Again, she leaned forward. Her face grew flushed as she said, "I wish I had."

"Don't say that, Helen." Mr. Grant looked at Bree. "My wife was with me Friday night, Detective. We were here, at home."

"Was anyone else with you?"

"We had a few friends over for dinner and our son Sam came by after. He was here until about midnight."

Mike jotted this information down in his notebook.

"And after he left?"

"It was just the two of us. Empty nest, you know." The corners of his mouth refused to hold the smile for more than a fraction of a second.

"We'll need your son's address so we can confirm with him too."

"Of course."

The longer the conversation went on, the more half-hearted Bree felt. Even if the Grants had murdered Peter Miles, she wouldn't want to send them to prison for it. If anyone deserved to get away with murder, it'd be Rebecca's parents.

She had nothing to worry about, she reminded herself. There wasn't any doubt in her mind that Sam's alibi would match up perfectly with his parents'. When it did, well, Bree wouldn't press too hard, even if she had suspicions. This wouldn't be the first time a murderer walked free because of a good alibi—Peter Miles certainly had.

And there was the witness who claimed she'd seen three women at the crime scene. Bree still hadn't told Mike about that.

While Mr. Grant dictated his son's address to her partner, she visualized her list of suspects. The Grants wouldn't be at the top. So, who was?

Her eyes traveled along the wall to the side cabinet. The middle shelf housed a china set behind clear glass doors. Liquor bottles lined the shelf below. On top were more framed photographs along with varied trinkets. A ceramic robin sat in the center, staring at her with beady black eyes.

Her gaze found the photograph at the far-right end of the cabinet and stopped there. Slowly, Bree got to her feet.

"Who's this?" she asked, motioning to the photo of a group of women standing side by side, wide grins on their faces. She'd seen a copy of it before (or could it be the same one?), taped to a car dashboard. That'd been, what, six, seven months ago?

Mr. Grant craned his head to see which one she meant. "Oh, that's Beck. And those girls are . . . were her best friends."

Three witches with a man as a sacrifice.

He rose and came to stand next to her. "That's Isabel," Mr. Grant said, pointing. "And Priya, and——"

Dylan, she mentally filled in the blank as he said the name.

CHAPTER TWENTY-EIGHT

Dylan occupied interview room 1 like she was sitting in her own living room—long legs stretched out beneath the table, arms crossed, posture relaxed. She was dressed in jeans and a dark green shirt, her black jacket hanging on the back of the chair. Her dark hair was up in a ponytail. Her kohl-lined eyes were bright.

"Good afternoon, Miss Darcy," Bree said. "Thank you for coming in."

Dylan nodded. "It's fine. Rather talk here than at the bar. People get buggy when there's cops around."

It was an understatement. The two customers in the otherwise empty bar had cleared out when Bree and Mike walked in the day before. The manager, Jason Hollis, acted jumpy too—up until he learned that they were there for the security footage from the night of Peter Miles's last visit, and not for some other reason. It made Bree wonder what he was hiding. A lapsed license? A penchant for serving alcohol to minors? Or something worse? Like using the bar as a front for dealing drugs?

She filed the questions away for another time and forced herself to focus on the task at hand. Her brain buzzed. Interviewing Dylan Darcy would be interesting.

"We appreciate it all the same." Lowering herself into the chair opposite, she turned on the recorder and spoke into it. "This is Detective Righetti and Detective O'Malley interviewing Dylan Darcy. The date is Wednesday, October twentieth, 1993."

Three days since they'd found Peter Miles.

Her eyes rose to meet Dylan's. "Do you know why you're here, Miss Darcy?"

"Well, you said it's about Beck."

"That's right."

Asking for her alibi was just a formality at this point. Bree knew she'd parrot the same story as the other two, Isabel and Priya. The night of Peter Miles's murder they were, allegedly, having a girls' night in at Dylan's house. Bree asked anyway.

"Where were you Friday night, October fifteenth, between the times of ten P.M. until two A.M. Saturday, Miss Darcy?"

Her blue eyes narrowed. "Why?"

"Please answer the question."

A few beats of silence passed before Dylan said, "Friday? I was at home. Some friends came over and spent the night. We watched a movie. Went to bed at around . . ." She paused. "I don't know, around one, I guess. Why?"

"Can anyone else vouch for that?"

"Like I said, I had friends over."

"Anyone other than your friends?"

"Why?" Dylan looked from her to Mike and back. "What's going on?"

"Just trying to get a timeline straight, Miss Darcy," Mike said. "Did you see anyone else that night besides your friends?"

"Uh, we ordered a pizza. Does that count?"

"What time did it get delivered?" Bree asked.

"A little after ten, I think. They were backed up on orders or something. We always order from the same pizza place. Gianni's."

"Gianni's. Delivered at around ten," Mike repeated, taking notes.

"Yeah." She crossed one leg over the other. "So, what's this all about?"

On the surface, she seemed relaxed enough, but Bree thought she could discern a current of tension running through her jawline, taut as a weighted fishing line. That didn't mean anything, she told herself. Police questioning would make anyone tense.

"You don't have any idea why you're here?" Bree asked.

"I can't imagine." Her tone was dry.

"Peter Miles is dead—did you know that?"

Dylan was expressionless as a gravestone. "Okay. Good for him. What does that have to do with me?"

"He was murdered," Mike added.

There was a slight movement around her eyes, as if she were about to blink but stopped herself.

"We believe it was personally motivated," Bree said.

Dylan was silent. Taking a photo from the folder in front of her on the table, Bree turned it around and slid it across. It was a photograph the crime scene tech had snapped after removing the sign from around Peter Miles's neck.

For a few moments Dylan stared at it, then she raised her eyes to meet Bree's.

Interesting. Isabel had covered the photo with her palm and looked like she was going to be sick. Priya had glanced at it, then quickly shifted her gaze away. Not Dylan. Dylan confronted the image without even flinching.

"You don't seem to mind that photo," Mike said. "Your friends could barely look at it."

"I work around drunks every day. I've got a strong stomach."

"Right," Mike said. Disbelief seemed to radiate from him like an odor. "Still, it's pretty gruesome."

Dylan's eyebrows lifted, but she said nothing.

"Do you think Peter Miles deserved to die, Miss Darcy?"

"Not my place to say," she answered.

"Did you want him dead?" Bree asked. This was the question she really wanted the answer to.

She flipped the photograph and slid it back toward them with a soft snort. "Pretty much everybody wanted him dead."

"What do you mean?"

"Ask her parents. Or her brothers. Ask anybody in her family. Or

her friends. We all thought he'd gotten away with it. I doubt anybody's going to be sad to hear he's dead."

"He was never officially charged with her murder."

Folding her arms across her chest, Dylan lifted her chin slightly
and answered, "That's on you, isn't it?"

It was hard not to admire her defiance, even if Dylan was too
much of a smart-ass for her own good. They *were* pushing her harder
on her alibi than Taylor and Santos—the two detectives assigned to
the Rebecca Grant murder case—had pushed Peter Miles on his. It
wasn't fair, and Dylan knew it.

"You work in a bar, don't you, Miss Darcy?" Bree asked. "The Ace
of Spades?"

"Aces."

"Pardon?"

"It's Aces of Spades. Plural."

"Right." She nodded. "You work at the Aces of Spades?"

"I think you already know the answer." Spoken like a challenge.

"Did you know Peter Miles sometimes frequented that same establishment?"

"Lots of people do. It's a busy bar."

Bree wouldn't say she'd seen Dylan and Peter interacting at Aces.
She'd keep that to herself for now.

"So, you don't remember him coming to the bar?" she asked.

Dylan shrugged.

"Maybe she needs a reminder of what he looked like alive," Mike
said. "People look different when they're dead," he told Dylan as he
flipped through the folder and pulled out another photograph.

Bree held back a wince when she saw it was one of Peter Miles in
his police uniform, posing for an official photo. She watched Dylan's
expression as Mike slid it across the table. Her brow furrowed a little.
A moment later the creases in her forehead flattened out.

"Yeah," she said. "He comes in a lot. But he doesn't look much
like that anymore."

Thinking she was comparing the live man to his corpse, Bree
sucked in a sharp breath.

Then Dylan continued, "He's changed a lot from that photo. He's just another sleazy drunk. Was another sleazy drunk." She looked at them as if expecting they'd contradict her.

Don't worry, you won't find anyone defending him in here.

"So, you're saying you've never seen a photo of Peter Miles until now?" Bree asked.

"Well, yeah, months ago, probably. When he was a suspect."

"But you didn't recognize him when he came into the bar?"

"I guess I didn't put two and two together. Like I said, he looked different. And the bar can get hectic. Doesn't always give me a lot of time to catch my breath."

"Let's go back to your alibi for a second," Mike said. "What time did you clock out from the bar on Friday?"

Again, she paused to think. "Around nine-thirty, I guess."

"Nine twenty-three, to be exact," Bree said. "We have the security footage from that night, Miss Darcy."

Another thing Bree didn't mention: that there was a suspiciously short time frame between when Peter Miles left Aces of Spades at eight-forty and Dylan's own departure. Bree had made sure to watch the footage alone—she told Mike she didn't mind the busywork and that he should focus on other aspects of the case—but even if he'd watched too, it wouldn't have mattered. Other than the tight timeline, there weren't any damning clues in the footage. The camera angle didn't even show who picked Peter up.

Dylan's expression gave nothing away. Which meant either she didn't have anything to do with the murder, or she knew the camera's blind spots and wasn't worried they'd seen anything incriminating.

"If you say so," Dylan said.

"The bar closes at, what, one?" Bree asked.

"Around there."

"Why didn't you work the full shift until closing?"

"My manager lets me leave early sometimes. Long as I can get somebody to cover for me, it's fine." She lifted her shoulders in a shrug. "Not a big deal. I do it every now and then."

"Okay." Mike stepped in. "So, you clocked out at nine twenty-three. What'd you do after?"

"I went home."

"Straight home? Didn't stop anywhere along the way? Not even for gas?"

Dylan shook her head. "Nope."

"What time did your friends come over?"

"They were already there when I got home. They both have keys to my place."

"Right." He flipped to a fresh page in his notepad and jotted this down. "What time did you say you went to bed?"

"Around one," she answered in a tone that implied he was testing her patience.

"What were you doing from ten to one?"

Another shrug. "Talking. Watching movies. I think *Top Gun* was on TV that night."

"Were you all together? In the same room?"

"Mostly, yeah. Except when somebody went to the kitchen or bathroom, I guess."

"Nobody left the house?"

"No."

"See"—Mike leaned forward—"that's not what your friend said."

Dylan's expression remained static. It seemed like it'd been a very long time since she'd blinked.

"Let's see." He made a show of checking the notepad in his lap. "Isabel Guerrero was there, right?"

"Yeah."

"Isabel Guerrero says you disappeared for two hours that night."

There it is. It lasted for less than a second, so quick Bree almost missed it, but the corners of Dylan's mouth jerked into a slight smirk. It was as if she couldn't control it.

"Are you allowed to lie like this?" Dylan asked. "Isn't it some kind of coercion?"

"Where were you those two hours you were gone?" he persisted.

"I wasn't gone. And I know Isabel didn't say that because it's not true. But I guess coercion is about what I should expect from the same police force that let my friend's murderer get away, right?"

Internally, Bree seethed. Dylan was right, Mike shouldn't have pulled that. Time to lead the conversation in a safer direction. Try a different tack.

Bree rested her elbows on the table and leveled her with a smile. "Miss Darcy, I know coming down here is probably inconvenient, so I'm going to be straight with you. If you know anything, or you're covering for someone, it's better to come forward now. The judge will be more lenient, especially taking into consideration what Peter Miles was suspected of."

"Am *I* a suspect?" Dylan said.

"Should you be?" Mike asked as if he held only the slightest curiosity for the answer.

She snorted. "I thought you were being straight with me. Am I a suspect or not?"

How could Bree answer the question honestly when she wasn't sure? Did she want Dylan as a suspect so she could have a solid lead? Or did she want Dylan to get away with it?

Get away with what? Don't get ahead of yourself.

"You may go, Miss Darcy," Bree said, clicking off the recorder. "Let us know if you plan to leave town. We'll probably have more questions at some point."

Dylan rose and took her time putting on her jacket, then walked out without another glance back. The two of them sat in silence for a few moments.

"Their stories are too similar," Mike said finally, shaking his head. "Rehearsed."

"That doesn't necessarily mean anything," she countered. "Dylan most likely knew we interviewed Isabel and Priya. They would have called her. She's probably been thinking over that night since yesterday, getting the details straight."

He nodded. "Could be."

Bree toyed with the corner of the manila folder. For now, she'd ignore the alarm bells going off in her gut. She'd pretend that Dylan's behavior didn't seem to be a confirmation of something sinister.

I'm staying objective. Though part of Bree knew this was a lie. It wasn't objectivity, it was denial.

"It's just a hunch," her partner said, getting to his feet. "But I think Dylan Darcy knows something."

"I'm not so sure, Mike."

He paused with his hand on the doorknob. "I guess we'll see."

Did this mean Bree had picked a side? If Dylan Darcy really had done it, would she be willing to let her walk away?

As she rose and followed her partner out into the hall, Bree wondered what answering *yes* to that question would say about her.

CHAPTER TWENTY-NINE

"We found traces of bleach under his fingernails," Ray told her.

Switching the phone from one ear to the other, Bree leaned back in her chair and crossed her legs. "So, the attacker cleaned him up."

"That's right. Whoever killed him, they did a good job. Oh, and turns out his fingers *were* broken."

"Any idea why?"

"I guess that's for you to find out. My theory is, the perp was trying to clean under his fingernails, he wasn't cooperating, so they broke a few fingers to show him who's boss."

She thought of how Dylan had looked yesterday when they interviewed her, then pictured her snapping his fingers one by one while Peter Miles screamed in agony. She imagined herself doing the same. Bree didn't hate the visual. Not as much as she should.

"Anything else?" she asked.

"We confirmed mode of death to be strangulation, but that's probably not news to you, Detective. What might be news is that it looks like there were multiple attempts to kill him."

"What?" She lowered the front legs of her chair onto solid ground.

"Well, there were multiple cord marks around his neck. My theory, and I know I'm not paid to theorize, but here goes: My theory is that the perp let go, then tried again. More than once."

Bree felt conflicting surges of satisfaction and horror. The idea was disturbing, even if it was Peter Miles at the receiving end of it.

Ray bit into something with a crunch and spoke through a full mouth. "Is it possible the attacker was a woman?"

Goosebumps rippled up her arms. "What makes you ask that?"

"Well, the evidence could point to a smaller attacker, possibly someone weaker than your typical male. It would explain the multiple cord marks. Maybe they didn't have the strength to get it done the first time and it took multiple tries to work it out. But again, not paid to theorize." Another crunch and more chewing. "One other thing. There were puncture wounds in his arm, from an IV it looks like. We also found a fair amount of saline in his system. Any chance he paid a visit to the hospital that night?"

This was an odd tidbit of information. "Not that we know of. Saline is for treating dehydration, right?"

"Mhm." She heard him swallow. When he spoke again, his voice was clearer. "Before you ask, you don't need medical knowledge to insert an IV. But whoever did it had practice. There's only one puncture wound, which tells me they knew what they were doing. That's why I asked if he'd been to the hospital."

Mentally, Bree cycled through her list of suspects. Who would know how to insert an IV, and do it well?

The nurse. Priya Shah.

"Thanks, Ray," she said. "Is that all?"

"Mhm." He was eating again. "Well, you know where to find me if you need me."

After they hung up, Bree sat tapping a pen on the desktop. Was this a real lead? It seemed flimsy. Sure, Priya could have inserted the IV, but from what Ray said, anyone with sufficient practice could have done it too.

She debated what to tell Mike. Her poor partner was probably feeling like a desperate EMT attempting to shock life back into a corpse with a defibrillator. The case kept threatening to go cold.

Multiple neighbors confirmed they'd seen all three cars outside Dylan's house on the night in question. Lethal blow number one. Then, they'd tracked down the employee from Gianni's Pizza who remembered making the delivery just after ten. Dylan had left an impression on him, apparently. Lethal blow number two.

Then there was Sam Grant, Rebecca's brother. He'd been livid when she and Mike arrived at his house to interview him. The entire Grant family had lawyered up, despite her reassurances that they weren't suspects.

Bree spotted Mike crossing the room, a Styrofoam coffee cup in his hands.

"Just got confirmation that Priya Shah drives a yellow Volkswagen Bug," he said as he got closer.

It took her a second to process what he meant. "Oh."

Shit, she thought.

Maxine Miles, Peter's mother, had mentioned it on Tuesday while showing them around the apartment in her basement where he'd been living. She claimed she'd seen a suspicious woman in a yellow car outside her house just weeks before her son was murdered. At the time, Bree brushed it off as unimportant. People did that sometimes; they felt pressured to provide clues and would remember pointless details that might or might not have really happened.

So, maybe Priya killed him on her own.

Not likely. Not with the description from the girl at the crime scene to consider. And then there were the multiple cord marks around Peter's neck.

As if they each took a turn strangling him.

The thought was bizarre and yet somehow still made sense. Bree couldn't see one woman being able to kidnap, subdue, and kill Peter Miles. But three . . .

Isabel Guerrero.

Priya Shah.

Dylan Darcy.

". . . her a visit," Mike was saying when she refocused.

"What was that, Mike?"

"We should pay Priya Shah another visit," he repeated.

"Yes, of course."

"Saw you talking on the phone when I came in," Mike said as she gathered her things. "Anything about the case?"

The lie came so quickly, Bree surprised herself. "Oh, no. That was just a personal call."

• • •

Isabel Guerrero.
Priya Shah.
Dylan Darcy.

Bree turned the names over in her mind as she drove. She couldn't stop herself from glancing at Mike every few minutes, wondering if he knew more than he was letting on. But as usual, her partner's expression betrayed nothing. Looking as if he were out for little more than a leisurely pleasure drive, Mike placidly gazed out the windshield in silence.

Although, she thought, he seemed unsurprised by life in general. It was hard to tell if he was being reserved about his theories or just being, well, *Mike.*

It wasn't too late to tell him everything. About the witness, what Ray had said on the phone, about her own suspicions of Dylan, Isabel, and Priya. But something stopped her.

I'll tell him tomorrow.

And if she just . . . didn't? Bree felt like a string tangled up in dozens of complicated knots. Surely Mike would figure some of it out eventually. Either he'd run into Ray and the forensics tech would mention it, or he'd go looking for answers on his own.

But maybe he wouldn't. There was a chance of that too.

Ignorance is bliss, she thought, glancing at her partner again.

Except, if Mike did find out she'd withheld information, he'd hate her. The one guy at the precinct who'd been halfway decent and always treated her with respect. She remembered the empanada she'd found on her desk that morning and swallowed back a lump in her throat.

But some things were more important than betrayal. The longer she worked the case, the more she believed it was better to let it go cold. Peter Miles didn't deserve to have his murder solved.

Not after what he did to Rebecca Grant.

Not after what he'd done to *her*.

CHAPTER
THIRTY

There was no response when they knocked on Priya Shah's apartment door. Cupping her hands around her eyes, Bree peered in through the small window. It looked down over an empty kitchen sink. The only sign someone lived there, or had been there recently, was a mug sitting on the white laminate countertop opposite the window, a tea bag string and tag dangling over the side like a flimsy anchor.

Mike knocked again.

"I guess she's at work," Bree said after they'd waited another minute.

"Yep. She works at . . ." He pulled his notepad from the front pocket of his shirt and flipped through it. "Wallis General."

They drove the ten minutes to the hospital and Mike stood outside while she went in to ask for Priya. Just as Bree was about to give up and go to the cafeteria for a coffee, the young woman finally emerged through the double doors. She wore light blue scrubs and a pair of well-used but immaculate white tennis shoes, her dark hair pulled into a neat, low bun.

A look flashed across her features as quickly as a mouse fleeing for cover. Fear perhaps? Whatever it was, by the time Priya crossed the lobby to where Bree stood, it had been replaced by annoyance.

She didn't slow her stride as she walked past and out through the sliding glass doors. Bree followed. Arms hugging her body, Priya continued a few steps farther down the walkway before turning to face them.

"You can't come to my place of work like this," she said. "If they think the police are coming around all the time, I could lose my job."

To her surprise, Priya's eyes were shining, as if she were about to cry.

"What is it?" she asked. "Can we do this quickly? I need to get back."

She stiffened, as if physically bracing herself for a wave of bad news to hit. For the first time Bree seriously thought, *She's hiding something.*

Judging by looks alone, Isabel should have been the weakest link. Isabel in her feminine blouses, skirts, and cardigans, with her soft pink lipstick and carefully styled bangs. But both times they'd interviewed her she'd been remote and absent-minded—as if she wasn't entirely sure why they'd sought her out. She left Bree with the distinct impression that Isabel was absolutely hiding something and that she didn't know anything about Peter Miles's death either. Both seemed equally likely.

In the few minutes they'd been talking, Priya Shah was already showing more emotion than Isabel Guerrero. Perhaps Bree was wrong to assume Isabel was the weak one. Maybe Priya would be the first to break instead.

Mentally, Bree ticked off what she knew. The murder was revenge motivated. Priya Shah had been outside Peter Miles's home just weeks before he was murdered. The girl witness had seen three suspicious characters inside the house who looked like women. It was just a little too convenient that Rebecca Grant happened to have three best friends who were one another's alibis for the night of his murder.

The real question was: Were Priya, Isabel, and Dylan capable of kidnapping and murder?

Then there was the timeline. Bree had driven the route from the bar to the crime scene earlier. It was roughly twenty minutes from one point to the other. Not doable without a car, and a neighbor from across the street had confirmed seeing both Isabel and Priya let themselves into Dylan's house that night. By all accounts that's where they were when Peter Miles went missing from in front of Aces of Spades.

Dylan could have asked him to meet her somewhere and picked him up once her shift ended. Possible, except she'd been home by ten to accept the pizza delivery. It was too narrow a window for her to kidnap Peter Miles, drive him to that remote, abandoned house, and tie him to the bolted-down chair. Considering the care given to the rest of the crime, it would have been much too risky.

She should have been relieved at how impossible it seemed for Dylan, Priya, and Isabel to commit the crime. Instead, she felt a sick disquiet. Bree was missing something vital. Or a clue would come to light later that would damn them all.

"We just have a few more questions, Miss Shah," Mike said, looking at his notepad.

"Do I need to call a lawyer?" she asked.

"You can if you'd like to," Bree said. "But we'd have to reschedule this chat for down at the station. It'll take more time and energy than it's probably worth. Is that what you want to do?"

Bree could almost see the mental back-and-forth happening in real time.

If I do call a lawyer, it makes me look guilty.

If I don't, I might say something I shouldn't.

This will all be done faster if I just get it over with.

They waited in silence while Priya thought it over.

Her hand found its way into the pocket of her scrubs and pulled out a lighter. Priya began passing it back and forth in her hands, periodically flicking open the cap and snapping it shut again. It was a nervous habit; she didn't even appear to notice she was fiddling with it.

"What do you want to know?" she asked finally.

"Come on." Bree crossed her arms. "You're a smart woman, I think you know."

Shaking her head, Priya sighed and looked down. Gold plating flashed as she moved the lighter with ease between her fingers, then transferred it to her other hand and repeated the movement.

"Well, you obviously have more questions about . . . him." Priya's eyes were trained on her fingers.

"Peter Miles."

Priya pursed her lips, her eyebrows furrowed.

"You don't seem to like hearing his name," Bree said.

"No, I don't. He murdered my best friend."

"Did your friends think that too? Dylan and Isabel?"

"We knew that."

"It must have been upsetting when he wasn't arrested," Bree said.

Priya sighed. "We already covered this the last time you interviewed me. No, it wasn't upsetting he hadn't been arrested. It was terrifying. The three of us knew what he was capable of."

The guilt, sharp and relentless.

"So, you thought you'd take matters into your own hands?" Mike asked.

Priya's brown eyes latched onto his face. "Excuse me?"

"What were you doing outside Peter Miles's house two weeks before he was killed? Casing it out?"

Bree half hoped Priya would deny it. It wasn't as if she and Mike could prove otherwise if she did. They'd gone around to all of Maxine Miles's neighbors to find out if anyone had noticed the yellow Volkswagen. Either too much time had gone by, or Maxine was more observant than most, because none of them had any helpful information to offer.

"Yes, I was there once, a while ago. I just wanted to see him," Priya said. "I wanted to know what kind of life he had after what he did. But it was just the one time. He scared me too much."

"How did you know where he lived?" Mike asked.

The lighter was back in her pocket and her hands hung motionless at her sides. "I saw him in a grocery store. I thought he looked familiar, so I followed him."

"You followed him?" Bree's voice rose in surprise. *He didn't hurt her,* she reminded herself, *he can't hurt anyone now.* "That seems risky."

"It's why I only did it once. It scared me."

"What store did you see him at?" Mike asked.

Squinting at her feet, she was silent for a beat. "Uh. Morrisson's. On Fifth."

They could ask Maxine if her son frequented that particular shop, but Bree suspected that, like with almost everything else related to her son's life, she wouldn't know.

"What were you doing there? The closest grocery store to your apartment oughta be the one on Whitby. Fresh Plus, right?" Mike appeared disinterested in the answer, his eyes on his notepad, but Bree knew his attention was honed to a dangerously sharp point.

"Morrisson's is cheaper."

"Still out of your way."

"Not if I'm coming from work."

She offered only as much information as needed, and not one iota more.

Smart girl.

Bree asked, "Why didn't you tell us this the last time we spoke, Miss Shah?"

"Because I knew this would happen." The lighter was out again, flipping end over end between her fingers. "That you'd think I was doing something wrong."

"You do realize it makes you look more suspicious, the fact that you hid it from us?"

The lighter clattered to the ground and all three of them started. Bree realized she'd been mesmerized by its rapid movements between the woman's fingers.

Priya lifted it from the pavement. Straightening up, she looked at them and said, "I need to get back. I was in the middle of rounds and I'm not sure why you're really here. I haven't done anything wrong. I followed him home one time. It's not a crime, is it?"

She was right. At the most, they could try to nail her for stalking. But Peter Miles was dead and couldn't file a complaint anymore. None of what they had would stick. Bree felt a whisper of relief.

There was no point in prolonging the interview. She could see in Priya's eyes she was one more question away from calling a lawyer. Bree glanced at Mike. He seemed to notice too because he nodded.

"Of course, Miss Shah," she said. "Thank you for your time."

CHAPTER THIRTY-ONE

"Heads have got to roll, Detective," the chief said. "Or *a* head. Are you telling me you've got hardly anything?"

Bree hesitated. She'd spent all weekend rehearsing what she'd say in their Monday morning meeting. Yet it still felt like she was navigating a minefield, trying not to blow herself up by revealing too much. Mike didn't know about the IV, or the multiple strangulation attempts, or the crime scene witness. If she was careful, neither would the chief.

It was too late anyway. Bree had waited, and the decision was made for her. It'd been exactly one week since Chief Hunter assigned her the case. She'd been hiding information for nearly as long. She couldn't tell her partner at this point. Or anyone.

Now, sitting in his office, Mike perched in the chair next to her like a demure grizzly bear, Bree felt a new strain of guilt. For the first time in her professional life, she wasn't doing her job right. Chief Hunter had taken a chance by putting her on the case and here she was intentionally blowing it.

She cleared her throat. "I wish I had something more concrete to give you, sir. Our only theory, and it's tentative, is that Rebecca Grant's three best friends are involved somehow. They had motive, and they're each other's alibis for the night of the murder."

Rubbing his jaw, the chief said, "All right. Explain."

"Isabel Guerrero. Priya Shah." Bree hesitated for a fraction of a second before adding, "Dylan Darcy. All three were close to Rebecca, very close. They're still a tight-knit group. More so now, I'd say, because they share a common purpose: avenging their friend's murder."

A sharp laugh shot from the chief's mouth. She felt a small sense of relief at the incredulity on his face.

"Avenging her murder?" Chief Hunter said. "Are you serious? What is this, some kind of flower-power fantasy?"

"Like I said, it's tentative."

"I think there's something there, Chief," Mike said.

"And this is all based on what evidence?"

Mike looked down at his notebook. "Dylan Darcy saw Peter Miles almost daily. He was a barfly at Aces of Spades, where she works. Aces of Spades was the last place he was seen alive, and Dylan was working a shift that night. There's also a camera out front, but"—he glanced briefly at Bree then back to his notes—"on the night in question, he's picked up outside the camera's range."

A chill tickled the back of Bree's neck as she recalled watching the last hours of Peter Miles's life play out in grainy black-and-white. By daylight he'd be dead, and in the video, he had absolutely no clue of what awaited him.

"Dylan Darcy would know the security camera's blind spots," Mike added.

His eyes narrowed, the chief said, "Go on."

"A few weeks before Peter Miles died, Maxine Miles—that's his mother—spotted Priya Shah outside their residence." He paused before delivering the reveal. "Priya Shah admitted herself that she was outside his house."

"Oh?" One bushy gray eyebrow rose quizzically.

"She claims she spotted him in a grocery store and followed him home," Bree made sure to add. "She said she wanted to see where he lived."

"We think she was casing his house." Her partner's tenacity for the truth had never annoyed Bree as much as it did in that moment.

"Priya Shah. Where does she work?"

"She's a nurse at Wallis General," Mike said.

"Right, right. Okay, I'll suspend my disbelief long enough to see where this is going. Go on, Detectives."

"Well, they all share the same alibi. All three claim they were at Dylan's house for a movie night. Isabel Guerrero lives with her fiancé, but all he knows is she was away that night and returned the next afternoon—after stopping by the college to finish some work. She's a TA," Mike explained. "Getting her master's."

"Okay."

"Priya lives alone, so there's no one to confirm she was away that night. She did show up for her seven A.M. shift the morning after, but prior to that her only alibis are Dylan Darcy and Isabel Guerrero. We talked to a few of her colleagues, and they remember her seeming tired that day—but they claim that's not unusual. ER nurses work long shifts and they're understaffed a lot. Apparently, exhaustion is a normal part of the job."

It was an uncomfortable discovery Bree would undoubtedly remember if she ever wound up in the ER. It'd been a surprise to learn how little sleep people in the healthcare industry were functioning on.

"Dylan Darcy's neighbors have anything to say?"

"No one noticed anything unusual." Bree fiddled with the button of her blazer, then forced her hands to still.

"It's an up-and-coming neighborhood, Chief," Mike said. "The kind of place where everybody keeps to their own business. People aren't jumping at the chance to talk to cops, if you know what I mean."

"I do, yeah. Did the vehicle check raise any red flags?"

"We're still waiting on a warrant," Bree said. "The judge isn't sure there's enough evidence to sign off on a search of their vehicles."

"Jesus. So, let me get this straight: The two of you've got nothing."

This was the part she'd been dreading. At least Mike was there to shoulder some of the blame, Bree thought bleakly.

"No hard proof. Just some flimsy evidence that these three women colluded to murder the man they think murdered their friend. Do I have that right?"

"Sir—"

"Do you have any other suspects?" he cut her off. "Any other lines of investigation?"

She bit back the desire to tell him everything. To reveal what else she knew and say, "See? I am taking this seriously." But Bree stayed quiet.

"We could get a handwriting expert in," Mike suggested. "Try to match the handwriting on the sign to one of them."

He shook his head. "You can't rely on that in court. And you know what it would look like if we dragged Rebecca Grant's three closest friends in here on charges of kidnapping and murder? Three women too? After what happened to Rebecca Grant, I can't see anyone being too eager to prosecute them, much less serve on the jury that puts them behind bars. If we could even scrounge up enough evidence to take it to court in the first place."

Except for the chief's finger tapping against the desktop, the office was silent.

Chief Hunter sighed. "I trust your instincts, Detectives, I'm not saying I don't. I just don't see how we can work this out without it turning into a circus. We can't arrest any of them, not without solid proof. Something more than Dylan Darcy working at the same bar he liked, or Priya Shah following him home. And the other one? Uh—"

"Isabel Guerrero, sir," Mike prompted.

"Isabel Guerrero. How does she figure into any of this?"

Bree didn't have the energy left to speak. She let her partner answer.

"Well, if the other two kidnapped and killed him, at the very least she provided a false alibi to help them cover it up. She's an accessory."

Massaging his temple, the chief shook his head. "Maybe so, but you can't prove any of it. Not unless one of them confesses."

"So, what do we do?" Bree asked, feeling like she'd just run a gauntlet.

"Well, somebody's got to pay for Peter Miles's murder."

That's more than you ever said for Rebecca Grant. She tried to quell the rebellious thought, but it glared bright as an industrial spotlight in her mind's eye.

The chief's gaze turned to the blinds obscuring the window. On the other side, police officers and detectives were going about their daily work. He shook his head again. "Somebody's got to go down for this or there'll be hell to pay," he said, and her heart sank. "No pressure, Detectives, but I don't think anyone here is going to appreciate it much if this case goes cold."

CHAPTER THIRTY-TWO

Before

It dawned a muggy eighty degrees on the day they buried Rebecca Grant.

By mid-morning, when Bree arrived at the church, the temperature was in the nineties, the air like a damp sponge in a microwave set on high. Officer Morales was already there, looking like he'd rather have needles shoved under his fingernails than be doing this.

He had to be wondering what lapse in judgment prompted her to volunteer for press patrol. It was a rookie job. But Chief Hunter claimed she wasn't objective enough to work Rebecca's case, so he'd agreed to funeral duty. A morbid and inadequate consolation prize.

"We're here at First Presbyterian Church where family and friends have gathered to mourn Rebecca Grant's passing." The peach-pantsuit-clad newscaster to Bree's left spoke into the camera. "She was reported missing in mid-March. The recovery of her body just last week was the result of an extensive police investigation into her disappearance."

That was giving them a bit too much credit, Bree thought. The only reason Taylor and Santos kept the case open so long without a body was because Rebecca's parents wouldn't let it go. Her father called the station so often that they'd labeled him "looney dad."

Tuning out the reporter, Bree watched the parking lot fill up. It would be a *packed service. Good. Rebecca Grant deserved that, at least. At eleven, some-one closed the church doors.*

She let twenty minutes crawl by before saying, "I'm going to take a look around."

"Sure." Officer Morales stared off into the distance, his expression vacant.

Moving her badge along her belt so it was hidden by her blazer, Bree crossed the street. Inside, the only sounds were the hum of the central air-conditioning and the murmur of the minister's voice—a soothing duet. Bree opened one of the glass doors separating the foyer from the sanctuary and slipped in. The seats were full, relegating people to stand along the side and back walls. She sidled into an empty spot behind the pew to her left.

The enlarged photo sitting on an easel next to the casket made Bree's heart stutter. In it, Rebecca stood before a mountain range looking radiant in a pink beanie and blue jacket. She was grinning as if she'd just won the lottery.

Then she came to me for help and I sent her to die.

I knew what he was.

I could have saved her life.

The last thought settled on her shoulders like a slab of concrete. Bree willed the tears back. Over the years, she'd taught herself to feel in increments, a jar full of hornets she released one at a time. But now, confronted with Rebecca Grant's smiling face, her ruined body encased in a coffin, Bree felt that carefully maintained control slipping through her fingers.

Memories rushed in, burning like mental sulfuric acid. Of twenty-one-year-old Briana waking up in a stranger's dorm room. Her mouth feeling like it was coated with sand. Her pulse pounding in her temples. A thick gauze draped over the previous night so she could only recall that third beer he'd given her. Not what happened after.

For weeks, she wore bandanas around her neck to hide the bruises, until they were reabsorbed back into her body. She wished the flashes of memory would disappear the same way. Again and again, she asked herself: How did this happen?

It was simple, really. He was visiting friends and joined them at an end-of-semester party. She was two beers in, relieved finals were over and high on the fact that she'd secured a scholarship to the University of Massachusetts. Her master's would be starting in the fall. Then . . . D.C.? A job in the FBI? Who knew?

So, Briana was friendlier than usual when she found out he happened to be from the same Texas town. They'd even gone to the same high school—though he was a few years behind her, so they'd never crossed paths. It seemed like a funny coincidence. She allowed herself to relax. Hadn't been paying attention when he slipped something into her beer.

It colored her whole life, that night. It was why she become a police officer. Why she moved home when the local PD started hiring. A part of her hoped she'd find him. That life had shrunk in on him, and one day she'd get to be there with the handcuffs. Delayed justice.

What she didn't count on was that he was one of the supposed good guys.

Six months into her new job, she walked into a briefing and spotted him amongst the new recruits. He didn't spare her a glance—she'd put on twenty pounds and cut her hair since their last encounter—but she recognized him right away. And Bree, who hadn't gone by Briana since that night nearly twelve years before, instinctively pressed her hand to her neck.

Now she was at Rebecca Grant's funeral crying. Hard.

What am I doing? She was being ridiculous, weeping at the funeral of a woman she barely knew.

"Next," the minister said, "a few words from a close friend of Rebecca's. Dylan Darcy."

A woman rose and made her way to the podium. Her blue eyes glittered in bright contrast against her sallow skin as she turned to the congregation. It was like looking into the face of someone who was slowly starving to death.

No, that wasn't right. Bree tried to capture the thought as it fluttered just out of reach.

Then it hit her. She was like a dormant volcano. Bree could sense the rage there, just below the surface. Dylan was one spark away from a full-on eruption. She looked like she wanted to do something about all this.

Bree's thoughts whirled. The silence grew taut as an overstretched guitar wire.

"Fuck this," Dylan murmured. The microphone amplified her voice and someone gasped. The congregation sat in stunned silence as Dylan retraced her steps to her seat.

That's when Bree knew. Really knew. The idea felt as if it had always existed, but she'd been unable to acknowledge it until this moment. She needed to do something. She should have years ago. Then maybe none of this would have happened.

From where she stood, Bree could make out the top of Dylan's head. Maybe what she needed was an ally. Someone like Dylan.

The revelation intensified, grew more luminous, a lighthouse signal cutting through a thick fog. Then the fog cleared, and the solution imprinted itself in startling clarity:

Peter Miles has to die.

PART
THREE

THE SCAPEGOAT

CHAPTER
THIRTY-THREE

ISABEL

It'd been thirteen days.

As Isabel sat at her parents' dining room table that Thursday morning, she avoided thinking about it with the diligence of an efficient pilot bypassing a turbulent air pocket. Instead, she focused on grading the last few papers for Professor Stahm's class, half-listening as her mother and father talked.

"¿Ya tienes fecha para la boda?" her mother asked suddenly from her place by the stove.

It was the soundtrack of Isabel's life, asked with increasing frequency whenever she came around. *Do you have a wedding date?*

"Sit down, mami, I told you I'd do that," Isabel said, her eyes skimming the paper in front of her.

"Your father is picky about his eggs."

From the opposite end of the table where he sat with his own coffee, Isabel's father waggled his eyebrows at her. She smiled, then quickly stifled it as her mother turned around, the skillet gripped in one hand.

"¿Entonces?" she asked her daughter, sliding the scrambled eggs from the pan onto her husband's plate. "Are you planning to wait forever?"

Her mother settled into her chair with a sigh, like a tired hen roosting, and took a tortilla from the warmer.

"Hm," Isabel answered, taking a sip from her mug of sweet, milky coffee.

"There's no hurry," Isabel's dad said. "You don't want to rush into marriage, mija, you need to live with that person for the rest of your life."

"What's that supposed to mean?" Her mother paused with a rolled piece of tortilla halfway to her mouth.

"That it's a big decision."

"Yes, but you said it like *that*. As if your father would be living in half as much comfort without me." This was directed at Isabel.

"She's right. Without your mother I'd be a sad old man living in a room surrounded by take-out containers," Isabel's dad said with a wink.

"And plagued by heart disease too, no doubt," her mother muttered before putting the food in her mouth.

"Of course!" He placed his hand on top of where hers rested on the table. "Most serious of all the ailments would be a broken heart."

It was like watching two beloved actors ad-lib the lines of a familiar play. As Isabel knew she would, her mother gave in and smiled. Her parents leaned toward each other and shared a quick kiss. Isabel tried to imagine her and Paul in thirty years. Would they be anything like this? It was hard to believe.

"Anyway, Isa is almost twenty-nine," her mother said, as if she were ancient. "If not now, when?"

"We're waiting for things to calm down at work for Paul before we set a date," Isabel said, turning her attention back to grading.

"Hm. You've been saying that since he started. Why can't you plan in the meantime? Set a date for six months from now?"

Isabel was glad Paul wasn't there to hear the conversation, because he'd made a similar observation when they'd gotten engaged last August. When he asked, down on one knee at Hill Park, the location of their first kiss, Isabel hadn't wanted to say yes. Not right away. She stammered something about the timing. Paul had just started his new job. Isabel was still in school.

"Don't worry, we can plan the wedding in the meantime," he said. "There's plenty of time to figure things out, bunny-boo."

What Isabel hadn't told him was that she'd been requesting brochures from PhD programs, and one of them was at NYU, another at Berkeley. How could she explain to Paul—reliable, immutable Paul—that she didn't know what she wanted to do with her life, with her degree?

In the end, Isabel was too afraid of hurting his feelings to say no. After sliding the small diamond onto her ring finger, he enveloped her in a hug. Immediately, she was filled with a mixture of excitement and regret.

As she sat at her parents' breakfast table drinking coffee and jotting notes in the essay margins, Isabel wondered what would happen if she admitted these doubts to her mother. She hadn't even mentioned them to Priya and Dylan. Not because they wouldn't listen and offer advice, but because she didn't think either one of them would fully understand.

They wouldn't understand that even though Isabel didn't want to be one of those married girls with an expensive degree she never used, she liked the idea of marriage. She just didn't like the baggage. Didn't want to make a man's meals. Didn't want to wash Paul's dirty underwear. Or fry his eggs. Or . . . did she want his children? Sometimes she did, sometimes she didn't. Yet, even while the idea of doing any of that sounded ludicrous, there was also a certain appeal to it all.

At her core, Isabel knew what the problem was. She was a reluctant traditionalist. A serial monogamist who wished she was brave enough to be something else. To be ninety and look back at a long list of love affairs stretched out through her life like a string of beautiful pearls. And yet she craved the other too. The comforts of the same relationship decade in and decade out. The same home. The security of knowing Paul would always be there. That if she married him, she wouldn't ever be alone.

Beck would understand.

The thought stung. If there was any big regret, it was that she hadn't shared these feelings with Beck. Dylan had never compromised in her life, and Priya's relationship with her parents had been shaky ever since she backed out of an arranged engagement two years ago. But Beck . . . she knew how to walk the line between what she wanted and what her parents wanted for her. Beck would have known what to say. She'd have the right diplomatic words to explain that all Isabel craved was to have her cake and eat it too.

And why shouldn't she? Men did it all the time.

It didn't matter now though. Beck was dead. And Priya and Dylan . . . they'd been different the past two weeks.

She was finishing the last essay when the phone went off.

"Probably Joe calling about that drill," her father said, carefully wiping his mustache before rising and going out into the hallway to answer.

"Hello?" he said. There was a long silence followed by the click of the receiver as he hung up.

His brow was furrowed when he came back into the kitchen.

"¿Qué pasó?" Isabel's mother asked, looking up.

Her father's gaze seemed to linger on Isabel for a moment too long. Suddenly, her mouth felt like sandpaper. Was it the police? Were they coming to arrest her?

No. They wouldn't call to warn her beforehand. And there was nothing to arrest her for anyway.

"Papá? What happened?" she echoed her mother's question, laying her pen aside. "Who was that?"

He shook his head. "No one. Prank caller."

Her mother tsked and began to stack the dirty dishes. "Kids these days. Nothing to do but waste time—"

The phone rang and all three of them jumped. Isabel's heart pounded and she had trouble gripping her pen. She laid it down again. Dread coiled inside her, a rattlesnake preparing to strike.

Again, her father picked up, listened for a moment, then hung up.

When he came back, her mother rose to her feet. "What's the matter?"

He shook his head. "Maybe you shouldn't answer the phone today."

"¿Qué? That's ridiculous. Lulu is supposed to call—"

The phone trilled, cutting her off. This time they were all still;

three actors frozen on the set of a charged domestic scene. Isabel moved first, rising quickly and crossing to the hall where the phone table was.

"Isabel!" her dad called. "No—"

"Hello?" Isabel spoke into the receiver.

In the beat of silence that followed, she could make out someone breathing heavily on the other end.

"Murderous spic bitch," a man's voice hissed. Then the line went dead.

"Te dije que no contestaras." Her father had followed her to the hallway, his face flushed. "What did they say to you?"

Slowly, Isabel lowered the receiver back in place. She shook her head. "Nothing."

The walls appeared gelatinous as she walked past him down the hall to the bathroom. She closed and locked the door, then lowered the toilet lid and sat. She just needed a second to think.

The phone rang in the hallway, and Isabel pressed a hand to her mouth. The ringing stopped abruptly, and her father's voice swam through the bathroom door as a murmur. "Leave it off the hook today, Magda. Understand?"

She stood and faced the mirror over the sink. For a moment, her expression contorted. There was a stirring at the back of her mind. A wheezing. A memory trying to worm its way to the top. Her breath came in stutters. She turned on the faucet as hot as it could go, lathered up her hands, and began to scrub. The repetitive movement and scalding water calmed Isabel. Mesmerized, she watched her hands turn bright red as tendrils of steam curled around them.

Turning off the tap, she looked back in the mirror. Her expression had settled into stone again.

I'm fine. Everything's fine.

Isabel mussed her bangs. They needed a trim. She'd do that this afternoon.

She dried her hands and retraced her steps back to the kitchen.

"—nothing better to do than call decent people's home and play pranks." Her mother was leaning against the sink, the white-and-red-checkered dish towel in her hands flapping as she gestured.

Gathering her papers, Isabel said, "I have to go. Professor Stahm needs these for his ten o'clock class. Today is the second part of his lecture on saltation in phonology, and the students are getting their papers back." Why was she sharing this mundane information? Why couldn't she simply say, *I need to go to work* and leave it at that?

"You look pale." Her mother pressed the back of her hand to Isabel's forehead and frowned. "And you're cold as ice! Are you not sleeping well?"

"I'm sleeping fine, mami," she answered, and it was true. For the first time in months, years probably, Isabel was sleeping peacefully through the night. Even Paul was pleasantly surprised by the sudden end to her nocturnal flailing. What Isabel couldn't understand was why she still felt exhausted. Why, after a night of deep, long sleep, she still woke up as tired as if she hadn't slept at all.

"I think you should call your professor and tell him you can't come," her mother said. "You really don't look well."

"I told you, I'm fine." Isabel motioned with her chin to the papers in her arms. "Anyway, I can't miss work."

Her mother crossed her arms and cocked her head.

"I'll just drop them off and then go home to rest." This was a fib, but Isabel knew from experience it was the only way she'd get out the door. "Thanks for breakfast, mami." She planted a kiss on her cheek.

"Call Paul when you get home. Tell him you're sick. He'll look after you," her mother said. "I'll bring you some caldo later, mi amor."

"Please be careful, mija," her father said.

How did they know—whoever *they* were—her parents' phone number? Isabel wondered as she walked down the driveway to her car. She paused to look up and down the street. Did *they* know where her parents lived too? Did *they* know where she lived?

It wasn't supposed to be like this, she thought.

Dylan promised.

It was supposed to set us free.

CHAPTER
THIRTY-FOUR

TEXAS STATE PENITENTIARY
Fall 1995

Today, someone died in the communal showers.

Although died seems like the wrong word. As if she passed from old age or an illness. Succumbed to something outside her control.

They lock us in the cafeteria so they can retrieve the body. A murmur ripples around the room, information passed from one inmate to the next like a baton in a relay race.

"I don't see Tammy." Petra, the nineteen-year-old who's here on drug charges, scans the room. "Where's Tammy?"

I don't have the heart to state the obvious, so I wait until the baton reaches us and Petra hears the news from someone else. She gasps and, pressing a hand to her mouth, begins to sob noiselessly, fat tears rolling down her cheeks.

I look away.

They work so hard to keep us alive in here. The cells don't have bars so we can't hang ourselves off them. Our cutlery, cups, and trays are made of plastic, so we can't use them to self-harm. At-risk inmates are put on watch.

No one says it, but we all think it. That it's kind of impressive Tammy managed to find a way anyway.

When they bring her out, everyone rushes to the window overlooking the corridor. People shove at one another for a better view. All of us ghouls with nothing better to do.

Some women bang on the plexiglass as they wheel the body bag past. My chest tightens, and suddenly breathing becomes a chore. I back up to take a seat at one of the tables. I grip the hem of my shirt hard, as if that will make the room stop spinning. One thought plays on repeat:

The only way I'm leaving here is in a body bag.

Will my death be a spectacle like this one? Will other inmates fight for the best view as they take my corpse away? Will anyone cry for me, the way Petra cries over Tammy?

Will anyone care?

CHAPTER
THIRTY-FIVE

PRIYA

It wasn't as hard as Priya thought it would be to adjust. She just had to pretend it was all a dream, and that the person in that dream was an alternate version of herself. It wasn't really *Priya*. Not the Priya with a stable job, a book club, and all the responsibilities of a pet owner. Not the Priya who watered her plants on a strict schedule, always did laundry on Saturdays, and never went longer than two weeks without deep cleaning her apartment.

The Priya in that dream, the Priya who stood in that dark, abandoned house and watched a man suffer, that was a distinctly different Priya altogether. She existed only in that particular time, in that particular dream.

Was it a healthy coping mechanism? To detach from herself, like a cell splitting in two? Priya wasn't sure. It wasn't as if she could go to a support group and ask. Well, she could, if Isabel and Dylan counted as a support group.

They'd met up a few times since. Dylan was adamant that they continue with the farce of girls' night once a week—just to keep up appearances for the two detectives who were poking around the case. It was almost comical how uncomfortable these meetings between the three of them were. Isabel could barely stand to look anyone in the eye and Dylan alternated between lecturing them about carrying on as normal and flipping on the TV to fill the silence.

Priya had been schooled from a young age in the art of enduring awkward family get-togethers. She already had to grit her teeth through awful weekly dinners with her parents where they asked her probing questions about marriage and career and always, always acted disappointed in her answers. Silently sipping a glass of red while watching Dylan channel surf and Isabel pretend to read a book seemed easy in comparison.

She almost wanted to rub it in Dylan's face how well she was coping. At their first meeting after *it* happened, Dylan had launched into a long speech about how difficult the months ahead would be.

"Especially the next few months while the police investigate," she'd said. "Acting normal is going to be the hardest thing you've ever done, but you have to if we want to get away with it. Get on with your life like always. Act normal. Do all the stuff you normally do. And if you panic, if you need to talk, call me."

She'd set up a code phrase in case the police decided to bug their phones: *I'm craving chicken wings*. Say the phrase, and they'd meet at Aces for actual chicken wings. If they needed to talk, it would only be in person. Never on the phone.

I'm craving chicken wings.

Dylan liked to think she'd thought of everything. That she knew the score and was in complete control.

She wasn't, Priya thought as she changed out of her scrubs and into jeans and a white oversized blouse. The last time they'd met, Priya sensed something was off. Dylan had been talking with more urgency than before, reminding them for the thousandth time to act normal, when Priya saw it. A brief shift in her expression. A crack, small as a hairline fracture, in her façade. She suspected Dylan wasn't keeping it together as well as she wanted everyone to believe.

Not my responsibility.

Priya's mind was already moving away from the topic, racing ahead to what she needed to do with the rest of her day. She felt oddly energized, even after her twelve-hour shift. Maybe she'd pick up Echo and they'd go for a nice long walk. As she slipped into her

Chanel espadrilles and pulled on her jacket, she debated what to have for dinner.

Chinese?

Had it on Monday.

Indian?

Too cliché.

Or not. It was comfort food, even if whatever Priya made couldn't measure up to the quality of her mother's cooking. She settled instead on grabbing a pizza on the way home. At reception, she stopped a moment to chat with the nurse on duty, hoping Call-Me-Rick would emerge and she'd have an excuse to walk out with him. The feeling of his hand on her waist still lingered from earlier when Priya turned a corner too fast and nearly collided with him.

"Whoa. Careful," Dr. Richard Schmidt said as his hand flashed out to steady her. He'd pressed it to her waist for less than a second before withdrawing it and leveling her with a dazzling smile. "Where's the fire, Priya?"

She thought she would melt right then and there. The hand on her waist was probably more instinct on his part than anything else, but then maybe it wasn't. Maybe he was hinting at something. The thought both excited and terrified her. Would the physical aspects of a relationship be easier with someone like him, someone she genuinely liked?

It didn't matter, she reminded herself. Call-Me-Rick was probably married and that was a moral boundary Priya could never cross.

I'm okay with murder but adultery is where I draw the line?

The thought made Priya snort as she crossed the parking lot.

No, Dream Priya is okay with murder. Real Priya isn't okay with murder or *adultery.*

She sidled around to the driver's door and stopped, one hand gripping the collar of her jacket, the other tight around her purse strap.

Someone had taken a key to the side of her Bug, scraping through the yellow paint to leave the words KILLER CUNT behind.

Priya's breath started coming short and fast. She backed up a few steps and looked around. Her heart felt like it was trying to claw its way out of her body through her mouth. Suddenly, in a perverse coincidence of bad timing, there was Rick, crossing the parking lot in her direction. He waved.

The first crazed thought through her mind was that she couldn't let him see it. Somehow, Rick would know it was true. He'd be able to read it in her expression and then any chance she had would be over. But she couldn't move, couldn't force her face into a smile that said, *Everything's fine here.*

"You okay, Priya?" he asked when he got closer. Behind his glasses, his blue eyes stared intently.

Snap out of it.

"Yes," she managed to say. But her voice sounded mangled.

"Oh, my word." Rick stopped next to her and stared. "Is this your car?"

For a brief second Priya debated saying *No.* But that would be pointless. She was sure he already knew the answer.

"Yes." Priya pressed a hand to her mouth, trying to stop it from happening, but it was too late. She started to cry.

"Oh, Priya." He wrapped an arm around her, and she pressed her forehead into his shoulder. "Who would do something like this? It's okay. It's going to be okay."

The logical part of Priya's brain warned her that she shouldn't be enjoying this as much as she was. Someone out there *knew,* and here she was pretending to cry—because the real tears had been over almost as quickly as they'd begun—so Call-Me-Rick would hold her and comfort her for just a moment longer.

She forced herself to step back (did he seem reluctant to let her go?) and wiped her fingers across her eyes.

"Angry ex-boyfriend?" he asked, then hurried to add, "You don't have to tell me anything, of course. Let me help you out. We'll get you taken care of."

He dug his wallet from the back pocket of his tan chinos and Priya caught a brief glimpse of the photograph inside the clear sleeve when he flipped it open. Call-Me-Rick in nothing but a pair of red swim trunks, his arm wrapped around a blond woman's shoulders.

For a moment, Priya thought he planned to give her money. Instead, Rick pulled out a business card and presented it to her. In bright red script against a neon yellow background it read: JIMMY'S CAR AND TRUCK REPAIR.

"Drive over there now," he said. "They'll buff it right off. You might have to go back for the paint job, but at least you won't be driving around town with . . . that on the side of your car. And tell them Dr. Schmidt recommended you. Jimmy's a good guy, he'll give you the friends and family discount." Rick winked at her.

"Thank you," Priya said. His decency made things worse. This man would break her heart and never even know it.

"Have you called the police yet?"

The question stopped her in her tracks. Priya's mind raced. "I'll drive to the nearest station to make a report in person. That way they can see it." She paused, trying to gauge if he believed her or not. "It seems more efficient that way."

"You've got a cool head on your shoulders, Priya. Efficient, even under pressure."

The compliment warmed her like a hot bubble bath.

She smiled. "Thanks."

"Again, I'm so sorry this happened. Can I give you another hug?"

As if she would say no to that. They hugged and when they pulled apart the two of them laughed in unison.

"Better get going," Rick said. "Jimmy's closes at seven."

"Okay. Thank you."

That can't be it, Priya thought as she turned away.

What would Dream Priya do? The question flashed through her head out of nowhere. She knew what Dream Priya would do, but the question was whether Dream Priya could overpower Real Priya long enough to do it.

She stopped and half-turned, her hand resting on the top of her car. Rick was already moving away, back to the parking spots reserved for doctors.

Before she could lose her nerve, she called, "Rick?" To her surprise, he both heard her and turned around. Now it was too late. Priya swallowed and forced the words out. "Maybe I could buy you a drink sometime? As a thank-you?"

There was a pause. Her cheeks grew warm. It felt like high school all over again, but somehow worse. They weren't two pimply teen-agers who would go their separate ways in a few years. He was her colleague, and now she'd have to face him—and this rejection—every day if she wanted to keep her job.

He ran a hand through his reddish hair. "You know what, Priya? I'd like that."

Her clenched jaw relaxed.

"But I'll buy," Rick added with a smile. "I'm old-fashioned like that."

"Okay." She had to battle to keep the giddiness out of her voice.

"Right now you need to focus on getting that taken care of." He motioned to her car. "We'll set a date later."

Somehow, Priya managed to smile and wave like this was normal. Like men agreed to dates with her all the time. She climbed into her car and sat there for a few moments, her heart doing a frantic tap dance. Then the foolish grin slowly faded as an old fear wriggled its way in.

What if she couldn't measure up to his expectations? What if he saw her for who she really was and didn't like it?

Across the street, the Texas flag outside the squat brick building housing the town's only Blockbuster hung limp, as if mimicking her mood. Priya forced herself to start her car and pull out. The same thought echoed again and again in her head as she drove.

That maybe Call-Me-Rick's *yes* wasn't such a victory after all.

CHAPTER
THIRTY-SIX

ISABEL

Isabel managed to get the graded papers handed over to Professor Stahm just a few minutes before class started. In his typical reserved way, the professor refrained from commenting on how last-minute the whole thing was, just leveled her with a stern look over the top of his glasses.

There'd been a few hours spent in the library afterward, trying to source an obscure reference to language development in the Middle Ages, followed by a meeting with her advisor about her thesis. It was a surprise to learn that, despite all the recent distractions in Isabel's life, he believed she was on the right track and making good progress. They fell into a discussion about the origins of fate (*fari, fatum*) and its application to modern life. Isabel had been fascinated by fate lately, and she plunged into the conversation so thoroughly that by the time she checked her watch nearly an hour and a half had gone by.

"Well," her advisor, Lucas, said. "As always, these chats are an immense pleasure, Isabel. I haven't any doubt you'll blow us all away once your thesis is finished."

"Thank you." Her mind raced as she tried to think of something else to say. She wished she could stay curled up in the conversation forever, eternally debating the philosophical nature of fate.

But before she was able to find a way to prolong their interaction, Lucas slapped his palms against his thighs and said, "Well! I have an appointment I'm already late for. So . . ."

There was nothing else for Isabel to do but take the hint. They exchanged goodbyes and vague pleasantries about meeting again soon. With as much enthusiasm as a barnacle detaching from the hull of a ship, she left his tiny basement office.

Outside, rays of afternoon sun coated the walkways like thick honey. The sights and sounds of daily academia soothed her, and as Isabel made her way to the campus parking lot, she felt herself relax. Students crossed the quad in pairs. Despite the chill, study groups sat in circles on the grass, thermoses of hot drinks pinning their books open on the ground. Her mind turned to home and the comfort of her green easy chair—the one new item she'd purchased for herself after she won the grant to study for her master's.

It'd been a long day, but there were still several hours of work left. At least she could do it from her favorite chair, a pot of mint tea at her elbow, and her cat, Señor Octavio Paws (named after the great Mexican poet), purring in her lap. Paul would be working late, and she was glad. Ever since the police dragged him into the precinct for questioning, her fiancé had been hovering around her like a concerned stage parent.

It was decidedly unsexy, but then they hadn't had sex in . . . how long? Isabel couldn't remember, which was even more concerning than if she had. She'd been distracted; he'd been worried. None of it was conducive to romance.

As she began the forty-minute drive back, Isabel went over her advisor's pointers, mentally working through each one and trying to come up with a plan. She was just pulling onto the main roadway through town when something caught her eye in the rearview mirror. Blue and red lights were flashing on the car behind her. She inhaled sharply. How long had the police car been there before she noticed?

It couldn't have been long, Isabel reassured herself as she signaled and prepared to pull over, otherwise they would have used the siren.

She turned onto a side street and angled the car up next to the curb. In her rearview mirror the other car copied her. That was when she noticed it wasn't the usual black-and-white police cruiser. The car was plain—except for the flashing lights it looked like any other ordinary car.

Isabel checked to make sure all her doors were locked before reaching for her purse. Someone appeared in the peripheral of her vision, an older, heavyset man in a button-up gray shirt and khaki trousers. She rolled down the window a few inches and peered up at him. His face was red, as if he'd been running.

"License," he barked before she could ask why she'd been pulled over.

It seemed to take an eternity to dig her wallet from her purse, then work her license free. The clear plastic card holder refused to relinquish its grip, her trembling hands only making matters worse. When she did get it out, she immediately dropped it and had to fish it from the floor on the passenger's side before handing it through the gap in her window with a soft, "Sorry."

He regarded the license in silence, his eyes moving from it to her and back. Isabel fidgeted and tried not to look guilty. There was a flash of movement on her right and she glanced over and jumped. Another man was standing on the passenger side. He was younger than the one holding her license and was peering through the window at her, as if observing a strange animal at the zoo.

Isabel's heart banged in her chest like a fist against a wood door. This wasn't how routine traffic stops went. Something wasn't right.

I can drive away at any time, she reminded herself, discreetly checking again to make sure her doors were locked.

"Why did you pull me over, Officer?" she asked. It suddenly occurred to her that these men might not be police. What was to stop someone from putting a blue light on their vehicle and pretending to be an officer of the law?

The man placed a hand on the top of her car and stood looking down at her.

"Could I see your badge, please?" she said. It was hard not to keep swiveling her head back and forth, looking from one side to the other, but she wanted to keep track of what the second man was doing.

The older man laughed. "No."

Her hand found the gear stick. "I'd like my license back, please."

"You're Isabel Guerrero, huh?"

She didn't say anything. The man leaned down and pressed his face to the driver's side window. Isabel recoiled. Fear gripped her chest so hard she could barely breathe, barely think.

"Where've I heard that name before, huh?" Tapping his forefinger against his chin, he mimed deep thought. "Oh yeah, you're a suspect in Peter Miles's murder. One of three, I hear. Isn't that right?"

His partner nodded. "Right."

"He was a good man, a good cop."

"Yep," the other man said.

"A good man's life ruined by three vindictive bitches." His brown eyes bored into Isabel. "A real shame."

"Yep," the younger man agreed.

"What do we do to cop killers in this town?"

His partner leaned down too and pressed his face close to the passenger's side window. The car seemed to be caving in on Isabel, the air growing compact. It was like trying to inhale water.

"Oh, cop killers get what they deserve. Sooner or later." The corners of his mouth lifted into a smile. It made him look almost boyish. If it weren't for the circumstances, it would have seemed like a welcoming grin.

"They do indeed," the older man said. "They do indeed."

The two of them straightened in unison and he tossed the license at her. It pinged off the window and fell to the pavement.

"We're just looking out for you, sweetheart. You and your friends be careful, you hear me?"

She watched in the mirror as they walked back to their car, got in, and pulled away from the curb. Neither one looked at her as they drove slowly past. At the end of the block the car turned left and disappeared. Gripping the steering wheel like a life raft, Isabel allowed her gaze to return to the rearview mirror.

You're okay. Everything's okay, she reassured her reflection.

Again, a rustle in the recess of her mind. Something trying to crawl free from the deep well where she'd thrown it. Cold, clammy fingers curled along the well's rim. It began to heave itself up over the side.

A shiver passed through Isabel's body. She laid her flattened palm against her cheek, then took some of the soft flesh between her thumb and index finger and twisted. Tears rose in her eyes, then receded. The thing released its hold and slipped back down into the well with a plop. Gradually, the pressure in Isabel's chest eased and her breathing slowed.

She dropped her hand back to the steering wheel. There was a red welt on her cheek, but it would fade. The others had. Isabel took a compact from her purse and dabbed some concealer over the mark anyway. Then she ran a finger beneath each eye to wipe away the smudged mascara. Smoothing down her bangs, she took a deep breath.

Checking and rechecking that the men were gone, Isabel finally worked up the courage to open her car door a few inches and reach down to grab her license. She locked the door again, checked all the windows, and twisted around in her seat to look out the back too. The street was quiet. Two boys cycled past, not seeming to notice the woman sitting in her car, looking like she'd met the devil.

Not the devil, Isabel thought. *His minions.* She crossed herself before putting the car into drive.

I haven't done anything wrong.

That's what she should have told them. Not that they'd believe her, but at least she would have defended herself.

She repeated it like an incantation. A prayer.

Hail Mary, full of grace, the Lord is with thee.

I haven't done anything wrong.

I haven't done anything wrong.

CHAPTER
THIRTY-SEVEN
PRIYA

Priya marched up Dylan's walk, her brain a boiling mass of fury. From inside the house, Echo began to bark.

"Hey, Pri," Dylan greeted her when she opened the door.

Echo bounced on his hind legs, faking jumping up to put his paws on Priya. Although she hadn't seen her dog since early this morning—when she dropped him off at Dylan's before her shift—Priya couldn't bring herself to mirror his excitement. As if sensing something was off, he stopped barking and backed up a few steps to stand, head cocked to one side, tail still wagging furiously.

"You're late. Everything okay?"

"Have you spoken to Isabel?" Priya asked. Seeing Echo usually brought a sense of immediate calm, but it wasn't the case today. It made her angrier. Dylan ruined everything.

"What? No. Why?" Her brow furrowed; her eyes needled Priya's face. She was like an alert spider, watching and waiting.

"She was threatened today, Dylan. By two cops."

Dylan glanced back and forth up the street then stepped back. "Why don't you come inside."

"What are we going to do?" she asked as she stepped into the foyer.

Even when she was mad, it was hard to disobey Dylan. "First, my car gets vandalized, then Isabel gets pulled over—"

"Your car was vandalized?" She closed the door too hard, and Priya jumped. "Why didn't you tell me?"

"Because I thought maybe it'd be an isolated incident. Then Isabel told me about what happened to her."

Echo weaved back and forth between them as they walked into the living room. Dylan took a seat on the couch, but Priya leaned against the doorframe and folded her arms across her chest.

"I'm guessing you don't know about the calls either." She felt a small surge of triumph when Dylan shook her head. For once, Priya was more in the loop. "Isabel's parents have been getting weird phone calls. These men calling them names then hanging up. This is serious."

"Okay." She sighed. "So, what are you here to say, Pri? That you feel guilty?"

"Guilty? Are you kidding? Of course I do, don't you? We killed someone!"

Resting her elbows on her knees, Dylan stared up at her. "He was a monster."

"Be that as it may, now it's too late. We've done this—this horrible thing." She found herself pacing back and forth, Echo at her side as if attached to her leg by an invisible lead. "We can't take it back. He's dead. We killed him. And the police know. They're just gathering enough evidence so they can arrest us. Oh, god." She stopped in her tracks and looked at Dylan. Her rage was gone. Horror took its place, like a cold blade pushed between her ribs. "Should we try to leave the country? Go to South America or something? Oh, god." She began to cry. "This is going to kill my parents."

"Priya. Pri," Dylan repeated more forcefully. "Sit down."

"I don't want to go to prison." Priya wiped her nose on the back of her hand and sank onto the love seat. "I don't think I can handle that. I'll kill myself first."

"Calm down. You're not going to jail." The weariness in Dylan's voice did nothing to ease Priya's anxiety.

"Gee, I wasn't aware you had magical powers that could keep us out of prison, Dylan. I'm *so* relieved."

The sarcasm prompted Dylan to roll her eyes. "Okay. Who pulled Isabel over? I'm betting it wasn't Bree." When Priya looked at her blankly, she added, "The woman detective. The one working his case."

"Well, no," she answered, reluctant. A logical explanation was coming, Priya could sense it. She just wasn't so sure she wanted to be explained to and calmed down.

"I'm also betting it wasn't Bree who vandalized your car. It's some guy in uniform. Some asshole looking out for his own."

"His own?"

"Male cops who do bad shit."

"Isabel said the guys who pulled her over weren't in uniform."

"Was she sure they were cops?" Dylan sat back and crossed her arms.

Echo lowered himself to the ground by Priya's feet and rested his head on his paws. She reached down and scratched his ear. Would her parents look after him if she went to prison for murder? *No.* Priya's dad was gentle, but Echo wouldn't care. To the dog, a man was a man.

They'd have to take him back to the animal shelter. The thought was an excruciating nail hammered straight into her heart. No one would be as patient with her dog, as willing to excuse his quirks, as she was.

"She said they had a police light on their car." Priya started the story at the beginning and repeated what Isabel had told her over the phone an hour earlier. Then she described the two horrible words she'd found scratched into the side of her own car. When Priya finished, there was a brief silence.

"Why didn't Isabel tell me about it herself?" Dylan asked.

"I don't know. I think she wanted to."

"But she didn't."

"Maybe she's scared of you, Dylan."

Her expression hardened. "You're not serious."

"Of course I'm serious! This is all serious! It's not a game."

"I know that." Her tone was flat. "It's just a little ridiculous coming from Isabel of all people. I knew she wasn't cut out for this."

Priya chose not to comment on Dylan's bloodshot eyes. Or the dark circles beneath them. When she'd come in, Priya had noticed the stack of neatly folded bedding at one end of the couch and wondered why Dylan was sleeping in her living room. Now she realized it was because the TV was there. The diagnosis became suddenly obvious: Dylan was battling insomnia.

For a long time neither one of them spoke. Dylan slumped back into the sofa like a deflated pool float and Priya sat hugging one of the square cushions against her stomach as if she wanted to absorb it.

"How is Isabel?" Dylan said finally. "Really?"

That's a good question. She squeezed the cushion tighter.

"Honestly? I think she's completely shut down."

"Shut down?"

"On the phone she sounded almost—" Priya struggled to find the right way to describe the near-catatonic rhythm of Isabel's speech. What was most disturbing was that she hadn't cried once while telling Priya the story. Isabel. Who cried over things like stray cats and St. Jude's Children's Hospital commercials. "It's like she's in denial. Like she's pretending it didn't happen. Or"—Priya lifted her shoulders in a shrug—"maybe she's really blocked it all out. I don't know. But I think she doesn't want to see you because she's afraid it'll all come to the surface."

"I didn't force her to do anything she didn't want to."

"I'm not saying you did. But you have this ability to . . . manipulate situations to suit your agenda."

"My agenda?" She sat up straight. "You're really going to play that card, Pri? I'm not some mastermind who manipulated you all into that house. Isabel volunteered to pick him up, remember? She practically begged to be the one to do it. And then . . ." Dylan stopped and turned her face away to stare at the wall for a moment. When she spoke next, her voice was like a newly sharpened scalpel. "All I'm saying is, maybe you and Isa should look at the fucking planks in your own eyes before you come fishing for the splinter in mine."

"Planks? What's that supposed to mean?"

"I forget you weren't raised with all that evangelical bullshit. It's from the Bible. It means don't judge me when you've got plenty to be judged about. You both do."

They stared at each other across the coffee table.

"You want a drink?" Dylan broke the thick silence, rising before Priya had the chance to answer. Echo's collar tags jingled as he lifted his head to watch her leave. Then he rested his snout back on his paws and sighed.

One thought after another whirled through Priya's mind. She couldn't decide what to do next. Would it be better to come forward and confess? If she did, she'd get a lighter sentence for being the first. But she couldn't, because that would mean Dylan and Isabel would suffer. And she'd have to leave Echo behind. Decades in a cell without pets or being able to wear pretty clothes or eat good food. She'd probably never see Call-Me-Rick again either. And for what? Revenge? Justice?

Suddenly she wasn't so sure it'd been worth it.

Against her will, Dream Priya and Real Priya had merged. It was foolish to assume it could be any other way. Even if Priya didn't go to prison, she'd live with those mental images for the rest of her life. His agony. His dignity gone. The way he—

The way he talked about Beck, like she was nothing to him. Like he didn't care what he'd done.

A glass appeared in her periphery. Priya took it and immediately felt comforted by its heft. She pressed her fingers into the intricate grooves in the crystal. It was weird, she thought, how Dylan didn't care about appearances. She wasn't embarrassed by how shabby her old house looked, and she never wore pretty things—at least not what Priya would consider pretty. But decent drinking glasses were the one luxury she seemed to allow herself.

Dylan set the bottle of Don Julio on the table and took a seat, a matching highball glass in her own hand. With a flutter of alarm, Priya noticed there was only a fourth of tequila left in the bottle.

"I thought you were going to return that to the bar," she said.

Dylan shrugged. "Special circumstances."

"You didn't—you didn't drink all that by yourself, right?"

Eyebrows raised, she shot Priya a loaded look. "I'm coping fine, Pri. Don't worry. Are you okay?"

Priya snorted. "Define 'okay.' I guess considering everything, yes, I'm okay." She tapped the side of her glass with her fingernails.

It was a little ironic, she realized suddenly, that the one person who probably had the right skill set to psychologically help them through this was dead.

We wouldn't even be in this situation if Beck were alive.

The thought sent a corkscrew of pain plummeting through her.

"So, what do we do now?" Priya asked. Was this what her life would be from now on, always looking to Dylan for direction?

"Nothing. We covered our tracks. The police may have suspicions, but they don't have evidence. If they did, they'd have already arrested us." She sipped her drink. "I know it's hard, but we have to wait it out. I'm sorry about what happened to you both, but we knew what we did would get a reaction. It was intended to. Why else did you suggest that sign?"

Priya nodded and took a pull of her drink. The tequila warmed the back of her throat.

"What about Isabel?" she asked.

"What about her." Dylan shrugged again. "Sounds like she's doing fine."

"I don't think she is, Dylan."

"Why? Because she's not acting emotional enough for you?"

"Come on." Priya shook her head. "This is Isabel we're talking about. She's always emotional. I'm worried this is the calm before the storm and she's going to have a breakdown."

Rubbing her fingers in a circular motion against her temple, Dylan appeared to consider this for a few moments. "Or, she's fine. We're all adults, and we all made choices. Now we have to make a few more to protect each other. If you're worried, remind Isabel that she just has to make one choice at a time, Pri. They all add up, but it's really one choice at a time."

"Thirty-three percent," she said softly.

"Thirty-three percent," Dylan agreed.

Where did that leave the remaining one percent, Priya wondered later as she guided Echo down the walk to the car. Because someone had to take responsibility for it, and it wasn't going to be her.

CHAPTER
THIRTY-EIGHT

DYLAN

On Tuesday afternoons Dylan cleaned the taps. There was usually a lull—the "dead zone" her manager liked to call it—when the bar got quiet. Even the drunks stayed away. She could never figure out why. Maybe there happened to be an AA meeting in the neighborhood. Or there was some unspoken superstition about drinking on Tuesdays.

Whatever it was, Dylan didn't mind. A quiet bar was meditative. She'd turn off the music and get carried away by the silence. The rich smell of leather stools, stale peanuts, and spilled beer mixed with the chemical lemon scent of the brass polish. The bartender's incense.

She drained and cleaned out the taps, then applied a coat of polish to the first one. Carefully, she wound the cloth through the small grooves and over the curves—like going through the motions of a familiar exercise routine. Dylan was polishing the final tap when the door creaked open and closed. Footsteps crossed the floor to the bar.

"Have a seat. I'll be with you in a sec," she said without looking up.

"Hi, Dylan."

Her eyes lifted. "Hey, Bree-Like-the-Cheese."

The detective didn't smile, not that she expected her to. Instead, she looked around the empty bar and said, "It's quiet today."

"It's Tuesday afternoon." Dylan didn't offer more of an explanation. She went back to work on the tap, trying to appear nonchalant. "You want a drink?" she asked when Bree slid onto a barstool.

"I can't. I'm on the job."

"Yeah?"

"Yes."

Dylan felt her pulse speed up slightly, but she resisted asking Bree why she was there. Let her come out and say so on her own.

"Rebecca Grant's father came into the station yesterday," Bree said after a few ticks of silence.

Eyes on the tap, Dylan didn't respond. She rubbed harder, gradually bringing her reflection into sharp focus on the gold brass.

"He wanted to confess to Peter Miles's murder," she continued.

As she worked the rag slowly back and forth around the pipe, Dylan willed her heart to match its rhythm. Her hands were steady. At least there was that.

"You think he did it?" she asked.

Bree took a cocktail napkin from the nearby caddy and flattened it on the bar top. "He was a mess. So drunk he could barely stay on his feet. We put him in holding overnight to sober him up, in case he wanted to change his tune."

This made Dylan pause. Mr. Grant so pissed he could barely stand? It was hard to imagine. She'd never seen him drunk, not even after Beck's funeral. He was a man of singulars, one glass of red wine, one vodka on the rocks, one bottle of beer.

"Sober and probably with a hangover the size of Texas this morning, and he still wanted to confess," Bree said.

"And?"

She shook her head. "I doubt he had anything to do with it. He'd certainly like to though. My guess is, he can't stand that he wasn't able to protect his daughter. He wants to feel like he did something about her death."

Extending her arms to each side, Dylan pressed her palms to the bar top. "Why are you telling me?"

"You were close to the Grants, I thought you'd want to know." She played with the cocktail napkin, curling the corner and flattening it out again. "I've been wondering about this a lot the past few weeks. Peter Miles's death—did it achieve what it was meant to? It can't undo the past. It won't bring Rebecca back." Her brow furrowed, and she paused and swallowed before continuing. "It just ends up hurting more people."

"Maybe. Or maybe it saved people from hurt. Eventually he would have done it to somebody else, you know. Another woman."

"Not if he'd gone to prison."

"You really believe he would've?"

Silence fell like dense snow. Bree kept her eyes on the napkin, folding and creasing each corner. Dylan could see her brain trying to work out a diplomatic answer. None seemed to come, because after a few more moments of thought the detective sighed and got to her feet.

"I don't know. Maybe there's no justice in this situation."

"I disagree." Their gazes locked in a silent combat.

Bree looked away first. "Sometimes it's like religion, isn't it?" she said. "This whole concept of justice. They tell you that you need to have faith. Faith in the system, faith that the bad guys will pay."

"Do you have faith the system works? That the bad guys pay?" Dylan asked. "Really?"

Squinting slightly, Bree lifted her shoulders in a weak shrug. "Sometimes. But what worries me in this particular case is that the wrong person is going to pay for Peter Miles's murder. The department just wants a suspect, and at this point I don't think they care who it is. If Mr. Grant tries to confess a second time . . . I can't guarantee he'll walk out again."

"They couldn't make it stick."

Bree exhaled softly through her nose. "They can make anything stick, Dylan. If they really want to."

Her boots clacked on the wood floor as she walked toward the door. There was a brief stab of sunlight, the detective nothing more than a dark silhouette in the doorway. Then it swung shut again, sealing Dylan back in the safe ecosystem of the bar.

For a few moments the only things moving were her racing thoughts. The cocktail napkin lay crumpled on the bar where Bree had left it like a discarded idea. The door swung open again, and Dylan's heart did a double leap at the thought that she was back. That she had something else to say. But the silhouette blended into the bloated features of a man in a cowboy hat—her first real customer of the day.

Dylan straightened up and adjusted her shoulders. *Act normal.* That was the advice she'd given to Priya and Isabel. No matter what Bree revealed, Dylan needed to stick to the plan. *Act normal. Reveal nothing.*

"Pull up a stool," Dylan told the customer, forcing a smile onto her face. She crumpled the napkin in her fist and dropped it into the trash can. "What can I get you?"

CHAPTER
THIRTY-NINE

DYLAN

The bar was so busy that Thursday night that Jason—who never voluntarily stepped up unless she was drowning—finally got off his ass to help. It infuriated Dylan that her manager could make her job easier all the time but chose not to. And even though he doled out his help like a miser giving pennies to a beggar, she couldn't complain because it was better than nothing at all.

They glided behind the bar like two dance partners intuitively picking up on each other's body language. She reached for a pint glass, he ducked to get more peanuts from the cupboard. She stepped back from the tap with a full glass in each hand, he moved smoothly in to set another beneath the still-running spout.

The weather had taken a surprise turn yesterday, a cold front rolling in and freezing everything overnight. Aces of Spades—like most bars in town—always got slammed on cold nights. People seemed to want to gather and socialize. It had to be some primitive instinct; the cave person's need to seek out warmth evolving into modern-day John and Jenny hitting up their local pub in search of liquor and conversation.

Isabel would probably know all about how socializing instincts had changed throughout history. It seemed right up her nerdy alley, not that Dylan could ask. Isabel didn't want to speak to her. Priya had agreed to reassure Isabel that things would settle down. But could Dylan trust her to communicate how urgent it was for them to be patient? She wasn't sure. It occurred to her that if they weren't careful, Isabel would be the one to turn on them, to take them all down. It was no good to start yet though. Space. Isabel just needed a little space to process everything.

Dylan was making a Tom Collins when Jason sidled up to her and said, "There's some customers looking for you."

She glanced in the direction he jerked his thumb. Two men had taken the last pair of stools and sat, elbows leaning on the bar, watching her. One was on the heavy side, his thick mustache in strong contrast to his bald head. He stared at her through small eyes set deep into his doughy face. The fabric of his gray button-down strained against the heft of his upper arms. He'd folded the sleeves to reveal thick, hairy wrists.

His companion was younger and trimmer with a clean-shaven jaw and a military-style buzz cut. He had that haunted look, though slightly more controlled, of a man who'd been in a war and seen some shit. Dylan could pick out the type right away—a few of those came into the bar regularly to get drunk. Vets from the Gulf War or, in one case, the Vietnam War. Even though Vietnam had ended nearly twenty years before, that particular veteran—a disheveled one-eyed man in his forties named Johnny—still had that drawn, preyed-upon look. As if he couldn't trust anyone around him to not start shooting.

When Johnny came in, usually on Wednesday afternoons, Dylan always felt sorry for him. She'd give him a free shot of whiskey and let him chat her up about Bernard who, from Johnny's descriptions, she'd deduced was an extremely overweight and astonishingly spoiled tuxedo cat.

This guy was the complete opposite of Johnny though. He put care into his appearance. As if his ironed shirt, navy blazer, and striped tie would keep the nightmares at bay. Maybe they did, some of the time. Maybe they all needed something different to fight off the demons. Johnny had his cat, and this guy had his tidy clothes.

Dylan thought of the bottle of tequila on her coffee table at home. She knew a thing or two about battling the monsters in her head.

She only got in a quick look before focusing again on the Tom Collins, but it was enough. Dylan could smell cop stink—even with her back turned and four feet of bar between her and them. It was like the way she could sniff out an undercover detective when she went through her shoplifting phase as a teen. Except for that one time, when they caught her walking out of the store with a few pairs of gold earrings and two lip gloss tubes. Her aunt had smacked her around a bit to put the fear of God in her, but that didn't cure Dylan. It just made her more careful.

Of course, she hadn't been able to sniff out Bree either. Somehow, Bree managed to completely disarm her. But, like she'd done when she got caught shoplifting, Dylan learned her lesson. She'd be more careful from now on.

As she topped off the glass with soda water, she ran through the options of who the two men could be. Cops, yes, but what were they here about? Why were they asking for her? The most logical answer was that Bree was no longer working the Peter Miles case. Maybe these two cops had taken over and were here to question her.

The idea irritated Dylan. The two goons couldn't have chosen a better time? When the bar wasn't so busy? Beneath the irritation, like a narrow stream, ran worry. Bree was unbiased. Or at the very least she evened out the score because she was a woman and a cop who believed women. It was going to turn into a real shit show, and fast, if there were two men in charge.

She placed the drink on a coaster and slid it across to Darla, the sweet sixty-something-year-old who came in on Thursdays for a Tom Collins and a hamburger. She called it her "date with Tom," which never failed to make Dylan laugh. She was a widow and her son lived in Florida, only coming home once a year to visit. Dylan knew all this because when the bar was quiet, she and Darla would talk. Last week, Darla had lamented that her son was pressuring her to move to Florida to live in his guesthouse.

"That sounds like hell," Dylan said.

"Oh, my dear," Darla replied. "Getting old is hell. Past a certain age, everyone starts treating you like your mind is going and you're infirm, whether you really are or not."

That's why I'm ending it all at sixty-five, Dylan thought. She didn't say it out loud—that would have been too depressing a thing to say to someone who probably *was* sixty-five. But it was something she'd always felt sure of. Dylan didn't want to be old—not because she was afraid her looks would go, or she'd get saggy, those were an accepted given—but because a family seemed implausible. She didn't want to wind up lonely and decrepit in a state nursing home.

"Thank you, hon," Darla said now, or at least that's what Dylan thought she said. It was hard to hear over the ruckus of laughter, talking, and clinking glasses coming from the tables behind her.

Dylan smiled and nodded, then mentally took a deep breath and turned around to face them. She hoped they'd be gone, but the two of them were still there sitting side by side, like pathetic Starsky and Hutch knockoffs.

As she walked the length of the bar to the end, Dylan tried to shake off her exhaustion. Staying one step ahead was proving more tiring than she'd anticipated.

She slapped two coasters down in front of them and said, "What can I do for you, fellas?"

"You Dylan Darcy?" the larger one asked.

"No." The answer slid off her tongue, smooth as melted ice cream. "Name's Sabrina. Dylan's not here today."

For a split second they both looked confused, and Dylan felt satisfaction at that. Then the slim one laughed. His laugh said, *I can't believe you'd fucking do that.*

"Can I get you a drink?" she asked, still not smiling.

"You know, we heard a lot about this bar." The slim one spoke, and she leaned forward slightly to catch his words. "And about a bartender named Dylan. Apparently, she does a great Sex on the Beach."

They both erupted into laughter, the skinny one slapping the larger one on the back. They thought they were so clever, Dylan thought. Like teenage boys.

"Are you deaf?" she said, a hard edge to her voice. "I said Dylan isn't here. Now, in case you haven't noticed, we're busy tonight, so

I'm gonna go deal with customers who are here to order drinks and not fuck around."

A hand gripped her wrist as she began to turn away, the fingers like steel. She swiveled back to find the older cop holding her arm pinned to the counter.

Yanking it from his grasp, Dylan practically shouted, "What the hell do you think you're doing?"

"You should watch that mouth," the older cop said. "A pretty woman like you using language like that . . . it's not attractive."

"Why don't you two shit-eating assholes fuck right the hell off."

The younger one didn't react, but the older one's eyes narrowed. "When you see Dylan next, *Sabrina,* how about you give her a message from us," he said.

"I'm not doing a fucking thing for either of you. Get out or I'm calling the cops." As she said it, she realized how ridiculous it sounded. They were the cops; she was pretty sure about that. They'd probably phone into the station themselves and say they happened to be at the location and would deal with the situation. What would she do then?

"Tell her we know what she did," he said.

The young guy nodded. "Tell her she better watch her back." The two of them were on their feet. "Don't go walking down any dark alleys by yourself, *Sabrina.*"

"Go to hell," she managed to say, but the words were lost in the tumult of the bar and the pounding of her heart. Without another word, without looking back, the two of them walked to the exit and pushed their way out into the frozen November night.

CHAPTER
FORTY

BECK

Before

Beck wasn't afraid. Just frustrated.

She thought she'd perfected the art of the breakup—how to leave a guy feeling like she'd done him a favor, like it was the right choice for them both.

But Pete was determined to win her over, to convince her to stay, even as she had one foot out the door. There were surprise visits to her apartment. Flowers he sent to her office. Notes she found tucked beneath her windshield wipers. It was all a little too intense.

"Dr. Grant?"

Melanie stood in the doorway, her eyes wide. Ever since she'd come to Beck for advice about a pill addiction a few weeks ago, things had been off between them. Beck had made the mistake of asking if Melanie herself was the one struggling.

"It's my cousin," the nurse snapped, just a little too defensively.

It made Beck wonder. Melanie was odd. One day she'd be efficiently checking off items on patient care lists, the next she'd forget to administer someone's medication. Beck couldn't put her finger on whether she was problematic or just eccentric.

"Your boyfriend's at the front," Melanie said, releasing the door handle with a twang that made Beck tense. "Should I tell him you'll be right out?"

"Oh. Sure, thanks. I just need to finish this." She indicated with her chin to the paperwork on the desk in front of her.

"You've snagged yourself a real cutie. I mean those blue eyes . . ." Melanie lingered.

Beck forced a smile. "I sure have."

Was she expecting Beck to elaborate on her boyfriend's other physical merits?

Barely a boyfriend. Almost an ex.

"Next time you can just call the office extension, Melanie. You don't have to go through all the trouble of walking over. I don't want to waste your time."

"I don't mind." The door handle vibrated. "I like visiting you."

Why couldn't anyone understand boundaries. It made Beck want to scream.

"That's sweet. I'll be out in a second." Beck turned her gaze downward.

"Sure, Dr. Grant." The door handle twanged a final time, then Melanie was gone.

She tried to focus, but her thoughts kept shifting away. Beck could picture him at reception, charming everyone. It was Pete's talent, chatting people up, making them like him.

What he wasn't so good at: understanding the word no.

· · ·

There he was, just like she'd imagined. Leaning on the reception desk laughing with Karen about something. Melanie hovered nearby, a hungry look in her eyes.

You can have him if you want him, Melanie, *she thought as she got closer.*

Pete straightened up with a grin. He was in uniform, his cap tucked beneath one arm.

"Hey, gorgeous." He kissed her on the cheek. "Hate to be a bother, but I need to speak to you real quick."

It was all show. And it was working. Karen and Melanie were staring at them like they were a pair of adorable penguin mates.

Beck fought hard to return his smile. "Okay, but I only have a few minutes."

The electric sliding door released them from the artificial cool of the center into the balmy womb of the spring afternoon. Insects droned incessantly, an anxiety-inducing backing track to a conversation Beck didn't want to have.

She faced him. "What's going on, Pete?"

He ran a hand through his dark hair. "I just really missed you today."

"That's sweet." Her annoyance began to thin, his charm diluting it.

"Do you miss me?"

"Of course." Always meet halfway. Make sure he knows you understand.

"It doesn't seem like it." He squinted off across the parking lot. "Especially lately."

Beck shifted from one foot to the other. She wouldn't say it aloud, not now. Beck was adventurous outside the bedroom and in . . . but the choking was too much. Maybe he needed to hear that directly. Not here though.

"We've talked about it, Pete." She kept her voice gentle. "We're not right together."

"I think we are." He moved closer.

She ordered her body to remain still. Stepping back felt like it'd be both a concession and a strike to his ego.

"Come on, Beck," he said. "You said you'd give this thing a fair shot."

A quick glance through the glass doors revealed both Karen and Melanie absorbed in the small drama playing out between the two of them.

"I can't have this conversation right now, Pete. I have to get back to work."

"Okay, okay." He put his hat on, and Beck felt the blood rush to her cheeks. He was cute, like Melanie said. "Maybe you can you come by after work? We can hash it out."

There wasn't anything to hash out. Beck was done, but she wasn't about to say it now.

"Sure, we'll talk."

In an old-fashioned gesture that would have melted her heart a few months ago, Pete briefly touched his thumb and forefinger to his hat's visor before walking away.

"By the way." He stopped. "I saw you at the station last week. What was that about?"

Relief morphed into anxiety so quickly she felt dizzy. It'd been a bad idea, Beck knew it as soon as she had stepped through the doors. But Pete was meant to be out on patrol that day.

"*Nothing.*" *She tried to keep her voice light as air.* "*I'm putting together a drug and alcohol information packet for one of the high schools. I needed a police perspective.*"

"*You could've asked me.*"

"*An objective perspective.*" *Beck made herself laugh.*

The half of his face visible to her pulled into a smile before he turned it away again. "*Sure. See you later, gorgeous.*"

Beck's heart slowed as she made her way inside.

In her office, she dug her wallet from her purse and took a seat. She extracted the neat square of paper from one of the credit card slots, unfolded it, then smoothed it out. Her eyes traced the name and number like they were a lucky talisman. Detective Righetti.

She'd performed this same ritual multiple times in the week since Detective Righetti had given it to her. And each time, she talked herself out of it, convinced herself she was overreacting. But Pete had shown up where she worked. *It felt like a step too far.*

Taking a deep breath, Beck reached for her office phone.

CHAPTER
FORTY-ONE

DYLAN

The temperature had dropped to the thirties by the time she closed the bar at two. Way too cold for north Texas, even if it was early November. Dylan looked around the parking lot. It was empty except for her Toyota Corolla sitting at the far end, gleaming with a thin layer of ice. The streetlamp's light extended only as far as the right-hand door of her car, the rest was cast in dark shadow.

Don't go walking down any dark alleys by yourself. The warning scurried through her brain like a nefarious rat. She took the small pistol from her bag and slid it into the pocket of her parka. Discount Starsky and Hutch were full of hot air. Empty threats. There was nothing to worry about.

That's what Beck believed too, until it was too late.

Fear coagulated in her chest at the thought. She and Jason had been the last employees to leave, and he was in such a hurry to get out the door—something about a friend waiting for him—that it seemed humiliating to ask him to stay and walk her to her car.

Now she regretted it.

Why didn't I park closer? Or swallow my pride and ask Jason to wait?

The answer to the first question was because she didn't want to take up spots customers would want. The answer to the second . . .

she didn't want to seem weak, to need a man's help. It made her angry to think that Jason of all people, by the sheer fortune of being born with a dick between his legs, could protect her better than she could herself.

She started across the parking lot. The ice squeaked beneath her Doc Martens. Her eyes darted from one shadow to the next.

You've killed a man, remember? You're not scared of anything.

The reminder did nothing to dilute the feeling that she was very small and very alone. Counting her breaths to calm herself, Dylan picked up the pace. Tomorrow she'd park closer, customers be damned. And tell Jason she couldn't close up anymore. She'd figure out what excuse to give him later—once she was safe at home. She fingered her car keys.

Almost there. Then you can go home, have a hot bath, relax.

"Excuse me," a voice called.

The hairs on the back of her neck rose. She tried to run, but her right foot slid on the ice and she almost lost her balance. Carefully Dylan righted herself and kept moving.

Don't fall. Don't fall. Don—

"Hey! I'm talking to you!"

Some mulish instinct made her glance over one shoulder. She clocked the large figure in a ski mask and broke into a run again, only to slam into something hard. Dylan's feet slid out from under her and she fell backward.

A cold, gloved hand covered her mouth before she had the chance to scream. A masked face loomed over her. Another appeared a second later. She fought back, scratching at his wrist and hand.

"Stop struggling," the larger figure ordered. Then a sharp, heavy pressure descended on her chest, and she couldn't breathe. She moved her head from side to side, panicked.

I'm going to die. I'm going to die.

"Give me your wallet, bitch, and nobody gets hurt."

It was only a mugging? That was good. That meant she just needed to stay calm and do what they said. Keep the situation from escalating and she'd walk away with nothing more than a few bruises. Dylan forced herself to stop moving and take shallow breaths. The weight of his knee between her breasts didn't let up, but it didn't get worse either.

She nudged her purse up against the larger attacker's foot and patted his leg to get his attention. Air flooded her lungs as he stood and moved away to rifle through it. Her eyes shifted to the other masked face, the one crouched over her with his hand pressed to her mouth.

"Don't try anything," he warned.

"Got it," the other one reported and threw her purse on top of her.

It's almost over, she thought. But the first masked figure lingered, his palm pressed to her mouth, scrutinizing her. Dylan could see it in his eyes. This was a man who wanted more than to just steal her wallet. He wanted to hurt her. Physically harm her. Slowly, she inched her hand into her parka pocket.

After a few more seconds of silent debate, he released her and got to his feet. Dylan could breathe fully again. She wasn't going to scream, not if they planned to leave her alone. No harm, no foul, other than a bruised ego, a hard lesson, and a vacant wallet. Her heart plummeted in her chest as she felt around in her pocket. It was empty.

Had she put the pistol in the other? No. Dylan had purposely slid it into her right pocket because that was her dominant hand.

It fell out.

Before she could fully process what that meant, her head snapped to one side, pinpricks of ice cutting into her cheek. Her face stung and tears immediately welled up. Dylan let out a loud gasp. He didn't give her the chance to react before hitting her again, punching down into her eye so that her head exploded with tendrils of excruciating pain.

"Let's go," the one with her wallet said.

Her assailant slapped her again then released her. Dylan managed to roll over onto her side and up to all fours. Something small and hard pressed against the side of her hand. She curled her fingers around it. It was the butt of her pistol. It must have been underneath her this whole time. What felt like a brick slammed into her ribs and she screamed, falling forward onto her face.

"Come on. Let's go before somebody sees."

"Take care of yourself, *Sabrina*," the other one hissed at her, kicking her in the rib cage again.

Dylan ground her teeth together hard to stop herself from screaming and rolled onto her back. Just like she'd practiced, she clicked the safety off in one smooth movement and fired multiple shots blindly in the direction of the voices.

"What the fuck! What the fuck!" one of them was yelling.

"What's the matter?" the other one asked, panic weaving in and out of his voice.

"She shot me! She fucking shot me!"

Tears and blood clouded her vision.

"I'm going to fucking kill the bitch!"

This is it. I'm going to die, Dylan thought. Is this what it'd felt like for Beck? Terror coupled with grim realization?

"I told you to leave her alone!"

They were cursing and arguing with each other, the conversation drifting in and out of focus like a faulty radio station.

Dylan tried to calm her thoughts, to accept what was coming. *Everybody dies. Maybe this time there'll be some justice. They can't let Beck get murdered by a cop and then me and not do something about it.*

She thought of Bree, of their one night together, and relaxed. Bree would take care of everything. She knew she would.

It took a little while for her to realize she was alone. That the cussing had grown more distant until there was silence.

Dylan lurched onto her side and gingerly pushed herself up. She brought her hand to her nose. The slightest touch drew more tears from her eyes. Her left eye socket screamed in agony and her jaw felt like it was disintegrating in acid.

She got to her feet and leaned against the car, taking deep breaths as the pain rose and receded. Her bag lay a few feet away like a dead animal. Looking down, Dylan was surprised to see she still held her keys in her left hand. She shuffled toward her purse. Leaning over brought with it another flood of pain and she groaned. She had the presence of mind to click the safety back on before dropping the pistol into the bag.

Come on. Hurry, Dylan. What if they come back?

The thought propelled her around the car to the driver's side. It took a few tries to get the key in. Dylan's hands were stiff with cold and her left eye had started to swell shut. She tried not to look around to see if they were coming back. It wouldn't do any good. If they did, it would be over for her—Dylan doubted she'd be able to get her little gun to fire again.

It felt like an eternity before she got the car door open and managed to climb inside. The engine spluttered and died the first time she turned the key.

Come on. Just this once don't give me trouble.

Her entire face was on fire, the hot tears running down her cheeks making it worse. It'd be too much to get this far, to survive all that, only for her car not to start.

Dylan turned the key again. The car protested like a diva making pre-show demands then gave in and rumbled to life. Clutching the steering wheel, she sat hunched for a few seconds, breathing and trying to get her bearings. She needed to go to the hospital, Dylan knew that much.

It must have been worse than she thought, she realized later when she walked into the emergency room. The nurse at the station looked frightened.

"I-I was attacked," Dylan managed to articulate, then she looked down, saw the front of her jacket covered in blood, and passed out.

CHAPTER FORTY-TWO

DYLAN

Dylan came to in a hospital bed, her body bellowing in protest. Gratitude surged and ebbed with the pain. As awful as it was, it meant she was alive. It was a reminder that things could have been worse. Much worse.

Gently she felt beneath her eye socket, along her jawline, then stopped just short of the middle of her face. Judging from the pain and how hard it was to breathe, her nose was broken.

Third time's the charm. Maybe this time they'd reset it so she wouldn't snore anymore. Her deviated septum—given to her courtesy of Jimmy Blythe, Mount Veil Junior High school bully, when she was thirteen—had never healed properly. Of course, she'd broken her nose for the first time when she was eight by ramming her bike full speed into a stop sign, so maybe it was just permanently messed up by now.

A portly nurse in blue scrubs pulled aside the privacy curtain.

"You're awake," she said pleasantly, as if Dylan were a B and B guest waiting for her breakfast. "I'm Nurse Sandra. How are you feeling?"

"Like shit."

"You poor thing. You were out for a while." The nurse was a lot older than the one Dylan had met at reception. Or at least it seemed like it—everything from her drive here to waking up in the hospital bed was a gooey blur. She wondered if they sent this grandmotherly nurse to soothe all assault victims. It seemed like an effective approach.

"You were attacked?" Sandra asked.

Two enraged rams bashed against Dylan's temples. She winced and nodded, wishing she could drift back into unconsciousness. At least that way nothing hurt.

"Was it a mugging?"

Again, Dylan nodded.

"Hm." Wheeling over a stool, the nurse took a seat next to the bed. Placing her warm hand on Dylan's arm, she gently asked, "Will you be needing a rape kit, dear?"

Dylan's entire body tensed, and she pushed herself up to a seated position. "God, no. I wasn't . . . That didn't happen. They roughed me up and took my wallet, that's it."

Why was she so defensive? As if getting mugged but not mugged *and* raped somehow meant she was a better victim.

Nurse Sandra appeared unsurprised by the reaction. "I'm so sorry that happened to you, it sounds terrifying. You're safe now. Okay?" She squeezed Dylan's arm.

As she sank back into the bed, Dylan felt a burst of nostalgia—for what, she didn't know. She'd certainly never had a grandma who fussed over her. And this nurse's lines sounded like they came straight from a training manual titled: *Communicating with Assault Victims.*

"The doctor will be in soon to check you over. Now that you're awake, I'm going to take another look at your wounds, all right?" Nurse Sandra said, pulling on a pair of latex gloves. She soaked a piece of gauze in clear solution and started dabbing at Dylan's face.

"Have you filed a police report yet?" the nurse asked after a few moments of silence.

"No."

"That's fine. I'll ask someone to call in. They'll send some officers over." She took Dylan's hand and flattened it out. Adjusting her red-framed glasses, Nurse Sandra leaned closer to inspect it. Razor-thin slashes crisscrossed Dylan's palms. She must have cut them on the ice. "It's best to file the report while it's all still fresh in your mind."

Dylan's fingers curled, her palm smarting from the hydrogen peroxide.

"Keep your hand open for me, dear."

Nurse Sandra's presence was relaxing, but she was treating Dylan like she was fragile. Like she was a victim. The thought made her seethe inside.

She's just being nice.

"I'm fine." She pulled her hand from the nurse's grasp. "It's not a big deal."

Sandra's pale eyes blinked back at her. "It's all right. You're safe now."

Dylan started to tremble. One more second of this babying and she'd scream. "Can you leave me alone please?"

The older woman hesitated, as if afraid of what Dylan might do once she was gone. To her relief, the nurse rose to her feet. "I'll go make that call to the police and check in on you in a bit. Your pain levels should decrease soon," she added, tapping the IV bag.

"Okay." Lowering her head back onto the pillow, Dylan let her eyes drift closed. The curtain swished. Dylan's eyes flew open again.

"Wait," she said. Sandra stopped and turned. "When you call the police, could you ask for Detective Righetti?"

"Detective Righetti," she repeated. She didn't seem at all surprised by the request, or the situation as a whole. Dylan didn't know if she should be calmed or alarmed by this. "Is he a friend of yours? Family?"

"She," Dylan corrected her wearily. "Bree Righetti."

"Ah. She." This seemed to be an adequate answer. "All right. I'll ask for Detective Bree Righetti."

"I won't talk to anyone else." She tried to sound determined. "I'll drive myself to the station to find her if I have to."

"That won't be necessary, dear. Don't you fret, I'll ask for her."

The privacy curtain swished shut behind her. Dylan lay down on her right side—the side that hurt less—and pulled the blanket up to her chin.

You fought back. You beat them.

Beck probably fought back too.

Dylan knew that the only reason she was lying here still breathing wasn't because she fought harder than Beck, or because she had a gun, or because she never dated the wrong sort of people (she did). It was because Dylan got lucky. That was the one thing separating her fate from her friend's.

The tears came faster, and her next thought was, *I'm glad Isabel isn't here to finally see me cry.* Isabel wouldn't judge her for it, but Dylan didn't want to show weakness in front of her or Priya. She was supposed to be the strong one of the group. The one with the plan, the answers.

By the time Sandra returned, Dylan had stopped crying and was sitting up again. A Dr. López appeared next and did a methodical examination of her wounds. Her nose was broken, he confirmed. They'd have to do an X-ray first, but it looked like she might have a cracked rib too.

Another nurse poked her head in through the partition.

"There are two detectives here, Doctor," she said.

"Thank you." He looked at Dylan. "Would you like to speak to them now?"

Not one detective. Two. Blood pounded in her ears. Her breath became short and quick.

"Is—Is one of them Detective Bree Righetti?" Dylan managed to ask. "Is one of them a woman?" she added sharply when he looked confused.

"Oh, yes, one of them is a woman." The nurse confirmed.

"We're done here for now," Dr. López said. "I'll have Nurse Sandra give you something more for the pain and I'll be back around once you've spoken to the detectives."

"Thanks."

She was impatient to see Bree. Anger paced inside her like a hungry leopard.

There were footsteps on the other side of the curtain, then a face poked through the break. "Here they are, dear," Nurse Sandra's disembodied head said.

A load lifted off Dylan as Bree stepped through the partition. Then a large man appeared behind her. She recognized him from the interview room. It was Bree's partner, Mark or Don or something.

"I don't want him here," Dylan said.

"Who? Detective O'Malley?" Bree looked around as if there was a crowd of men standing by the hospital bed for Dylan to choose from.

"I'll only talk to you."

"Yes, of course." She glanced up at her partner. "Do you mind waiting in the cafeteria, Mike?"

He shrugged. "Call me when you need me."

After he'd gone, Bree pulled the gap in the curtain shut and faced Dylan.

"Crap. What happened, Dylan?" She looked about ready to cry.

Well, that confirms I look worse than I thought.

"You should see the other guy," Dylan tried to joke, but it fell flat and neither one of them laughed.

Pulling out a notebook, Bree took a seat on the stool the doctor had occupied not too long before. "The precinct called me at home."

"Oh."

"The minute they told me Dylan Darcy was in the hospital asking to see me . . ." Bree shook her head. "It gave me the scare of my life. I got here as fast as I could. I'm sorry if I made you wait."

"Don't mind me, dears." Grandmotherly Nurse Sandra was back. "I'm just going to check this real quick." She did something with the IV, then excused herself.

Bree flipped the notebook open to a clean page. "Do you think you can tell me what happened?"

Dylan cleared her throat. "I was attacked in the bar parking lot."

"Mhm. You mean Aces of Spades."

"Yeah."

Nodding, she continued to make notes. "About what time?"

"Around two. Two-fifteen. It was my turn to close up."

"Okay. So you closed up. Did you see anyone suspicious hanging around?"

Dylan stopped mid-shake, curlicues of pain radiating across her face. Her nose was the axis, sending signals to her eyes, jaws, fore-head, and cheekbones. *When are these meds going to kick in?*

As if waiting for the internal cue, the discomfort began to recede.

"No. The parking lot was empty," Dylan said.

"Okay. You're doing great. Just keep telling me what you remem-ber."

Settling back in the bed, she felt herself relax a little.

"Then what happened?" Bree asked. Her brown eyes were soft, gentle. Dylan wanted to pull her onto the hospital bed and kiss her.

Instead, she answered, "I was walking to my car when I heard someone come up behind me. I don't know—I freaked, I guess. I started to run."

"Good instincts. Your brain knew you were in danger."

"Then, the other one was there in front of me all of a sudden. I ran into him pretty hard. Knocked me on my back."

Bree nodded, her pen moving quickly across the page.

"They—he put his hand over my mouth so I couldn't scream and the other one." Her chest ached as if his knee were still there; a phan-tom limb pressing down on her. "The other one kneeled on my chest so I couldn't . . . It was hard to breathe."

The detective said nothing as Dylan detailed the rest of the attack up to the moment when the first attacker released her. She stopped and Bree looked up.

"So, they fled the scene?" she asked.

Dylan shook her head. "He kicked me." Her hand moved to hover over her rib cage. "A few times. And then I shot one of them."

Her gaze snapped from her notebook to Dylan's face. "Jesus. Really?"

"Yeah," she said with a nod. "Pretty sure I hit him too, because he was screaming about it."

"Okay." Bree made a note. "Suspect has a potential gunshot wound. If it's anything more than a graze, he'd have to go to the hos-pital. We might be able to identify him that way. Any other unique markers you can think of? Were they tall? Short? Fat? Slim?"

"One was overweight, the other slim. Both about . . ." Dylan thought for a second, rooting through her memory. "I'd say five ten or eleven."

"But they were both wearing masks so you can't say for sure what they look like."

"I know exactly what they look like."

Again, Bree's eyes met hers.

"I can do you one better," Dylan said. Her hands curled into fists. "I can tell you exactly where to find them."

"You are full of surprises, Dylan Darcy," she said softly. "Where?"

"At the police station. I was attacked by two cops."

Bree's eyebrows rose.

Dylan laid a hand on her stomach and leaned her head back to look at the ceiling. Exhaustion settled over her like a heavy blanket. She would say this one last thing, then she would sleep. She deserved to sleep.

"You need to check the bar's security camera," Dylan said. Then she closed her eyes.

CHAPTER
FORTY-THREE

TEXAS STATE PENITENTIARY

Fall 1994

"You got five choices as a lifer," Dory, the fifty-something former hippie from two cells over, says.

She holds up a hand, her stubby fingers outstretched.

"You can go crazy." Her ring finger curls. "You can get yourself killed." Her pinky is next. "You can kill somebody else." Two fingers left. "You can off yourself." The index finger folds. "Or you can accept it and grow old in here." She presses her thumb against her other fingers, forming a fist.

Dory lets it sink in for a few seconds, then turns her attention back to her breakfast.

"At first, everybody thinks two and four are the best choices," she continues after polishing off her grits. "But trust me, there's no way to do either that ain't painful or messy. And if you survive . . . things will get worse. You think they can't, but in here there's always a lower level of hell."

Using her finger, Dory scrapes up the leftover syrup from the canned fruit portion of the tray.

"Personally, CK, I'd choose number five. Take some classes. Get buff. Join a family." She eyes me. "You never know, maybe I'll have an opening in mine, depends what you can offer. You gonna finish that?"

As I slide my tray of half-eaten food over, I can feel the many decades left of my life bearing down on me, heavy as a boulder. Wouldn't it be easier to let it go? To allow it to crush me?

Dory nudges my foot, forcing my focus back. Her brown eyes are small and hard as flint.

"Take it from somebody who knows, CK." She lifts her plastic coffee mug in a sort of salute. "Go with number five. Don't even bother with the others."

She makes it sound as easy as placing an order at a drive-thru. It isn't.

How can I not think about ways to die when all I've got is time to kill?

CHAPTER FORTY-FOUR

BREE

Bree left Dylan waiting to go into X-rays and walked to the cafeteria. Guilt nipped at her heels like a pack of angry stray dogs as she wound her way through the hospital halls.

Stay levelheaded.

It was hard. Hard not to be angry at herself, to not feel as if Dylan was here because of some oversight on Bree's part. She *knew* what he was. She *knew* how the justice system worked. How rare a good outcome was for female victims. And yet, instead of taking matters into her own hands years ago, she stalled. And again, after Beck died, she hesitated. Now Dylan was lying in a hospital bed because Bree had waited too long.

She found Mike sitting at a round table in the cafeteria, a paper cup of coffee in front of him. When she came up, he wedged his pencil into the spine of his puzzle book and closed it.

"You don't look so good," he said.

If she looked the way she felt, Bree couldn't disagree. Her head ached like she hadn't slept in three months.

"Thanks for the honesty, Mike." She collapsed more than sat in the chair beside his.

"She give a description?"

"In a way." Bree paused. "It's bad, Mike. Really bad."

"Huh."

They fell silent. Flecks of leftover food dotted the side of the table closest to Bree. She stared at the crumbs, trying to decipher what dish they'd formerly belonged to. Pie? Casserole?

Her mind moved on to a more pressing issue: whether to get a coffee. Judging by the slush in Mike's cup, it probably wasn't a good idea. Her stomach had been ornery lately, and it wasn't like she needed anything else keeping her up at night. But she was so tired too.

The coffee station—commercial silver vats, flimsy cups, packets of bright pink Sweet'N Low and all—called to her like a mirage in the desert.

"According to Dylan's account, two cops showed up at Aces and threatened her." The words stuck in her throat like painful burrs. "Then they waited until closing and attacked her in the bar parking lot. Cops, Mike. Cops did this." She wanted to walk into the precinct and burn the whole place down. *Protect and Serve.* That was what they were supposed to do, wasn't it?

Give a man even a little bit of power and most of the time he'll abuse it. Bree couldn't remember who had told her that, but it never rang truer than right now.

"Maybe the security camera outside that bar caught it," Mike said. "It'll finally be good for something."

"Exactly what I was thinking." She nodded. "We'll wait until she's back from X-rays and talk to her again. I need you there this time, Mike. There needs to be another witness. If this . . ." Bree hesitated. "If this goes the way I think it will, I'll need you to back me up."

Which really meant that she needed a male colleague from the department to corroborate the story. Keep the baboons happy. At first, Dylan had refused to see Mike. But Bree managed to talk her down. It was more a combination of the drugs mellowing her out and the scare from her attack than common sense, she suspected. Dylan seemed like she'd be much more stubborn otherwise.

"I think I'm going to have to do something I really don't want to," she told Mike.

"That's what this job is, ain't it?"

Bree raised her gaze to him. He had an honest face, she thought. A good cop's face. "Yeah."

Especially for people like you and me.

His eyes were fixed on the cafeteria windows that lined the far end of the room. Outside, the sky was easing into the black-blue sheen of an approaching dawn. The clock on the wall over the coffee station showed a few minutes after five.

"Ready?" Mike got to his feet. His hands fidgeted with his belt, adjusting it and searching for a wayward shirttail to tuck in.

Scratch that, I don't need coffee, I need a stiff drink. These sorts of thoughts always frightened her. Wasn't that how it all started for Dad? Hard liquor to get through a hard time. Then death at the bottom of a bottle.

"Yeah, okay," Bree said as she got to her feet too.

She let out a deep sigh and felt it all the way to her core.

• • •

She woke hours later in her own bed. It was barely a quarter past eight, but Bree forced herself up and to the phone. She dialed the hospital, and a nurse informed her that, once the doctor had treated her wounds and reset her nose, Dylan insisted on going home. They gave her a prescription for pain meds and hopefully she'd fill them, the nurse added, sounding peeved.

It didn't surprise Bree. Dylan would want to take care of herself and being in the hospital probably made her feel vulnerable. She hung up and dialed Dylan's house.

Dylan picked up after only a few rings.

"Sorry to wake you," Bree said.

"I was awake." She didn't offer any more information.

"Okay. Well, we dragged your manager out of bed early this morning and went down to Aces for the security footage. They're on the tape, Dylan. Both of them. One even removed his mask—from the looks of it, it was after you shot him."

She paused to give Dylan a chance to respond, but she stayed silent.

"We've been able to identify him, but I need you to come down to the station to look at some photos. The other attacker kept his mask on, so . . ." she trailed off.

"Okay," Dylan said.

"Can you do it this morning? I'll swing by to pick you up."

"That's okay. I can drive myself."

"You're in no state to drive, Dylan."

There was a sharp exhale. "I'm fine. I drove home, I can drive to the station."

Bree couldn't bring herself to insist. It seemed kinder to let Dylan hold on to some semblance of control. They agreed to meet there.

She dressed in blue slacks and a white blouse and scrunched some mousse into her unruly curly hair. As Bree drove, she sipped coffee from her travel mug and wondered when her exhaustion would finally hit rock bottom.

At the station, she dropped her purse at her workstation and carried her mug to the break room. She refilled it with coffee, then fixed a cup of black tea, added sugar, and walked to reception.

"Oh, thank you, honey." The secretary smiled and accepted Bree's offering, cupping her hands around the mug. "Read my mind. Can I do anything for you?"

"Is Mike in yet?" Bree said, easing her way into the question she really wanted to ask.

"Mike O'Malley?" Laura consulted the chart on her desk. "Haven't seen him yet, no. But it says here he's not due in 'til nine." She glanced up. "Thought you knew that."

"Oh, yeah. We must have gotten our wires crossed."

Bree panned her gaze around the room. A few officers were seated at their desks, working. And there'd been two in the break room, loudly comparing how much they'd drunk the night before. It was hard to tell who wasn't here because they weren't supposed to be and who was supposed to be here but wasn't.

"I don't see Detective Taylor either," Bree said, trying to sound as casual as she could. "I'm supposed to rendezvous with him on this case I'm working. He hasn't called in sick, has he?"

"I don't think so." Again Laura consulted her spreadsheet. "Oh, wait." Heart skipping, Bree watched her finger travel along the document. "That's right, he called in a little while ago."

"Oh, no. Taylor called in sick, huh?" Bree smiled and leaned forward conspiratorially. "Do you think he was out late last night, raising hell? There are a few guys in the break room going on about a pretty crazy night."

Her long blond ponytail swung back and forth as she shook her head and laughed. "Wouldn't put it past him. But he didn't call in sick."

Good girl, Bree thought. It always annoyed her before how much of a gossip Laura was, but now it was proving useful.

"He said he had some family matter to take care of," Laura said, lowering her voice. "I heard he's going through a bad divorce. Wife's trying to take the house *and* the kids and make sure he never sees either one again."

"Really? I can't say he doesn't deserve it."

They exchanged a knowing look.

"Ain't that the truth," the secretary said.

There'd been rumors about Taylor floating around for years. About how he demanded sexual favors from local pros in exchange for not busting them for prostitution. About how he'd skim a little off when there was a drug bust. About how he was paid by certain businesses to look the other way when it came to suspicious dealings. About how he viewed the police force as a special club whose members protected one another. *Even at the cost of their victims,* Bree thought bitterly.

It didn't seem at all far-fetched to believe Mrs. Taylor had gotten sick of his antics and finally pulled the plug on their marriage. Bree remembered meeting her at the last precinct Christmas party. She was a slim woman dressed in an outdated baby-blue dress with white pockets and collar—as if she hadn't had the time to go shopping in the last decade or so. It was probably an accurate assumption, Bree realized later that evening after she was somehow relegated to the "women's side" of the room. She stood nursing a cup of overly sweet punch and listening to the detectives' wives talk. Mrs. Taylor had birthed four children in as many years. Even though she tried to infuse her voice with a modicum of enthusiasm, Bree suspected she was tired of staying home day in and day out to wipe noses and clean up vomit while her husband roamed about town.

"Thanks, Laura," Bree told the secretary. "I suppose I'll have to catch up with Detective Taylor another day."

"Sure thing, honey. I'll let you know if he calls to say he's coming in."

Just then, Dylan pushed her way through the precinct doors. She looked like a stray cat that had accidentally wandered into a dog pound. A bandage covered her nose, and her left eye was swollen shut. Small gashes marked up one side of her face, and her bottom lip was split and bloated.

Perfect timing. Bree wanted Laura to get a full look at what Dylan had been through. She needed another woman in the precinct to be able to confirm the damage because the men might just pretend they'd never seen it.

"Oh my word," Laura said softly.

"This is Dylan Darcy. She's here to identify the men who attacked her last night. I'll talk to you later, Laura," Bree said, rapping her knuckles twice on the desktop. "This way, Miss Darcy."

There was a low murmur as Dylan followed her to her desk. More than once, Bree caught the other officers on duty sneaking a look.

"Can I get you coffee or anything?" Bree asked.

"No." She cleared her throat. "Thanks."

Bree had finished taking photographs of Dylan's wounds when Mario Santos walked by. Except for a slight widening of her undamaged eye, Dylan didn't react. There was a swagger to Santos's step that Bree didn't like—or maybe she was biased.

Then Dylan nodded and Bree leaned in to catch the words falling like stones from her mouth.

"That's him. That's one of them."

In a split second Bree made the decision to rise and hurry to catch up. Santos shot her a look when she fell in step beside him.

"What do you want?" he asked in a way that didn't invite a response.

"I heard Taylor's out sick. That's a shame, I was hoping to run something by him on the Peter Miles case. Hope he doesn't have that bug that's been going around," she added, trying to sound nonchalant.

Bree felt his sharp glance land back on her but kept her eyes trained ahead, as if Santos and Taylor were mere afterthoughts.

"Nah, just food poisoning. Had some funny Chinese last night, almost called in sick this morning myself."

Liar, liar . . .

"Hm." She debated saying something like, *I hope he feels better,* but decided against it. Bree had never shown an ounce of concern for Taylor before, and it might be overkill.

"If you got a question about the case, I can help you," Santos said, coming to a stop next to his desk. Was it her, or did he sound a trifle condescending?

"Great." She flashed him a smile. "Thanks. I'll be around later."

Before he could answer, she peeled away and hurried back in the direction of her own desk.

Bree wasn't entirely sure, but she thought she could sense his eyes lingering on her for longer than was comfortable as she took her seat across from Dylan again.

CHAPTER FORTY-FIVE

BREE

At nine on the dot Mike came in looking tired and unkempt in a wrinkled blue shirt and tan chinos. He set a brown paper bag in front of her, then lowered himself into his chair with a grunt.

"Thanks, Mike," she said, opening the bag to find a concha inside.

"Mhm." He took a sip of his coffee. "You been here long?"

"A little while." She pulled her chair around to his side of the desk so she could sit next to him.

Her partner's wispy, barely there hair was squashed to one side, like grass caught in a strong wind. Suppressing the urge to reach out and smooth it down, she filled him in on Dylan's visit in a low voice.

After she finished, he sat in silence for a few minutes, nursing his cup of coffee.

"You gotta tell the chief," he said.

"Yes."

His gaze traveled across the room to a point behind Bree.

"Santos is here," he reported. "And Taylor?"

"He called Laura and told her he had a family issue to take care of. And get this: Not five minutes later Santos informs me he's out sick with food poisoning."

"So, he's covering for Taylor."

"Maybe." She leaned in closer, afraid her voice would carry. "Santos kept his mask on, which means we can't get a positive identification on him, right? And we can't be completely sure it's Taylor in the video either—not beyond a reasonable doubt."

"It sure looked like him."

"It's not solid proof, though. You saw the security footage; any half-decent lawyer could argue it's someone who bears a passing resemblance to Taylor."

"True." Mike took a sip of coffee and squinted at his desktop.

"So," Bree continued. "Maybe Taylor really is home with the stomach flu. Or, much more likely, the two of them were out last night intimidating people and he got shot." She really wanted to add *and got what he deserved too,* but didn't. "The thing is, I need more proof before I take it to the chief, Mike. These two goons visiting the bar and Dylan Darcy getting attacked on the same night seems like more than just coincidence, but we need something concrete to tie the two events together."

One nagging thought Bree didn't want to voice aloud was the question of whether she could trust the chief. Sure, in a bid for objectivity he'd put her on the Peter Miles case, but did that mean he'd take a complaint like this seriously? What if he tipped off Taylor and Santos? There were days she doubted she could trust Mike, and he'd more than proven himself a decent partner over the past few years.

"How about we call Ellen," Mike said. "There's no love lost between the two of them. I bet she'd tell us straight up why he's not here today."

"Oh. That's a good idea, Mike."

He grinned and eyed his coffee cup. "Yeah, well, even a broke clock's right twice a day. You better do it." Mike got to his feet. "Pretend to be Laura," he said before heading in the direction of the break room.

Back when Bree started in the department, Laura had given her a list of all the other detectives' home and pager numbers. It was for if she ever needed to reach them in a large-scale emergency—a hostage situation, or a Manson Family–type multiple murder. Bree had yet to use it. It lived in its own folder in her desk drawer just in case though. She suspected most of the other detectives had lost their lists by now—not a promising thought considering the shit show that had just taken place in Waco earlier that year.

Bree pulled her chair back around to her side of the desk and took out the folder. After locating *Thomas Taylor* on the list, she looked around the room. Everyone seemed to be out of earshot. Feeling like a cashier about to rob the till right under a manager's nose, Bree lifted the receiver and dialed. It rang for a long time before someone picked up.

"Hello?" a woman's voice demanded. In the background a baby was screaming. Or crying. Or both.

"Hi, Mrs. Taylor." Bree forced her voice into a higher register. Hopefully Ellen Taylor hadn't spent enough time with Laura to be able to tell off the cuff if it was really her. "This is Laura? From the station?"

"He's not here." Mrs. Taylor cut her off before she could follow it up with a real question. Sounding like a woman who'd just walked twenty-five miles and was being asked to do one more, she added, "Like I told you before, he's at the Ruby Motel. Number eighteen."

"Thanks, Mrs.—"

Ellen Taylor hung up, cutting the wailing baby short.

Ruby Motel, 18, Bree scribbled on her notepad. Elephantine footsteps alerted her to Mike's approach. He held out a cup of coffee. The offering warmed her, but it was quickly followed by a sense of imbalance. As if they were on opposite ends of a seesaw and Mike's acts of kindness buoyed him upward, while her lies by omission weighed her down.

Feeling like a traitor, Bree took it. "Thanks," she said. "He's at the Ruby Motel."

"All right. Oughta take a look, I guess."

Bree eyed the coffee. Even though she trusted her partner more than most, she struggled to drink anything she hadn't prepared herself.

Just to be polite, she took a sip, then cocked her head at him in surprise. "Mike, this is exactly how I like my coffee."

"I know."

"It's like I made it myself." She took another small sip and set it to one side. "A little sugar, a little cream."

He didn't seem to see the need to respond. Would Mike ever stop surprising her?

Still, the burst of affection she felt for her partner was quickly dampened by worry. Mike noticed small details. Like how she drank her coffee. How much longer would it be before he figured out what she was hiding about the Peter Miles case?

Resting her elbows on her desk, Bree lowered her head into her hands for a moment before looking up. Mike loomed nearby, like a stone lion standing guard.

If she'd had doubts before about letting Dylan get away with whatever role she'd played in Peter Miles's murder, she had a lot fewer now. The woman had almost been killed by two corrupt cops, Bree didn't think she had the stomach to send her to prison too.

Focus on right now.

The least she could do was solve this case.

"It's a mess, Mike," Bree said. "I'm worried about showing up at the Ruby Motel. I don't want the reputation of a cop who can't keep her nose out of her colleague's private business. It's already hard enough for me here as it is. I don't want that for you either."

Mike nodded but didn't respond. He looked like he was thinking, so Bree stayed quiet too.

She'd finished half the concha by the time he spoke.

"Do you believe her?" he asked.

"Who, Dylan Darcy?"

"Yep."

"Well, she's walking evidence of a physical assault. And there's the security footage. It's impossible not to believe her."

"Not that part, the first part. The part where they came into her bar and threatened her."

This same thought had been circling Bree's brain nonstop. *Do I believe Dylan Darcy?* There was no doubt she could lie when it suited her. It didn't seem implausible Dylan might have a vendetta against everyone involved in Rebecca Grant's murder—including the two detectives who'd failed to bring her killer to justice.

At the same time, Bree's instincts were screaming that Dylan was telling the truth.

Trust your gut.

"Yes," she said finally. "I believe her."

"Then we do our jobs. No matter who's on the other end of it, even if they're cops too."

"Ruby Motel?"

"Ruby Motel," he said with a nod.

CHAPTER
FORTY-SIX

BREE

The Ruby Motel was a single-story structure curled around a central parking lot like a diseased dog laid down to die. Rows of faded green doors sat back from a short concrete walkway. Some of the outer screen doors were missing, others hung open on lopsided, rusted hinges. The exterior needed a good scraping and a new coat of paint, and the roof showed bare spots where shingles were missing.

The one thing the motel did have going for it was a decent-sized swimming pool. Not that the size mattered, considering the pool wasn't in use anyway. It sat in the center of the parking lot, harboring a look of neglect, dead leaves accumulating on its winter cover.

Despite the chill, Bree wished she could strip off her clothes, lift the cover, and slide underneath into the water. Submerge herself and block out the world. Forget about Peter Miles. Forget any of this was happening.

A headache had started to brew on the drive over. Punishment for her attempt to compensate for too little sleep with too much caffeine. Maybe all she really needed was a hot bath, Bree thought as they sat in the car staring past the swimming pool to room 18 at the other end of the lot.

The curtains on the window were drawn tight and the only movement they'd seen in the last twenty minutes was a trucker coming out of a room three doors down.

"We should have called first," Bree said. "Checked to see if he was in."

Mike shrugged. "And if he picked up? He would've known something was off. Better to catch him by surprise."

She'd agreed with him, but that was twenty-five minutes ago. Now Bree wasn't so sure. This could turn into a career-ending move. A you're-stuck-at-your-desk-until-you-retire move. Even if the chief did see their side of things, she doubted he'd tolerate spying on other detectives in the precinct.

A bit late to start worrying about career-ending moves.

Bree had already accumulated plenty of those. If she didn't find a satisfactory resolution to the Peter Miles case, if the information she was hiding came to light, her career would be over anyway.

An image of Dylan's bruised and battered face flashed through Bree's mind. She'd looked so small and fragile lying in that hospital bed. So vulnerable. Outrage reared up like a pissed-off scorpion ready to attack. It'd be meaningless if Bree came this far and turned right around, too afraid to rock the boat because it might ruin her career prospects.

They were doomed before she even set foot in the precinct. She knew she'd never work her way up to chief, never get promoted far—if at all—in the male-dominated world. The deck was already stacked against her on her first day. The opportunities to take control, to push the narrative of a case in the direction she needed it to go, were few and far between. The least Bree could do was see this through. For Dylan. She'd be a fool not to.

"Let's knock," she said.

They climbed out of the car and crossed the parking lot. Bree felt like she was approaching a bomb, knowing there was less than a minute before it'd go off. The doors didn't have peepholes, a lucky coincidence. She wiped her palms on her slacks and pulled open the screen door. As if to reassure herself he was still there, Bree glanced quickly at Mike then rapped twice on the fiberboard.

"Housekeeping!" she called.

There was silence.

Bree knocked harder. "Housekeeping!"

"I don't need anything," a voice barked from the other side of the motel door.

Instinctually, she took a step back, her shoulder still propping the screen door open. Mike rocked back and forth on his heels, hands jammed in his pockets.

Taking a deep breath, she stepped up to the door again and rapped three times. "I got those towels you asked for!" Bree shouted.

"Jesus Christ," came the muffled response. Something fell and he swore again. A moment later the knob jiggled and the door flew open, revealing Taylor's red, puffy face. "I said I don't need any—" He stopped, his small eyes widening in surprise.

Behold, a hungover baboon in its natural habitat.

He was shirtless and her gaze immediately landed on the sling encasing his right arm and bandaged shoulder.

Mike's foot slid forward at the same time as he tried to slam the door.

"Fuck!" Taylor threw the door open again. "What the fuck do you two morons want?"

"What happened to your arm?" Bree asked.

"Fuck you." He spat the words out.

"Looks like you hurt yourself pretty badly."

"Fu—"

Mike advanced into the room and Taylor stumbled backward until his ass landed squarely on the bed.

"What the hell do you think you're doing?" he demanded, but Bree thought she could detect a note of fear in his voice.

"Just looking around," Bree said. The stench of cigarette smoke, dirty laundry, and rotten food layered the room like thick, invisible silt.

Taylor opened his mouth to say something, then snapped it shut again. Mike towered over him, arms folded, his eyes scanning the area. She saw it at the same time he did because Mike grunted.

In a few swift steps she crossed the room to where the shirt lay crumpled on the threadbare carpet. The blood had dried to a dull copper color. She took a pen from her jacket pocket and used it to lift the shirt by its collar. The right shoulder and part of the sleeve were stiff with blood. It took her a moment, but she found it—a hole, the edges charred a slight black, near the shoulder. It seemed impossible that such a small hole could cause that much blood. Bree felt an unexpected surge of pride for Dylan.

She did that to him.

Carefully holding the shirt at the end of her pen, she turned to Taylor.

"Looks like you lost a lot of blood, Detective," she said.

He sat silent, his small rodent eyes shooting flames at her.

"Which is funny because your partner said you were out with food poisoning."

"Don't look like food poisoning to me," Mike said.

"You need to come down to the station for a chat," she said.

Taylor laughed. Actually laughed. "I'm not going anywhere."

"We can take you in cuffs, or you can keep some of your dignity and come in voluntarily. It's your choice," Bree said, even though Taylor didn't deserve the option. She wanted to drag him in cuffed, just to make a point, but if she humiliated him in front of the whole precinct they'd all, the chief included, rally to his side. Loyalty to the Brotherhood in Blue trumped everything else. In the end, Dylan would be the one who'd pay for a mistake like that. She and Mike needed to play things carefully.

"What the hell does that mean? I didn't do nothing," he said.

"Unless you pulled this bullet out yourself, which judging by those bandages I'm guessing you didn't, we can trace which hospital you went to. We can retrieve that bullet." She kept her eyes locked to his. *I'm not afraid of you.* "And I bet that bullet matches a certain gun belonging to a woman who used it to defend herself early this morning."

"Don't know what you're talking about."

"Ah, of course," Bree said. "I'll try to be clearer. Two men attacked a woman outside Aces of Spades at around two this morning. Funny thing is"—she cocked her head to one side—"the bar has a security camera."

With some satisfaction she watched Taylor's eyes widen.

"And guess who's on the footage?" Bree paused to let this sink in. "I think you know you're in trouble, Taylor. Your partner is too. So, the question is, who gets ahead of this, you or Santos? I'm offering you the first chance."

Taylor considered this in silence. He'd started to sweat—probably from the pain in his shoulder and his hangover finally dropping the hammer on him. Bree could picture a hamster in his brain sprinting the idea wheel, debating whether betraying his partner would be worth it.

"I need a shirt," he said finally.

No honor among thieves.

So, he was going to risk it. Not a bad tactic considering the police department didn't have the best record of punishing its own, but she didn't want to think about that now.

She laid the bloodied garment carefully on the brown polyester bedspread and looked around. A flash of blue slumped next to the dingy coffee maker caught her eye and she lifted it with her thumb and forefinger. Luckily, it proved to be just what he needed—a semi-clean shirt.

Even though she'd already seen Taylor shirtless, Bree turned away to give him a sense of privacy as he dressed. While he grunted and sweated his way into the shirt, she took in the stack of Chinese take-out containers and the half-full bottle of Johnnie Walker Black on the desk.

"I need coffee," Taylor announced as they filed through the motel room's narrow door. "Your treat."

Mike said nothing and Bree, who was walking behind them carrying the bloody shirt, felt the fingers of her free hand tense into a half-fist.

"Sure," she said. "Just for you, we'll stop by the best coffee place in town. It's called the station break room."

CHAPTER FORTY-SEVEN

BREE

"What the hell were you thinking?" The chief paced back and forth across the four feet of space behind his desk. "You two have really crossed a line."

Bree and Mike exchanged a look. *The chief's in a rage.* It was a phrase thrown around the precinct as a joke, but there wasn't any humor in it now. Chief Hunter's mustache seemed to bristle with an angry intensity of its own. His face looked like he'd somehow gotten sunburned in the fifteen minutes they'd been in his office.

Glancing toward the window, Bree was glad he'd closed the blinds when they came in. She could picture the other detectives in the precinct standing around gleefully eavesdropping outside.

"Let me see if I understand." He dropped into his chair. "You have Detectives Taylor and Santos in separate interrogation rooms, and you're holding them for questioning."

"Yes, sir," Bree said.

"You are questioning them in the attack on a woman who is also a person of interest in the murder of Peter Miles."

"A potential person of interest, sir." The distinction seemed necessary.

His glare could have melted ice. "That's not what you implied last week. You made it clear she's more than just a potential person of interest." In the tone of a man juggling one too many balls, he added, "Am I to understand this woman shot one of them?"

Who was it, Bree wondered. *Who was it that came in here and tattled to him like an angry little boy?*

"In self-defense, yes."

"And you believe this? She could have—no, she probably does have a vendetta against the police department. It's possible she killed one cop and now she's shot another. The woman is dangerous."

"You need to see her, Chief." Mike spoke up. "She's beat up pretty bad. They could have killed her. Firing that gun probably saved her life."

The chief ran a hand over his head and sighed. "Any other witnesses to this alleged attack?"

"The two of them came into her place of work and threatened her just hours before," Bree said. "I'm sure we could find a witness who saw them there or overheard something."

She tried to sound more confident than she felt. Taylor and Santos were cops and Aces of Spades was a dive bar. The barflies at establishments like that weren't the types to give witness statements.

"There's also a security camera outside her workplace, where the attack happened. We've identified Taylor from the footage. And we called around to both the local hospitals," Bree continued. "One of them treated a man for a gunshot wound early this morning. Apparently, he flashed his badge, and they agreed not to call the *real* cops. Luckily for us, one of the nurses caved and admitted to helping treat him. And they kept the bullet. I suspect the patient will match Thomas Taylor's description and the bullet will match Dylan Darcy's gun. We'll probably even find witnesses who can describe the man who drove Taylor to the hospital—Santos."

"Jesus." Eyes boring into Bree, he shook his head.

"They were trying to intimidate her without actual proof that she'd committed a crime, Chief," she said. "This is serious."

"No need to remind me, Detective." Chief Hunter's tone was shot through with irritation.

Sensing his patience—and her chance to make her point—was

quickly slipping away, Bree hurried to add, "If this was an attack on a cop, why didn't Taylor or Santos report it right away? Detective Taylor called in sick. He didn't want anyone to know he'd been shot. That's suspicious."

"I know it. Jesus." The chief brought his fists down on the desk and Bree jumped. "This is a mess. First, I have a cop believed to have raped and murdered a young woman. Then he's murdered. Then two more of my detectives are accused of attacking a woman. Now they're in holding, one of them with a gunshot wound." He was up out of his chair pacing again. "When the commissioner hears about this. Jesus Christ."

She felt sorry for him. All in all, Chief Hunter wasn't a bad guy. He had enough foresight to assign her to Peter Miles's case, which said something about his personal moral code. She didn't want to be the catalyst to him potentially losing his job.

"This could be a chance for you, Chief," Mike said.

"Oh? How's that, Detective O'Malley?" The question was loaded with sarcasm.

"Frame it as cleaning house. Stamping out corruption in the police department."

Silently, Bree was grateful to her partner for saying what she knew the chief wouldn't take seriously if it came from her. Although, stamping out corruption now technically included her too, didn't it?

"Rebecca Grant's murder made a lot of people lose trust in the police," he continued. "You can regain that trust. And if you were gonna run for office someday . . ." Mike stopped there. It was an open secret that the chief harbored bigger political ambitions.

Hands thrust into his pockets, Chief Hunter considered this in silence for a few moments.

"You got enough evidence to charge the two of them with assault?" he asked.

"That's a yes on Taylor," Bree said. "Santos, I'm not so sure. He could wriggle his way out of it, claim it was someone else who carried out the attack."

"Well then, you'll have to get Taylor to turn on him."

"Yes, sir," Bree said.

As if he'd used up his word quota for the week, Mike was quiet.

"Okay. Let's start there. Tie up the loose ends. Make this airtight."

For a few beats he looked at Bree, then shifted his gaze to Mike. "Jesus," the chief said. "The two of you are going to kill me."

They rose from their seats. Bree's heart was sprinting—she couldn't tell if she was scared or excited.

"If you're going to try to do this, you need to get results on the Peter Miles case too," he said. "I don't want it looking like you're biased. Get me results. Get me an arrest."

"Yes, Chief," Mike said.

Barely managing to hold back a grimace, Bree echoed, "Yes, Chief."

"Oh, and, Detectives?"

Hand on the doorknob, she half turned to look at him. She knew what was coming.

Do not screw this up.

To her surprise, Chief Hunter said instead, "Be careful out there."

CHAPTER
FORTY-EIGHT

BECK

Before

Beck's cheeks warmed when she entered the Coffee Pot and spotted Detective Righetti seated in a booth by the window. She almost regretted asking to meet and, for a second, considered walking right back out. Before she could, the detective saw her and waved.

They shook hands and Beck slid into the seat opposite.

"Thanks for meeting me outside the police station," she said.

"No problem. Actually gives me an excuse to get away from the desk, which is nice."

The reassurance warmed Beck through like a shot of vodka after a dip in a cold lake. She studied Detective Righetti as they placed their coffee orders. Today she wore her dark chin-length hair half up in a small butterfly clip and, like when they'd met just over a week ago, minimal makeup. Only a hint of mascara, her nails as unadorned as her face.

Beck suspected the lack of outward femininity was a protective armor.

"So, what did you need to talk about?" the detective asked after the waitress walked away. "You mentioned before that there's a guy causing you trouble. Is that still the case?"

"A little bit," Beck said and felt immediately dishonest. "I guess I was hoping to talk more about my options. You know, get some advice."

"Sure." She nodded. "Is he still showing up uninvited to places? I guess *that's a 'yes,'"* the detective said in response to Beck's wince. *"Have you con-sidered a restraining order?"*

Beck shook her head. *"I think that would make it worse. Upset him."*

"Okay. Are you sure you don't want to tell me who it is?"

Suddenly, Beck's gaze was bolted to the table. She'd seen Pete at the station, not far from Detective Righetti's desk. Surely that meant they knew each other. Revealing his name seemed like it would open one more avenue for potential embarrassment.

Turning a sugar packet over between her fingers, Beck said, *"I'd rather not."*

A silence solid as an iron anchor fell. Beck looked up to find the detective staring out the window. Her eyebrows drew together, a narrow ridge forming between them.

"Okay. That's your prerogative." Detective Righetti faced Beck again. *"But I have to ask: Has he ever hurt you?"*

"Oh, no, of course not." The light dabbling in BDSM didn't count, did it? It was just the one time, and Beck had consented beforehand. She just didn't know it'd be . . . like that. *"He wouldn't intentionally hurt me or anything. He's just emotionally intense."*

"Emotional abuse is still abuse."

"I'm a psychiatrist." Beck laughed, even though it wasn't funny. *"Or I will be once I finish my residency. I know he's using love to manipulate me. Though I'm not the most objective person to determine that."*

Their coffees arrived and the detective waited until the waitress walked away again before asking, *"Does he have keys to your place?"*

"No."

"I'd get the locks changed anyway. Just in case. That's the first thing you do."

"Okay."

"Did you call that number I gave you? For the self-defense classes?"

Beck's face grew hot. She was failing this safety checklist. *"Not yet."*

"Right. Well, you should sign up. They're good skills to have."

"Okay."

"Come up with a breakup plan," she continued. *"Write out what you want to say, and practice saying it. Be clear but nonconfrontational. Do it in a safe*

place. Make plans with a friend after so there's someone expecting you. And make sure he knows you have plans."

"I feel like I need to take notes," Beck said, half-joking.

"I've got you covered." Pulling a pen from her blazer pocket, the detective took a diner napkin and flipped it over. She repeated everything, writing it down as she said it. "But." Her gaze met Beck's. The intensity was like a flashlight to the eyes. "If he refuses to take the hint, you need to get the police involved. These things can escalate quickly. Okay?"

Beck nodded. "Okay."

By the time they finished their coffees, Beck was sick of talking about it. The more they discussed it, the more frivolous it seemed. After the waitress refilled their mugs, she carefully shifted the conversation away. She told Detective Righetti about her work at the rehab center. This seemed to pique the detective's interest, and soon she in turn was telling Beck about how her father struggled with alcoholism up until it killed him. Beck was used to this, to near-strangers revealing intimate details of their lives. There was just something about her that made people want to share.

A half hour later, they made their way out to the parking lot together.

"Thanks for treating me to coffee," Detective Righetti said. "You didn't have to."

"It's the least I could do. You've been really helpful, thank you."

"It's mutual. I rarely talk about my dad." She tucked a strand of unruly hair up into her half-ponytail. "It's nice to get a professional opinion."

The connection was there, waiting for Beck to seize it. "How about I give you one of my cards? You can call if you have questions. There's some in my car." Then, because she knew how it might sound to a cop, Beck added as a joke, "This isn't a ploy to kidnap you. Promise."

The detective laughed and followed her to her cherry-red BMW—a med school graduation gift from her parents and one of Beck's favorite possessions. She slid into the driver's seat and began rummaging through the glove compartment.

"I really should be more organized with these," she said, producing the box.

She turned to find Detective Righetti standing with one hand on her car roof, peering inside. Beck followed her gaze to the photograph taped just above the radio.

Their eyes met and the detective smiled. "Nice photo."

"My non-related sisters." She laughed. "Dylan, Isabel, and Priya. You'd like Dylan." She tapped her face in the photo. "In another life I could see her becoming a cop. She has that same protective quality." Beck held out the card. "Here you go."

Detective Righetti took it, her expression thoughtful. "Dr. Rebecca Grant," she read aloud.

"Call me Beck." She realized right then that she didn't know Detective Righetti's first name. It hadn't come up during the time they'd spent chatting in the diner.

Detective Righetti seemed to read her mind. "Okay, Beck." She smiled. "Well, you can call me Bree."

"Like the cheese?" Beck asked and Bree laughed.

CHAPTER
FORTY-NINE

PRIYA

Isabel gasped and took a step back when Dylan opened the door. Priya's own throat constricted, and she wanted to turn around, get back in her car, and go home. Pretend none of this was happening. Dylan looked like she'd been through fifteen rounds in a boxing ring. Even Echo was strangely subdued, as if confused about how to react. He whined, then tentatively licked Dylan's hand.

"Would have been nice to have you there, Maneater." Dylan scratched the dog's head. "You would've taught them a lesson, wouldn't you?"

"Oh my god, Dylan," Isabel said.

"It looks worse than it is." She stepped back to hold the door open. "Come on in. Hey, Pri."

All Priya could manage was a nod. She unhooked Echo's leash and he circled once between them, tail wagging, before trotting off down the hall.

"What happened?" Isabel asked. "On the phone you made it sound like it wasn't that bad."

"Come on." Dylan closed the door and, grasping her elbow, gently steered her down the hallway. In a daze, Priya followed. It all had the feel of a terrible dream come to life. Here she thought the horrible words scrawled on the side of her car would be the worst of it. Obviously, it could get a lot worse.

One of us is going to end up dead.

The thought turned her body to ice.

In the living room, Isabel yanked her arm free from Dylan's grasp and pivoted to face her.

"How could you do this?" she said. The flat register of her voice was unnerving.

"Whoa. What?" Dylan said, stepping back.

"I hope you're happy now that you've dragged me and Priya into . . . this." Isabel waved a hand at Dylan's battered face.

"Come on, Isabel. I think you've been more than capable of dragging yourself into it." There was a dangerous edge to her voice. A warning.

"I didn't even want to do it in the first place. And now look what happened. Priya and I don't deserve this."

"And I do? I deserve to get attacked in a bar parking lot, is that it?"

"No. Of course not." Isabel took a deep breath and looked around the room, as if the words she needed might be written on a wall somewhere. She brought her gaze back to Dylan. "That's not what I meant. What happened to you is awful. It's just that . . . Well, you wanted this. And we didn't."

A film reel of different emotions flickered across Dylan's face. Her expression settled on determination and Priya's heart sank.

Don't, she mouthed at Dylan from behind Isabel's back. But if she saw, she chose to ignore her. Next to Priya's leg, as if he could sense an incoming storm, Echo whined and shifted from one paw to the other. Priya lay a hand on his head, more to steady herself than to comfort the dog.

"Sure, the plan was my idea. But you're the one who finished it," Dylan said.

"What's that supposed to mean?" Isabel stared at her.

"You killed him. Or did you conveniently forget that?"

For a moment, Priya felt dizzy. A grating hum filled her ears, as if a throng of mosquitos were trapped in her brain.

So, we're doing this now. Just airing it all out.

Isabel retreated a few steps until the backs of her legs hit the love seat.

"I don't know what you mean," she said, arms hugging her waist.

"It's a good thing, Isa." Dylan stepped within arm's reach and Isabel flinched, as if preempting a blow. Instead, Dylan gently took her by the shoulders and leaned down so her swollen face was eye level with Isabel's. "You did good. Priya freaked out, remember? I freaked too. We couldn't have done it without you. You're the one who got us across the finish line."

In the silence that followed, Priya could hear Isabel's breath begin to rise in volume and speed. The tension was palpably increasing, as if she and Dylan were pulling an elastic band tighter and tighter between the two of them. Then it snapped.

"I don't know what you're talking about." Isabel jerked away. "Let go of me!"

Priya jumped, Echo barked once, and Dylan dropped her arms to her sides, her eyes wide.

"Isa."

"Don't call me that!" She threw her hands, palms out, toward Dylan, then pressed them to her cheeks. Something strange was happening with her face. It kept contorting into a horrible grimace, then smoothing out again—as if two sides of Isabel were at war for control. Squeezing her eyes tightly shut, Isabel opened her mouth in a sharp, abrupt scream.

Instinctively, Priya's hands flew to her ears. Sobs began to rack Isabel's body. She rubbed her hands violently up and down her cheeks as if she'd just walked into a sticky spiderweb and was desperately trying to get it off.

For a second, Priya didn't know what to do. Then her ER nurse instincts took over.

"Isabel." She crossed the room and gently grasped Isabel's wrists. Her hands went slack, and Priya helped lower them to her sides. Isabel was shaking, a sparrow caught in a storm, but at least she'd stopped crying.

"It's okay," Priya said. A sour taste rose to the back of her throat, as if she were about to be sick. She wasn't equipped to deal with this, none of them were. "Here, sit down."

Slowly, Isabel obeyed. Dark trails of mascara ran down her cheeks. In the dim living room light, it looked as if she'd clawed at her face, drawing blood. Echo was barking, weaving his way between the three of them.

"Echo, stop," Priya shushed him, and grasped his collar to hold him in place. He whined again, then settled back on his haunches.

She turned to find Dylan staring at Isabel as if she were a wild animal with its paw caught in a trap. Skirting the coffee table, Priya came to a stop beside her.

"Come on, Dylan," she said. "You need to sit down too."

Silently she took a seat, gaze locked on Isabel.

"It's not true." Isabel looked at Priya, her eyes begging her to agree. "I'm not—I'm not a killer."

"Except you are," Dylan said.

"Dylan!" Priya glared at her. "Think you can ease off for just a minute?"

"What? It's true." She let out a breath and shrugged. "We all are."

"We have to make it right," Isabel said. "Right, Priya?"

"Isabel . . ." Priya's brain went blank, and she didn't know what else to say. Echo poked his damp nose into her palm.

"You." Isabel turned on Dylan again. Her delicate fingers curled into tight fists in her lap. "This was your plan! Do something!"

"Cut it out." Dylan's tone was hard and cool.

Always so hard and cool. Right then, Priya realized she wasn't just afraid of his friends, of the cop buddies who wanted to avenge his death. She was also afraid of her friends. Of what Dylan could, and would, do to survive. Of what Isabel had done.

"You're sure holding on to that selective memory, Isabel," Dylan said. A dam was let loose, and the words began to tumble out faster. "I wasn't the last one to put that wire around his neck, remember?"

Priya didn't want to relive that moment, but it came rushing back at her anyway. The way *he* simply refused to die. How Dylan tried.

Then she tried. And, just when he—his voice full of gravel from their two attempts with the wire—was taunting them for their failure and describing all the horrible ways he'd make them pay later, Isabel snapped. Priya had never seen her lose control like that. Even now, she wasn't sure if her five-foot-two friend was a powerhouse of hidden strength, or if it all came down to determination; Isabel's sheer will to hold on even when he was jerking back and forth like a flayed horse.

Isabel pressed her hands to her ears, her shoulders hunched. "That's not true! I didn't do anything."

"No one asked you to be in the room at the end." Dylan seemed determined to drive the knife in all the way to the hilt. "But you insisted. You know what? I think you wanted to be the one to kill him, you—"

"Dylan, stop," Priya said. Her jaw felt too tight, as if it'd been wired nearly shut.

"Why? She needs to face up to it," she said, motioning in Isabel's direction. "I'm sick of you two blaming me for everything. We all need to take responsibility for our part in this."

"Responsibility? You think I'm more guilty than you?" Isabel wiped her nose with the back of her hand. The movement was rough, so unlike her usual studied motions.

"Will you both just shut up!" Priya shouted. They stopped and looked at her. Dylan's jaw clenched and unclenched, as if working herself up to respond. Before she could, Priya said in a more level voice, "We all need to calm down. This isn't helping."

How had she and Isabel switched roles and she'd ended up as the peacemaker?

"You know what?" Dylan leaned forward. Priya had to hand it to Isabel, she didn't recoil—though from her expression it looked like she wanted to. "You need to get a grip and stop feeling sorry for yourself. We're all equally to blame."

Not me. The rebellious thought surprised Priya. Technically, though, it was true. Dylan had made the plan. Isabel had ended it. Priya had only been along for the ride.

"I didn't mean to." Isabel's voice was low. She stared at the ground, as if afraid to look at them. "That—that's not me. I'm not a murderer."

Priya shot Dylan a loaded glance.

Don't you dare contradict her.

"You're not," Dylan said, for once backing down. "It doesn't count. He was a monster."

"But it still wasn't our decision to make," Isabel said. "We weren't supposed to be the judge"—she motioned to Priya—"the jury"—she looked at Dylan, then pressed her hand against her own heart—"or the executioner."

Silence unspooled between them.

When Dylan spoke, her voice was gentler. "Someone had to be, Isabel. He would have done what he did to Beck to someone else if it wasn't for us. He would have never faced any real consequences. You know that."

Isabel sniffed and said, "I know. I just don't know if I can live with this for the rest of my life."

Dylan rose and crossed the room. Wincing, she gingerly lowered herself to crouch in front of Isabel. Placing both hands on her knees, she said, "You shouldn't feel bad for what we did, Isa. For any of it. He did worse to Beck."

Echo whined and pulled against his collar and Priya released him. He trotted across the room and nosed his snout into Isabel's lap. She ran her hand over his head.

"I don't know how to live with this." Isabel's voice had calmed and the stiffness in Priya's shoulders slackened slightly.

"It'll get easier."

The two of them swiveled their heads to look at her. Excited at the change in direction, Echo charged back toward Priya and burrowed his nose against her palm. They seemed surprised, Priya thought with a prickle of irritation, as if they'd forgotten she was even in the room.

"Over time, it'll get easier," Priya repeated, working her fingers beneath Echo's collar and scratching. "Right?"

"Yeah." Dylan nodded.

"But what are we going to do about them? Those cops?" Isabel asked. "They're not going to leave us alone."

"She's right." Priya sank down next to Isabel on the love seat. She was suddenly very tired. Concentrating at work had been nearly impossible the past few weeks. *It'll get easier.* She held the phrase close, turning it over and over in her mind like a treasured lucky talisman. "It's getting more dangerous."

Dylan returned to her seat on the couch. Now that the three of them were settled, Echo took it as his cue to do the same. He leapt up on the love seat between her and Isabel and draped his body across Priya's lap like a giant furry seatbelt.

"My parents had to unplug their phone," Isabel said. "Those men kept calling and saying awful things." Her voice fell to a whisper. "It's horrible."

"I think I might get fired," Priya blurted out.

Dylan's good eye widened in surprise.

"I don't know how I know, I just do," she continued. "People treat me differently now than before."

It was a relief to say out loud what she'd been turning over and dissecting in her mind all these weeks. Word traveled, it always did, and most of her colleagues knew she'd been close to Rebecca Grant. *His* death only complicated things. It meant more detectives coming around to ask questions. More reporters showing up at the hospital hoping to speak with her. More newspaper articles with less-than-subtle hints at revenge as the motive. Everyone loved a good revenge story. Except for the people involved.

It could have been her paranoia, but Priya suspected her fellow nurses were starting to avoid her. As if she were an ill omen wandering the hospital halls and her bad luck was contagious. Even Emma, the head nurse she always got along with best, would pretend she was too busy when Priya asked if she wanted to go for coffee. It was only a matter of time before Richard—her beloved Call-Me-Rick—decided enough was enough and told hospital HR to gently sever the cord tying her to the job.

"That's bullshit," Dylan said. "They can't fire you because of an assumption."

"Yes, they can." Priya's laugh was sharp. "People get fired for less. If it keeps disrupting my job, they won't have a choice. Things are getting out of hand."

"They're already out of hand," Isabel said. "I mean look at Dylan."

It was hard not to. One eye was the color of a ripe plum and swollen almost completely shut. A cut traveled from her cheekbone to her ear. Underneath the bandage, Priya pictured Dylan's nose as a mass of bloody cartilage poured into a mold and slowly drying into its original form.

"You're lucky you didn't lose an eye," Priya said. She couldn't resist a lighthearted dig. "You'd pull off the pirate look though. There's still time to get you a jaunty eye patch."

A smile tugged at the corners of Dylan's mouth. "Outstanding bedside manner, Pri. You always know exactly what to say."

"How can you joke about this?" Isabel asked. "You could have died, Dylan."

"But I didn't," Dylan said. "And I think we're in the clear now. Your parents won't be getting any more calls, Isabel. And you won't lose your job." She looked at Priya.

"You can't guarantee that," Priya said. The tension was back, gnawing at her gut. Isabel seemed calm now, but Priya felt the new stress of wondering when she'd melt down again. What if the next time it happened in public? Or in front of Paul or Isabel's parents?

"No, but they arrested the cops who attacked me. If they're the ones who've been harassing the two of you, it'll stop now."

Priya sucked in a breath. "What?"

The tip of the cut sunk into her dimple when Dylan grinned, like the end of a fishing line hooked deep beneath the surface.

"I shot one of them," she said. "Those motherfuckers messed with the wrong woman."

"As opposed to the rest of us." Priya knew Dylan didn't mean it in that way. She knew she was picking a fight over nothing, but she couldn't help herself. "We're too weak to fight back, right? Not like you."

"That's not what I meant, Pri." The smile was gone. The triumph fading away.

"You shot someone?" Isabel asked, slow on the uptake.

It didn't make sense for her to sound so shocked by it, Priya thought. After all Dylan had done? How could it surprise Isabel that she was capable of shooting someone too?

"It was self-defense," Dylan said.

"Do you think they really wanted to kill you?"

"I don't know. It wasn't headed any place good though."

"Why does it matter?" Priya interrupted Isabel before she could form whatever inane question she planned to ask next. "The police protected the officer who murdered Beck. What makes you think they're going to punish the ones who hurt you?"

"Well, the bullet wound, for one thing." Dylan sat back with a wince, her hand pressed against her side.

From the way she was favoring it, Priya suspected there might be a cracked rib Dylan hadn't told them about. Probably because she was afraid of freaking Isabel out more.

"It's evidence he can't get rid of," Dylan continued. "Before the attack, those two goons came into Aces and threatened me. There's motive. And Bree—Detective Righetti told me they turned on each other once they interviewed them separately. It's different when a crime involves two people."

What about when a crime involves three? If she, Dylan, and Isabel were put under intense interrogation, who'd be the first to turn on the others?

"Detective Righetti," Priya said softly. The name tugged at the corner of her mind. Why did it sound so familiar?

"Wait," Isabel said after a beat. "Is that—is that the detective working his case too? The one that questioned us?"

"Yeah." Dylan nodded.

"Isn't that a conflict of interest?"

"I don't know," she said after a pause. "I guess not if there's a connection between the two cases."

"Can we trust her? Detective Righetti?" Priya asked, working her hands into Echo's fur. The dog's body was hot and heavy in her lap, but she didn't want him to move. He was a security blanket, pinning her down, keeping her grounded.

Dylan shrugged. "I don't know. But she's a woman. And that makes her the best chance I have of somebody taking me seriously."

"I don't like it." She shook her head. As if in agreement, Echo stirred and sighed. "She's getting too close."

"To me, Pri. Not to you, not to Isabel. This will make things better." Dylan turned her gaze to Isabel. "You can plug your phone back in now, I bet you won't get any more of those phone calls." She looked at Priya. "And you don't have to be scared every time you walk to your car. I wish I could help you both more, but I can't. You'll just have to wait it out."

"It'll get easier," Priya repeated the mantra from earlier.

Again, the dimple appeared, sucking the tip of the cut inward. "Yeah," Dylan said. "It will."

CHAPTER
FIFTY

DYLAN

Aces was picking up that Friday evening when she spotted her. Bree-Like-the-Cheese sitting on a stool at the end of the bar, as if she'd always been there. It was the same spot she'd sat in the first time she came in. Dylan locked eyes with her and nodded.

She finished pouring the two pints and took payment. On the way to the end of the bar, Dylan grabbed a coaster.

Placing it in front of Bree, she leaned both palms on the counter and said, "We're out of Kozel. Not back in stock until next week."

Bree nodded slowly. "I see."

The bar roared with life around them.

Welcome to the Hotel California, the speakers sang.

"Your face looks better," Bree said.

"Thanks. It is."

Dr. López had said it would take around six weeks for her nose to heal, but Dylan could already see the difference. The swelling in her face had gone down and the cuts were starting to harden and scab over. The cut across her cheek would probably never fully disappear, but it gave her some character.

Holy shit, what's the other guy look like? was the most common quip from her customers. *Or gal,* they'd add, as if it were clever.

Over the past few weeks, Dylan had earned more in tip money than she ever had in her five years working at Aces. Some customers joked that the tips were for her hospital bills or to pay a hit man to finish off whoever'd done that to her. Her wounded face, she realized, was its own type of currency. It made Aces of Spades seem tough. Gritty—like the kind of place where the bartender took part in underground fights in her spare time.

She did nothing to dispel the air of mystery surrounding her. Nothing except to tell Jason on her first day back that she wouldn't close up anymore, not unless another employee was there with her. He had the gall to look right at her brutalized face, roll his eyes, and mutter something about how dramatic she was. Dylan wanted to punch him.

But he agreed, which was all that mattered. It wouldn't help with the nightmares. But it'd help during her waking hours. After talking to him, she went home, poured what was left of the Don Julio down the sink, and tossed the bottle in the trash. The attack seemed to accomplish one good thing at least; it absolved her of what little guilt she had.

"I need to talk to you, Dylan," Bree said, bringing her attention back.

Something shifted inside her at the way Bree said her name, sad and a little apologetic.

"So, talk," Dylan answered.

Bree looked around the bar. "Maybe somewhere quieter?"

Glancing up at the clock, she did a quick mental calculation. "I'm on break in ten."

"Sure."

"You want anything to drink?"

"Soda water."

"Any whiskey with that?" Dylan watched for a smile, but Bree wasn't biting.

"Just the soda water's fine."

Dylan filled a glass and set it in front of her, then turned away and got back to work. Her mind buzzed with theories and questions. Why was she here? What did she want? While she mixed a batch of margaritas, Dylan thought about the first time she and Bree had met. And each time after that.

The copy of *Selected Poems* by Dylan Thomas had a permanent spot on the shelf beneath the bar. It was dog-eared and the spine swollen from the time she spilled beer on it a few weeks ago. Whenever things were slow, Dylan liked to take it out. She'd never read poetry before and was surprised by how much she enjoyed it. Dylan Thomas wrote like a man who'd constantly walked the very edge of life, who understood that death was never far away. She liked that. Too many people lived in denial, as if death were a myth. Or a choice.

Had Bree given it to her the same night they kissed? No, that came later. It seemed distant—as if it'd happened in another life, or so long ago the memory had become worn, like a much-used knit blanket.

But it hadn't. It was only five weeks ago (or was it six now?). The air had smelled of early autumn and just a hint of rain. Dylan couldn't remember what they talked about—it didn't seem important—just that at one point she stepped forward and, sliding one hand along Bree's neck so her thumb rested against her cheek, Dylan kissed her. She tasted of maraschino cherries. This detail stood out because she didn't remember Bree eating cherries in the bar. She'd drunk half a beer as usual and eaten a few peanuts, so where did the cherry flavor come from?

It was a great kiss, Dylan thought now. Even if that kiss happened on the night they killed Peter Miles, and even though she only did it so Bree would forget he was at the bar at all. It was a shame it had to be the last.

Nearly twenty minutes passed before there was a lull that allowed Dylan to take her break. She leaned across the bar and rapped on it to get Jason's attention. He'd sequestered himself in his usual side booth with a friend and they were on their second round of beers.

"It's slowed down a bit so I'm gonna take my break now," Dylan called.

Jason nodded and returned his attention to what his friend was saying.

Asshole, she thought as she grabbed her jacket from the row of hooks at the back and motioned to Bree.

Putting on the jacket, Dylan exited the bar, the detective right behind her. The same calm she'd felt when she helped kill *him* draped itself over Dylan now like a comforting shawl. Whatever was going to happen would happen. There would be no stopping it. She was ready.

The weather had warmed enough the past week to melt the ice and transform the parking lot back into grimy black gravel. It would be a warm holiday season this year. Thanksgiving was coming up and Dylan made a mental note to dig out the Christmas lights from the bar's storage shed tomorrow. Jason would want her to hang them on Black Friday.

Her eyes traveled to where her car was parked opposite the Aces entrance. It was a prime location she would have left open for customers before, but she didn't care anymore. Was that how she would think of everything now? As *before* and *after* the attack? Her life divided into a series of *befores* and *afters*. *Before* her mother overdosed. *After* she moved to live with her aunt. *Before* Beck's death. *After* Peter Miles's death. *Before* her attack. *After*.

She pressed her fingers to her cheekbone. Parts of her face were still tender, her nose especially. Despite the warmer weather, a chill worked its way into her limbs and Dylan shivered. She turned to Bree.

The detective leaned against the wall, her car keys in her hands. She stared at them, as if they were an oracle communicating some important information. Then she slid the keys into her jacket pocket, nodded once as if she'd decided something, and brought her gaze up to meet Dylan's.

So, talk, Dylan wanted to say, but remained silent.

"Thank you for coming in to identify your attackers," Bree said.

"Sure."

"We're aiming for aggravated assault. I suspect their lawyers will try to get them off with just assault, claiming all they did was threaten you. But we're going to try to make it stick."

Did she expect a show of gratitude? Dylan said nothing. She'd read the newspaper headlines. CHIEF OF POLICE CLEANING HOUSE and other similar titles had dominated the local front page for the past few days. They were making an example of the two cops who'd attacked her. It should have felt like a victory, but it was too little too late.

They should have done this months ago, after he killed Beck.

"Dylan." Her tone reeled Dylan's mind back into the conversation. "I'm under a lot of pressure to close the Peter Miles case too."

Bree stared across the parking lot and sighed. Her focus honed to a needle-sharp point on the detective, Dylan waited.

"I know you've met Peter Miles before, Dylan. I've seen you talk to him. More than once."

"Okay."

"One night at the bar I remember you running out after him. I think you thought he'd done something to the woman he was buying drinks for all night."

"Huh." Dylan nodded slowly, once, then again.

"I guess my question is," Bree continued. "Why, when we showed you his photograph, did you act like you didn't recognize him?"

"Like I said, he didn't make much of an impression. He was just another drunk in a bar."

"Was he?" She shot her a look that could have cut granite. "Just another drunk in a bar? Or was he a *specific* drunk in *your* bar?"

Dylan stiffened. "It wasn't an accident, was it. Your coming here, to *my bar*."

"What makes you say that?"

She shrugged. "Call it a hunch. Like the one you seem to have about me."

"I think mine is more than just a hunch."

"Look, I'm not sorry he's dead. But it's not a crime to feel that way. I'm not even sorry about the way he died. Murder seems fair for a man like him. What I don't get is why you keep trying to pull me into it. I had as much to do with his death as you did."

"Dylan." Bree sighed and shook her head. "You're strong. I can tell. It's probably one of the reasons I'm attracted to you. Was attracted to you." She corrected herself even though Dylan didn't believe for a second she meant it. "So, fine. Maybe you can stand up under scrutiny, maybe not."

A chill began to climb Dylan's spine like a spider.

"Your friend Isabel though," Bree continued. "I'm not so sure she can. I saw her earlier this week."

Dylan's heartbeat seemed to slow ever so minutely.

"She's not doing very well, is she?" The detective didn't wait for an answer. Her eyes rose to match with Dylan's, and she added gently, "Aren't you worried?"

There was another pause while Bree waited for an answer. When Dylan didn't speak, she said, "I have a fairly good idea of what happened to Peter Miles and why. And I have a fairly good idea of who did it. I haven't told anyone else what I know, but . . ."

Her voice trailed off. What did Bree want? A *thank you*?

Dylan's pulse was steady. Her expression didn't change—or at least she didn't think it did. She was lucky not to be as expressive as Priya or Isabel. Anxiety flared in her mind.

Isabel. Who wears her emotions on the surface for anyone to see.

It was a mistake to let her get involved that night at Dylan's house—that first time they talked about killing Peter Miles. She should have known Isabel would be the weakest link. The rusted coupling that would eventually snap under consistently applied pressure.

"I can't give this case up, Dylan. I wish I could." Bree crossed her arms tight. The look in her eyes seemed almost pleading. "I know you believe Peter Miles got what he deserved, and I can't say I disagree." Her gaze shifted to focus on a shadowy corner of the parking lot. "He hurt me too. Years ago. In college." She stopped, swallowed, and took a deep breath before continuing. "He drugged and assaulted me."

A sharp inhale stung Dylan's nostrils. Bree's expression was filled with pain and regret. Without thinking twice, Dylan stepped forward and wrapped both arms around her.

"Damn. I'm so sorry, Bree." She spoke into her hair.

They stood like this for some time, Bree relaxing into her, her breath warm against Dylan's shirt. Someone exited the bar, breaking the spell. Immediately they stepped away from each other, as if remembering their roles in this drama. Cop and criminal. Repelling magnetic poles.

They watched the man cross the lot to his truck, then turned their eyes back to each other.

"I just want you to know that I understand where you—where the three of you are coming from," Bree said. Her smile very nearly broke Dylan's heart.

A beat of silence filled the space between them.

"You know," she continued. "After that night, when you followed Peter's girlfriend out of the bar? I started sitting in my car in the parking lot, waiting for him to leave so I could make sure there wasn't a woman with him."

Fear exhaled its cold, damp breath over Dylan. Did that mean she was out here the night Isabel picked up Peter Miles? She forced herself to stay calm, to focus on the unspoken meaning in Bree's words.

"Of course, I couldn't do it every night. But when I did, I'd sit there and I'd . . . well, I'd imagine things." She paused, as if giving the words time to sink in. "I guess what I'm saying is, I'm not immune to thoughts of revenge."

One idea after another surged to the surface of Dylan's racing mind. For the first time, she wasn't sure what to do next. Bree didn't know everything, but it seemed clear now that she knew enough.

"Sounds like you had just as much reason to kill him as me," Dylan said finally. "Hypothetically."

The laugh surprised her. It was short and flat, like a sigh or a harsh exhale. "That's probably true." Bree dug her thumb and forefinger into the corners of her eyes and sighed. "Look, I need you to understand something, Dylan. Someone will go to prison for his murder, one way or the other. If I don't get results, they'll just put another detective on the case. The powers that be won't let this one go cold. I have to close it, or someone else will."

The manipulation surprised Dylan, but she couldn't begrudge her that either. You did what you had to do to survive. She couldn't imagine what it was like to carry that trauma. To face *him,* that man, every single day. Bree was just doing what was needed to get by. She was trying to survive, even now—just like any of them were.

Just like Dylan would if she were in her place.

CHAPTER FIFTY-ONE

TEXAS STATE PENITENTIARY
Spring 1994

I'm the cop killer.

Word gets around the cellblock right away. Some women don't care. They carry on doing their time as if I'm not here. Others have heard of me—after all, my arrest and conviction made national news. They find ways to cross paths, to get a good look.

It's my saving grace. These two words garner me both an immediate respect and a nickname: CK. Part of me is relieved. For now, my crime distracts from other things that might draw the wrong sort of attention in here. Becoming a target is a terrifying possibility I don't want to confront.

Not that I'm the only one sent up for murder. There are others.

But I am the only cop killer.

If there's anyone the other inmates hate more than the men in their lives who hurt them and set them on this road to decay, it's cops. No matter what circumstances led them to their crimes, there was always a cop—usually a man too—who didn't believe or help them when they needed it. But once it was too late, and everything had gone wrong, that cop was all too eager to slap on the cuffs and turn the key.

The other inmates act like I've evened some score. I realize too late that I haven't. Even though he's dead, it's still in his favor.

Because he took her life, and now he's taken mine too.

CHAPTER
FIFTY-TWO

ISABEL

A swarm of discontented bees droned in Isabel's ears. She blinked and looked around, then lowered the receiver. The bees moved off into the distance. The phone was heavy against her palm. Her other hand was poised as if about to dial a number, but she couldn't recall whose. When had she gotten up to make a call? Who was meant to be on the other end of the line?

It was like awakening from a dream to find she'd sleepwalked. Except this was much worse because reality was the nightmare she wanted to escape from. And she never would. She couldn't wake up from this.

Who did I want to call?

Oh, that's right. Dylan.

She had something to tell her. Didn't she? Isabel wasn't sure. The desire to figure it out drained away like water into parched ground. Slowly, she replaced the receiver and peeked around the corner into the kitchen. From the clock over the sink, Mickey Mouse's disproportionate arms ticked out the minutes and the hours.

A quarter after ten, Mickey said.

But what day?

A weekday, it dawned on her a moment later as she shuffled, barefoot, back to bed. She knew this because Paul had gotten up and gone to work this morning.

The nights of deep, uninterrupted slumber were over for her. Isabel now found sleep impossible. Instead, she spent those long hours lying next to a gently snoring Paul, her eyes wide open and her thoughts spinning like a windmill caught in a gale. The sleeping pills from Priya called out to her from the drawer in her bedside table. But Isabel was too afraid to take them. What if she confessed in her sleep? What if, in a pill-induced haze, she tried to kill Paul? They all knew what they were capable of now. How could anyone be safe around any of them ever again?

Only once Paul left in the morning was Isabel able to fall into a relieved sleep. It wasn't necessary for her to go through the motions of getting up herself; he was working long hours and wouldn't find it strange that she stayed in bed when he left early or was already beneath the covers when he came in late in the night.

He hadn't noticed anything yet. But the big case he was working on would end eventually. Then what would she do? Already, Isabel had fielded two calls from her parents asking why she hadn't made it to breakfast the day before. If Paul didn't notice, they would. The university had, mercifully, accepted her excuse that she was down with a bad flu, but that couldn't last forever either. Eventually, everyone would pick up on her strange behavior. They'd all start to suspect something was terribly wrong. How long would it be before someone drew a line between Isabel and *his* death? Before they figured out what she'd done?

She felt helpless. A gazelle with a broken leg waiting, shivering and terrified, for the lion lurking in the nearby trees to finish her off. Isabel wished she could return to the early days, when she blocked his death, and her role in it, from her mind. Denial was preferable to this crushing guilt.

Maybe she ought to call Priya. No. She'd probably be at work too. But she, Dylan, and Priya had all exchanged work numbers for this very reason, hadn't they? To be reachable no matter what?

It was yet another precaution after Beck's death; one more brick added to a wall meant to protect them. Except, Isabel suspected, it wasn't really doing anything at all. If one of them went missing or was attacked or killed, why would it matter if they had one another's work phone numbers? Why would it matter if the rest of them were "reachable"? The entire wall crumbled, like teeth caving in under the impact of a fist.

Curled beneath the comforter with Señor Octavio Paws next to her, Isabel dozed. The bang of the front door plummeted her back into reality. The cat scattered and Isabel fell from the bed in a panic. Her heart surged up her throat, desperate to flee.

"What the— Isabel?" Paul's voice sounded through the house. "You left the chain on the door. Isabel? Honey?"

There wasn't time to change out of her pajamas. Isabel got to her feet and stood frozen in the center of the bedroom.

"Honey?" His tone grew louder, more urgent. "I can't get in."

"Sorry!" she called back. "Coming!"

Running her fingers through her hair and smoothing down her pajama top—as if this could possibly make her look more presentable— Isabel hurried down the hall. One of Paul's skinny arms flailed through the cracked door in a bizarre attempt to unhook the chain. Without a word, Isabel shoved the arm, and it retreated. She closed the door, undid the lock, and opened it again.

Paul took in her disheveled appearance as he stepped inside. "What are you doing home?"

"What are you doing home?" Isabel echoed.

"I forgot my brief." He was looking around, but she could sense he was distracted by her, by the state of her. "Seriously? Why are you home? You're always at school on Tuesdays."

Taking a seat at the kitchen table, she glanced at Mickey Mouse. Two o'clock. She'd lost hours of the day without realizing it. Señor Octavio Paws jumped onto the table and bumped his face against hers.

Floating around like an unmoored boat caught in a river current, Paul opened and closed cupboards and picked up and put things down again. He bumped from one end of the room to the other, his attention always, always snagged by her.

"Isabel? Bunny?" He finally drifted to the table and took the seat opposite. "What's wrong? Is this—is this some kind of . . . prolonged grief? Is it Beck?"

Isabel felt tired.

Would it be so bad if she just gave in, confessed everything to him? Maybe then he'd stop asking so many questions and she wouldn't have to keep coming up with answers. But she couldn't. She'd promised Priya. And Dylan.

"I wasn't feeling well this morning," she forced herself to say. "But I'm better now. I was just about to get dressed to go to work."

"Okay." Paul didn't move. Why was he looking at her so intently?

A second later she realized he was waiting for her to do what she'd just said: Get dressed and leave.

"Did you find your brief?" she prompted. "Don't you have to get back?"

"I have a few minutes."

For a long moment, the only sound in the kitchen was Mickey Mouse marking the time. Señor Octavio Paws mewed and jumped off the table. Isabel relented and got to her feet too. In the bedroom, she put on the same jeans and sweater she'd worn yesterday. If she still lived at home, dressing this late would have warranted a lecture from her parents. To her mother, who put on makeup and a good dress just to go to the grocery store, wearing pajamas after seven A.M. was a cardinal sin.

When she emerged from the bedroom, she found Paul standing by the door.

"Found it," he said, holding up the thick folder. "Ready?"

They stood like two strangers at the end of an awkward date. He wasn't going to leave first. She gave in. Slipping into her clogs, Isabel grabbed her purse and—more out of habit than because she actually wanted it—picked up a book from the coffee table.

Paul followed her out like an irritating guardian. He locked the door, then trailed her to her car.

"Love you, bunny-boo," he said, leaning in for a kiss. Feeling like a chagrined child, she climbed in and let him close the door for her too. Without knowing where she was going, she started the car and backed out. When she checked her rearview mirror, he was still standing in the driveway, watching her go.

CHAPTER FIFTY-THREE

ISABEL

Isabel's mind was a blank as she drove aimlessly, not sure where to go or what to do. Usually, whenever she had spare time, she would opt to go to the library. Isabel could get lost for hours in those stacks or spend half a day reading in one of the plush window chairs. But she had no appetite for that today and it scared her. Books had always been a refuge, ever since she was a little girl. What did it mean to lose that desire, that safety net?

Somehow, she found herself on the south side of town. On a sign up ahead white letters against a deep blue background spelled out ACES OF SPADES. Just below it hung a smaller sign—this one black letters against white—announcing COLD BEER. She spotted Dylan's car and turned sharply into the parking lot, cutting off someone in the right lane. The driver laid on their horn for a few seconds before speeding away and Isabel lifted her hand in a half-hearted apology.

Except for Dylan's car and a decrepit-looking Chevy pickup the color of dirty river water, the parking lot was empty. She eased into the spot next to Dylan's and sat for a moment, her hands squeezing and releasing the steering wheel. Before she could change her mind, Isabel grabbed her purse and crossed the lot to push open the windowless bar door.

Inside was quiet as a church. Slowly her eyes adjusted to the dim lighting. Dylan was behind the bar, her forearms resting on the counter. Across from her sat a man in a scuffed red trucker hat—presumably the owner of the brown Chevy. A bottle of beer and a glass of something walnut colored were lined up in front of him. They both turned their heads to look in the direction of the door, and Dylan's eyebrows rose.

"Wave me down if you need anything else, Bill," Dylan said, patting her flattened hand against the bar top.

She crossed and met Isabel at the opposite corner. They sized each other up for a second, then Isabel slid onto a stool and laid her book and purse on the counter.

"I'd like a drink," she announced, just a little too loudly.

Bill, who had just lifted his glass to his lips, snorted into his drink and muttered, "Amen."

Dylan studied her for a few more seconds. She was trying to figure out what Isabel was doing here, what she wanted.

When you figure it out, let me know, Isabel would have liked to say. She too wished to know what she was doing here and what she wanted.

"Aren't you supposed to be at school?" Dylan asked in a low voice.

She shrugged. "I'm playing hooky."

Dylan's eyebrows shot up again. Her face still showed bruising and signs of the attack, but it was healing quickly.

"That doesn't sound like you, Isa," she said.

"It doesn't? That's strange. I guess I'm trying out a new me."

"Get the woman a damn drink, Dylan," Bill called from across the bar, making them both start. "Looks like she needs it."

Dylan turned back to her. "He's not wrong. You look like hell," she said.

Did she? Isabel patted her hair and tried to remember if, in the viscous haze of that morning, she'd even looked in a mirror.

"What do you want?" Dylan asked. Then added a beat later, "To drink."

Isabel couldn't tell if she was asking what she wanted to drink or informing her that what she wanted was to drink. Both seemed equally likely.

What do I want? To drink?

The two questions immobilized her for a moment. She'd never drunk at Aces of Spades. It didn't seem like the type of establishment where Isabel could order a glass of wine. If she could, it would probably come in a tumbler, taste like car oil, and strip the enamel off her teeth.

Normally, when she was unable to make up her mind, Isabel would ask for a recommendation. But for some reason she didn't want Dylan to recommend her anything, and she didn't want Bill to hear her ask. She settled on what seemed safest.

"A beer?" She blushed at the uncertainty in her own voice. "A beer," Isabel clarified, only to realize with a burst of mortification that she would have to specify which beer next. Her parents didn't drink. Paul drank Scotch, but only on special occasions. White wine was Isabel's poison of choice, but she mostly drank it at home. She had no idea how to order beer.

To her immense relief, Dylan didn't ask. With a nod, she took a glass from beneath the counter and tossed it up. It flipped once in the air before she caught it. Bill whistled from the other end of the bar.

Angling the glass, Dylan flicked the tap handle and stared off toward the door as she waited. The foam had just reached the glass rim when, without looking, Dylan closed the tap. It all seemed like second nature.

She didn't meet Isabel's eye as she placed the drink in front of her.

Silence spun a web between the three of them. Dylan busied herself washing glasses, and Bill seemed happy to stare at his drinks, occasionally emptying one or the other a little more. Isabel looked at the contents of her own glass. Golden as honey, little bubbles rising to the surface, beads of condensation budding on the sides. She ran her thumb down the glass then rubbed the wet off on her index finger.

What am I doing?

She didn't want a drink, didn't want to be here. She wanted to burrow beneath her comforter and never have to get up again.

"Isabel?" Dylan was standing in front of her, biting the edge of her bottom lip.

A warm droplet of water landed on the back of Isabel's hand. She looked down then wiped the tears from her face.

"Go to my house and try to get some sleep," she said. "I just changed my sheets yesterday and you're welcome to the bed. You have your key, Isa?" When Isabel didn't say anything, Dylan dug in the pocket of her jeans and pulled out a key ring. She worked a key loose and set it on the counter next to Isabel's untouched drink. "Just wait for me there, I'll try to get off my shift early today. Think you can do that?"

In answer, Isabel laid her hand flat over the key and pulled it toward her.

As she got off the stool, Dylan said, "You'll be there, right?" The question barely concealed the concern in her voice. Did she think Isabel was going to drive off a bridge instead?

"How much do I owe you for the beer?" Isabel asked, rummaging in her purse for her wallet.

"Don't worry, I'll take care of it," Dylan said, and the words seemed to encompass the entire world.

CHAPTER FIFTY-FOUR

PRIYA

Dylan pinged her pager at work, telling her to call the bar. As soon as she was free, Priya went to the pay phone by the hospital cafeteria and dialed Aces.

It rang for a long time before anyone answered.

"Hello, Aces." Dylan sounded as if she'd sprinted across the room to pick up the receiver.

"Dylan, it's me," Priya said.

"I'll have another margarita when you're free, Dylan honey," a woman's voice called out in the background.

"Sure thing. Think you can come over later?" Dylan asked.

Unsure if the question was aimed at her, Priya waited to see whether the bar customer would answer. She pictured a leathery-looking woman with an overly teased perm and wearing a lot of denim. That seemed like the general type of clientele at Aces of Spades.

"Priya, you there? Can you come over later?" Dylan repeated.

Priya pressed the phone closer to her ear and angled away from the two nurses passing on their way to the coffee cart.

"Oh, sorry. I thought you were talking to one of your . . . customers," Priya said.

At the end of the hall, Call-Me-Rick appeared. Priya's heart began to beat faster. He stopped to have a conversation with another doctor, his hands miming out some fascinating story.

"Nope. Talking to you. So?"

"I don't know." In the distance, the two doctors broke into laughter. "I'm off at five, but I'm worn out, Dylan. Can we do it another day?"

The other doctor patted Call-Me-Rick on the shoulder before disappearing around the corner.

"Sorry, Pri, it has to be today. It's—" Dylan paused, as if unsure of how much to say over the phone. "It's important."

Rick glanced briefly down the hall, but either he didn't see her or didn't want to, because he continued on without so much as a smile in her direction. It'd been like that ever since their date. Priya couldn't decide if she had set herself up for failure or if they were doomed no matter what, but it'd been an agonizing hour of drinks at the Tipsy Cow. She'd shown a lot of restraint too, stopping herself at two cocktails even though she desperately wanted a third, just to take the edge off the long, awkward pauses. It was like finding a puzzle piece that looked like it should fit but somehow didn't, no matter how hard she tried.

And now he was distancing himself from her. There was less teasing and flirting, and he seemed to wince when she called him Rick.

It felt like falling out of favor with the king. It shouldn't have bothered Priya, yet it did.

To make things less awkward, she went back to calling him Dr. Schmidt, hoping he'd see what she was doing, how she was trying to accommodate for his feelings. Maybe he'd ask her to call him Rick again. Suggest they give it another try with a second date. But he didn't. He accepted the change without comment and, to make matters worse, stopped calling her his favorite nurse. Now it was Irma. *Irma.* Who was at least fifty-five, had thick, veiny ankles, and smelled like sauerkraut. It would be insulting if it wasn't so depressing.

"Pri?" Dylan prompted.

Taking a deep breath, Priya pressed her fingers into the corners of her eyes.

"Yeah, all right. What time?"

"I'm off at seven, so see you there at seven-thirty," Dylan said before hanging up.

The invite seemed monumental, though Priya hated the feeling of being summoned.

The Court of Dylan.

After her shift ended, Priya picked up Echo and took him for a long walk. Better to get some of his energy out now, in case the meeting at Dylan's ran long. The two of them spent a blissful hour together walking along the river, the dog straining at the leash and whining whenever he saw a bird. Later, they found a bench and sat looking at the water. It was murky, the color of milky coffee. Winter water. The river rushed on, gathering leaves and soil and swirling it together.

Priya checked her watch. They had a little time before they needed to make the thirty-minute drive back.

A low growl erupted in Echo's throat. Immediately alert, Priya glanced left then right. A man was walking down the running trail, bundled up in a black jacket, a wool cap pulled so low over his forehead and ears that his face was almost obscured. Priya's fingers tightened around the dog leash, and she checked her surroundings. It was a well-lit area, and there were plenty of people around. Behind her a woman smoked a cigarette while her three boys played football. A couple occupied the next bench over and were cozied up to each other. A jogger passed the man, sidestepped a puddle, and continued down the pathway. The backs of his yellow sweatpants were splattered with mud.

"Shh, it's okay," Priya whispered to Echo, scratching his ears. Her dog's muscles were stiff as iron rods. He growled again.

The man passed without acknowledging them, though Priya could have sworn she felt him watching her from the corner of his eye.

She waited a few more minutes before rising and looping Echo's leash around her hand. Quickly, she crossed the green toward her car, yanking on the leash whenever Echo stopped to sniff at something. At the entrance to the parking lot, she paused. The man in the black jacket was there, leaning against a dark Ford truck.

How did he get here so fast?

Had he somehow cut across from the other end of the park? Motionless, he stared off toward the playground where a woman was walking a pair of nervous-looking Chihuahuas. The man didn't acknowledge Priya, didn't even glance in her direction, but it was obvious he noticed her.

Echo was oddly silent, but when she glanced down she saw that his ears were perked, his eyes alert. Priya could always read her dog's moods by his tail. Most of the time it moved incessantly, a sign (she liked to believe) of Echo's zest for life. But now it was as still as a limp flag in the terrible calm before a storm.

In the few moments she'd been standing there, the man's shadow seemed to lengthen and unfurl fangs. Priya's scalp tingled, and she felt in her pocket for her Mace.

Everything's fine. Everything's fine.

Forcing her gait to remain calm and steady, Priya started across the lot. Echo growled as they passed the man. Her car wasn't far, just a few more paces and they'd be there. She'd get Echo in as quickly as possible, then lock the doors.

Priya drew the Mace from her pocket and held it pressed to her thigh.

Nearly there.

"Miss?"

Her heart leapt at the man's voice. Priya walked faster.

"Excuse me, miss?" He seemed to be following them.

Panic squeezed her heart in a viselike grip.

"Hey!"

Echo swung around so suddenly she almost lost hold of the leash. He strained against it, his front paws lifting from the ground as he barked furiously. The man stumbled back a few steps, his eyes wide and his hands held up in surrender.

"What the hell! Calm your dog, lady. I was just trying to tell you you dropped your keys." The familiar palm tree keychain she'd bought on a family trip to Goa dangled from one of his fingers.

"Just set them down!" she said. "My dog's very protective. Leave them there."

"Okay, okay." He set the keys on the trunk of a nearby car and began to back away. Echo's barks transformed to growls as the man moved farther off. "Last time I do anybody a favor," he said in a low voice. Priya thought she heard him add a "Bitch."

She didn't care. Waiting until he was back by the truck, she darted forward and grabbed the keys. Glancing over her shoulder every few seconds to make sure the man hadn't moved, she walked the rest of the way to her car. She quickly climbed in after Echo and locked the door.

It wasn't until she was almost to Dylan's house that Priya felt the tension in her shoulders melt away. Had she overreacted? Was it likely the man hadn't meant her any harm?

Yes and yes, Priya thought.

And yet, the interaction was a reminder that distrust should be her default. Because you never knew what kind of man you were faced with until it was too late.

CHAPTER
FIFTY-FIVE

BECK

Before

Ah, look at me

I'm shatt—

The sharp honk of a horn cut through the music. Beck hit stop on her Walkman and Mick Jagger's voice died away. Feeling in her pocket for the folding knife, she turned.

"Hey, Beck." It was Pete, grinning at her from the cab of his pickup. "Need a ride?"

Simultaneous bursts of relief and irritation spread through her like dye in water. Relief that it wasn't some stranger trying to pick her up. Irritation that, two weeks after their breakup, she was running into Pete of all people.

"That's okay," she said, jogging in place to stay warm. "I'd rather run back."

He reached over and opened the passenger-side door. "Come on. It's getting dark."

Beck looked around. She had gone a little farther than usual today and he was right. It was still daylight, but probably wouldn't be for much longer. Still . . .

"I don't think that's a good idea," she said.

The corners of his sharp blue eyes crinkled as he laughed. "Come on. I know we broke up. Doesn't mean I can't do something nice for you."

Hand pressed to her sweaty forehead, she considered this.

"I'm not trying to win you back, promise." Pete lifted both hands from the steering wheel. "Just want to give you a ride. For my peace of mind and old time's sake."

She shifted from foot to foot, trying to calculate how long it'd take her to run home. Her stomach growled, a reminder that, as usual, she'd forgotten to eat before setting out.

Her eyes rose to meet his. Their breakup had been amicable—it surprised and embarrassed her how well Pete took it. He'd given her plenty of space since then; no more impromptu visits, calls, or notes. Beck had wasted poor Bree's time for nothing.

"Come on, Beck. Let me protect and serve for once," he said with a wink.

Maybe a ride was fine. Who said they couldn't be, if not friends, at least friendly?

"All right," she said and hoisted herself into the passenger's seat.

He started driving almost as soon as she closed the door. Warm air flowed through the open window and washed over her, raising goosebumps on her sweaty face and neck. On the radio, George Strait sang the opening lines of "Amarillo by Morning."

"Know what?" Pete said. "Just picked this up at the gas station." One hand on the wheel, he lifted the bright yellow Gatorade from the cupholder. "Your favorite flavor too. Almost like I sensed I'd run into you. I haven't drunk any yet. You should have it."

"Thanks," she said, unscrewing the cap.

"What are you doing so far from home anyway?"

She took a long drink and let the taste of artificial lemon coat her mouth and throat before responding. "I'm training. For Everest Base Camp. I read about it in a magazine." It was hard not to sound excited, even when telling him about it. "It's a two-week trek from this town in Nepal to the base of Everest and back."

"Oh, I thought you meant you were climbing Everest."

"God, no. I wish I could, but I'd probably die."

"And you don't have a death wish," he said. Beck thought she sensed a hint of derision in his tone. As if he were saying: What you're doing isn't all that hard, then.

She took another drink. "Base Camp is still eighteen thousand feet above sea level."

"*Is it, now?*" *He didn't seem impressed.*

Beck's grip tightened around the bottle. See? *She wanted to say.* This is why we didn't work out. You were never supportive.

Silence fell. She didn't try to revive the conversation. Scratching the cap's ridges with her thumbnail, she mentally laid out the next thirteen months, checking off training goals. Everest Base Camp would be a challenge, no matter what someone like Pete said.

Her gaze rose, searching for a familiar landmark to tell her how much farther they had to go. Maybe she could walk from here. It took a moment to orientate herself. With a start, Beck realized that he was driving the wrong way. They were almost out of town.

"*Pete, turn around.*" *Tension rose in her voice.* "*My apartment's the other way.*"

"*You think you're so special, huh?*" *His question was like a well-aimed uppercut.*

"*What?*" *Instantly, her body grew heavy as a sack of wet sand. God, she was tired of this. Of him. She should have never gotten in this truck.*

"*Fucking Everest Base Camp,*" *he said in a high-pitched voice.*

"*Pete . . .*" *But the rest of the sentence danced out of reach and her voice trailed off.*

Why was she so tired? Beck's eyes locked on the Gatorade bottle and a muffled warning sounded in the back of her mind. Prompted by a soft and unconvincing panic, she hurled the bottle out the window. An arc of neon liquid spread through the air, a few droplets blowing back to strike her in the face. The bottle landed and within seconds became a speck in the rearview mirror.

"*What the hell, Beck?*"

She fumbled at the door, her other hand working her seatbelt. The vehicle swerved right as her fingers found the lever and pulled. On the second try the door sprang open.

"*What the fuck are you doing?*" *he shouted, slowing to a crawl.*

Beck spilled from the still-moving vehicle, the unforgiving Texas clay hard as cement against her hands and knees. She bit down on her tongue and tasted blood. She needed to get it out. Whatever he put in the bottle. Wavering on the edge of unconsciousness, Beck jammed her index and middle fingers into her mouth. They tasted like earth and salt.

Suddenly, Pete's face loomed large in front of hers. He yanked her hand down and grabbed the other wrist, folding her body together as easily as if she were a pocketknife.

Two words emerged from the mist in her mind: My knife.

But her limbs were heavy as lead weights, her vision already blinking in and out.

"Easy now," he whispered.

She tried to speak, but her tongue was an immovable brick. Her head dipped forward to rest against his chest. Fear flared briefly then died; a short-burning sparkler.

"It's okay, Beck. It's okay," he murmured in her ear. "I've got you."

One last monumental effort and she managed to lift her head, to look him in the face. For a second, they hovered there, discordant lovers in a deathly embrace. The future seemed to expand before her, two distinct pathways reflected in his blue eyes. Then he closed the space between them, and it all collapsed in on her like a dying star.

CHAPTER FIFTY-SIX

PRIYA

Priya's shoulder ached with the effort of keeping her grip on the leash as Echo dragged her up the walk to Dylan's house. He liked it here, probably because he associated it with treats and a big backyard. Dylan's car wasn't in the driveway, but Priya spotted Isabel's blue Honda parked by the curb.

The yard had undergone yet another change since she was last here—part of Dylan's ongoing quest to prepare it for reseeding in the spring. The stubbly grass and weeds were gone, and there was a layer of fresh earth on top. Dylan had probably done it all herself too. Just thinking about it made Priya tired. Wouldn't it be easier to pay someone to lay one of those ready-grown lawns? Not cheaper, but less of a headache at least.

Avoiding the second step as always, Priya climbed the stairs to the porch. Her copy of Dylan's house key was somewhere in her purse, but it felt like too much effort to dig out. Instead, she knocked and counted silently to ten. No one came to the door. Maybe that wasn't Isabel's car, and no one was home. Priya was about to knock again when a tremulous voice called from the other side, "Who is it?"

"It's me. Priya."

There was a pause, as if Isabel wasn't quite sure whether she ought to believe her or not.

Priya sighed. "Come on, Isabel. Just check the window." It came out a little more pointed than she intended. But after the incident in the park, Priya was in no mood to be patient. "It's me. Let me in."

A second later, there was a click and the doorknob turned. Isabel appeared. Her hair was mussed, and her mascara had smudged around her eyes.

"Sorry, I was asleep," she said.

That explained her flushed face and the soft outline of a pillow seam running from forehead to chin.

"What are you doing here?" Priya asked. What she really wanted to say was, *Since when are you and Dylan so close that you come to her place to nap?*

"Did Dylan tell you to come over?" Isabel opened the door wider, allowing Priya and Echo to crowd into the foyer. "Oh, hello there. Good boy. Yes, good boy," she crooned at the dog, ruffling his ears and planting a kiss on his head. Echo's tail whipped back and forth like an ecstatic windshield wiper.

"Yeah. Dylan's not here yet?"

"No." Isabel looked at her watch. "I guess she's running late." She yawned.

As if on cue, they heard a car pull into the drive. Priya opened the door again. Dylan was crossing her lawn, head bowed. Despite the cold, she was coatless and wore the sleeves of her plaid shirt rolled up to her elbows. On the second step Dylan paused and bounced her foot up and down as if to test its sturdiness. Then she nodded and climbed the rest of the way to the porch.

The second step was brand new, Priya saw with a start. The half-rotted wood was gone, a new plank put in its place. How had she not noticed it before?

"You fixed the step," she said.

Dylan smiled. "I fixed the step. A nice coat of paint and it'll be good as new." Her gaze moved to Isabel. "Get some rest?"

Eyes on the floor, Isabel cleared her throat and murmured, "Yes. Thank you."

"Good." She patted Echo on the head and closed the door behind her.

There was something different about Dylan. It wasn't just the yellowed bruises, the stitches along her hairline, the still-healing nose. It was a look in her eyes. *Manic* was the word that came to Priya's mind.

"Who's in the mood for Chinese?" Dylan asked, continuing down the hall.

Priya unclipped Echo's leash and he dashed after her. She and Isabel followed. Again, Isabel yawned, and this time Priya copied her. It was catching. And she was tired.

In the kitchen, Dylan was shaking dog treats out onto the floor and Echo was inhaling them almost as soon as they left the package. Straightening, she asked, "So, Chinese?"

"Sure," Priya said.

"Okay," Isabel said.

"White wine's in the fridge, red's on the counter." She took the receiver from the wall and dialed. A moment later, she said into the phone, "Oh, hey, Mr. Chen. It's Dylan, from one twelve—yeah, that's right. Good. How are you?"

Priya tried to exchange a look with Isabel, but she was busy opening the bottle of white.

Want some? Isabel mouthed, holding up the wine. Shaking her head, Priya pointed to the cabernet sauvignon next to the coffee maker.

The small talk over, Dylan started dictating their order by a series of numbers.

"Oh, and throw in a number three." She laughed. "Thanks, Mr. Chen." She hung up and faced them. "Need a professional to help with that, Isa?"

Isabel was wrestling with the corkscrew on the bottle of white, her bottom lip caught between her teeth. As efficient as always, Dylan took it from her and had it open in less than fifteen seconds.

"Red for you, Pri?"

She nodded. Something was off about Dylan, about the way she spoke, but Priya couldn't point to what. It wasn't until Dylan handed her a half-filled glass of wine and asked, "That enough?" that it dawned on her. Dylan was speaking to them the way someone would if they were about to break some very bad news. It was how Mr. Grant had sounded when he'd called to ask—his voice infused with a bare modicum of hope—if Priya had seen Beck, then told her she was missing.

Carrying a glass of water, Dylan led the way down the hall. As she followed her to the living room, Priya began to steel herself.

What has Dylan done now?

CHAPTER FIFTY-SEVEN

ISABEL

Was she the only one falling apart? That's what Isabel wanted to know. They sat in the living room—Priya on the love seat, Dylan at the opposite end of the sofa from Isabel—staring off in different directions, avoiding eye contact and not saying anything. They stayed like this for so long the silence became a fourth entity, like a ghost hovering in the center of the room.

Beck's ghost, waiting for them to make things right.

"The Chinese food should be here in about fifteen minutes." Dylan broke the silence. "Mr. Chen's pretty fast most of the time."

"We know, Dylan. We all know Mr. Chen, we've ordered from him before," Priya said with a roll of her eyes. Then she added, "I'm actually not that hungry."

"Better to have it for when we do get hungry." Dylan sounded uncharacteristically gentle. Like a doctor about to break news of a cancer diagnosis to a patient. "Would you rather talk about this now, or later?" she asked after a pause, looking from Isabel to Priya. As if that were their cue, all three of them took a sip from their drinks.

She didn't need to say what *this* was. They all knew.

"The phone calls stopped," Isabel said. "Like you said they would."

"So, it was those two cops," Priya said. "Not that we doubted it before. But good to know, I guess."

"That's good, Isa," Dylan said.

"What's going to happen to them?"

"Who?"

"The cops who attacked you," Isabel said.

Echo rose from his bed between the sofa and the love seat, stretched, and turned around three times before settling again.

"They're charging them with aggravated assault," Dylan said. "But they're out on bail now."

"Can you go to jail for aggravated assault?" Priya asked.

She nodded. "Yeah. A few years, I think."

"Good." A clamp tightened in Isabel's throat. Was it relief she felt? Or fear? Would she be thinking about them in two or three years when they were out, wondering if they still hated her and wanted to make her pay? "You should pay for the crimes you commit." Her voice broke.

"Isabel, come on," Priya said softly.

"It's true." She sniffed and cleared her throat. "Fair is fair, isn't it? They're doing the time, we should—"

"What?" Dylan asked.

Shaking her head, Isabel unfolded and refolded her legs beneath her. What was she trying to say?

"Turn ourselves in?" Priya asked.

The question fell like a two-ton slab of cement. Isabel's gaze shifted between her friends, trying to decipher what their expressions meant.

"We were all there," Isabel said. "We should all take responsibility."

"Yes," Priya said. "We were all there."

There seemed to be something Priya wasn't saying. But what? That they weren't all equally responsible?

As usual, Dylan's expression was unreadable. "Don't beat around the bush, Isa. Say what you mean."

"I think we should turn ourselves in for his murder," Isabel said, and she felt as if a load had lifted.

"No—" The sound of the doorbell cut Priya short.

For a second, no one moved. Then Dylan rose and disappeared down the hallway. There was a muffled verbal exchange and a few moments later she reappeared holding a plastic bag full of take-out boxes.

"Food's here," Dylan announced unnecessarily. She deposited the containers on the wood chest. *Need to find a coffee table for Dylan for Christmas,* Isabel remembered, then stopped herself. It wouldn't matter now.

Dylan left the room and returned carrying plates and cutlery, a bottle of wine wedged under each armpit.

"Since when do you have a doorbell?" Priya asked.

"Just installed it." Dylan set everything down and took a seat.

There was a beat of silence. Should she repeat what she'd said? Isabel wanted to talk about it, she didn't want it to get swept out of the way like so many other things did.

But Priya saved her from that by saying, "I'm not going to turn myself in. I'm sorry, but why should I ruin my life over him?"

"Because what we did was wrong." Isabel heard the plea in her tone and flushed.

I shouldn't have to convince you of that.

"Why? I didn't kill anyone." Her eyes flicked to Isabel and away, as if afraid to look at her for too long.

"Not technically, but . . ."

Why wasn't Dylan helping her, Isabel thought. When it came to technicalities, Dylan was the guiltiest of them all. But she was motionless and mute as a statue.

Isabel forged onward. "I mean, you helped kidnap him, Priya."

Priya's eyes widened and it took her a moment to understand why. Dylan wasn't supposed to know they were both there when Isabel picked him up at the bar.

It doesn't matter anymore.

But Dylan either didn't care or didn't understand what Isabel meant, because she didn't move, didn't say anything. If not for the occasional blink, Isabel would have thought she'd actually turned to stone.

"We would go to jail." Echo's collar jingled as he lifted his head in response to Priya's brittle tone. "Over *him*. Our lives would be wasted, ruined, for *him*. How does that make any sense?" Her eyes turned to Dylan and her voice tightened like a stretched elastic band. "Why aren't you saying anything? Or don't you care?"

Finally, Dylan moved. She took a long drink of water and nodded slowly. "She's right, Isa. It's no use ruining your life over him. He's not worth it."

The two of them were making it sound like they were discussing nothing more than a bad breakup.

"That cop. She isn't going to let up. I can tell." Goosebumps rose on Isabel's skin. She shivered and pulled the navy wool throw across her legs. "I have to turn myself in. It's okay if you don't want to, I'll take responsibility for everything, so don't worry. I just can't—I can't let this go."

"Come on," Dylan said. "Do you really think anyone's going to believe you kidnapped and murdered him on your own?"

Was it so hard for Dylan to think her capable of something like that?

Yes.

After all, she was the one who begged to be a part of it, and look at her now, practically holding her friends hostage.

I should have listened to Dylan when she told me to stay out of it.

"I picked him up outside the bar and drove him to that house. He was too drunk to resist when I tied him up. Once he was restrained, killing him was easy. See?" Isabel gestured with both hands. The wine rose up the side of her glass and came dangerously close to sloshing over the rim. "It's all true, I've just left out a few details. Why wouldn't they believe that?"

Priya was staring at her like she'd sprouted a pair of horns out the top of her head. Dylan's expression was a little more complex. She seemed to be wavering between thinking Isabel had a point and complete incredulity.

"Okay," Dylan said. "Let's say you do that. Then what?"

"Then I guess I go to trial for his murder." Saying it out loud made it more real, and suddenly she was queasy.

"You're a terrible liar, Isabel. I'm sorry, but it's true," Priya said.

"Your story would fall apart before you even made it to the courtroom. You'll have to tell it over and over again. Even if you plead guilty. And a confession isn't enough, the police will want to back it up with actual evidence."

"No. I could—" She stopped. A pebble of disappointment spiraled and sank to the bottom of her gut. Her shoulders slumped. Priya was right. She might be able to effectively lie once. But if she had to retell the story? There was a reason she'd gone into academia. Books were honest. Open to interpretation, yes, but never deceptive.

"I mean, look at Beck's dad," Dylan said. "Objectively, he'd make a better suspect than you. He's bigger, stronger, has more of a motive. And what happened when he tried to confess? All it took was one night in a cell and they knew he couldn't have done it."

They were all quiet. After a while, Dylan rose to refill their glasses.

As she poured wine into Isabel's, she asked, "What is it you want, Isa? Really?"

"To do the right thing," she answered right away.

"You want some sort of justice?"

"Yes. I guess so."

Dylan sat down. "Do you think destroying your family is justice?"

"What?"

Angling her body to half-face Isabel, she extended one arm along the back of the sofa. "Let's say you confess, and they believe you. What'll happen to your family if you're put away for murder?"

This silenced Isabel. She felt a wave of embarrassment at the realization that she hadn't even considered it.

"It'll destroy your mom, your dad, your sister too," Dylan said. "Look at Beck, at the collateral damage to the people around her when she died. It'll be worse for you. Your parents will have to accept that you are capable of killing someone. That's a kind of slow torture. Worse than if you died."

On the love seat Priya sat as if transfixed by a fascinating story. Dylan took another long drink.

"Now," she continued. "Look at him. At Peter Miles. Do you think his death destroyed anyone? Really destroyed them?"

"His parents?" Isabel whispered.

Her friend cocked her head to one side. "Maybe. But think about it: Would someone as evil as Peter Miles have parents who love him? He murdered our friend, Isa. For no other reason than because he could. Does that sound like someone who's cherished and loved?"

"No." Her voice was small, almost inaudible.

"No," Dylan repeated. "No one cares that he's gone, not really. In fact, I bet some people are relieved. But you . . . spending twenty years in prison for murder, getting out when you're almost fifty and your life has passed you by, there's lots of people around you that will care. Lots of people will be destroyed. And for what? For a monster? Does that seem like an even trade to you?"

"She's right, Isa," Priya said.

A weariness found its way into the sinews and muscles of her body. They'd worn her down, Isabel thought, staring into her wineglass.

"Isa." Dylan scooted over, closing the distance between them. She laid a hand on Isabel's arm. "I know this has been tough on you. Think you can give me a little time to figure something out?"

They held each other's gaze. Something flitted behind Dylan's eyes, an unidentifiable sea creature passing just beneath the dark surface of the water.

"Okay," Isabel said finally.

"Priya?" She looked over to the love seat.

Priya nodded. "I agree, we need time to think about our options."

"I'll figure something out," Dylan said, patting Isabel's arm.

You always do.

But now Isabel wasn't so sure that was a good thing.

FIFTY-EIGHT

After

I don't remember much from my sentencing, but I do remember her.

Everything else is a watery blur. I come up for air from time to time and catch snatches of the judge's speech.

"Severity of the crime."

Sink back under.

"Concerning lack of remorse."

Sink back under.

"A cold disregard for human life."

Sink back under.

It doesn't matter. The judge won't mention my wasted potential. He won't talk about the promising future I could have if I hadn't resorted to murder. About what a loss to society my incarceration is.

No, those phrases are reserved for the Ted Bundys of the world. People expect, maybe even accept, that violence from men. But a woman? It confuses them. Throws their worldview off-kilter. Upsets the status quo. Makes them question everything.

There's no such thing as a bright young woman. Only an irredeemable one. And I am irrevocably the latter.

A murmur ripples through the jam-packed courtroom when the judge hands me a life sentence. Immediately, guards gather around me like a protective armor. *They want to make sure I reach the prison and serve my time. That I get what I deserve.*

I rise to my feet and search for her through the crowd. Our eyes meet. She's standing too. An unspoken conversation flashes between us as the guards cuff me. The moment seems to stretch for an eternity and yet lasts no time at all. I read a single question in her eyes: Why?

Someday, I'll explain to her that I'm not doing this because I think I deserve the punishment. Yes, I failed Beck, but her death isn't on me. It's not on any of us. Peter Miles made his choices. And he died for them.

Just as the guard takes hold of my arm to steer me away, I notice the tears streaming down her cheeks.

The way she looked that last time I saw her is engraved in my mind. I think of it as they book me, transport me, and lock me in my new cage. Her first letter arrives the following month, asking the same question: Why? *A few weeks later another. Then another.*

I want her to understand how grateful I am. How I couldn't have asked for a better end for Peter Miles. I want to explain to her that what I'm giving her is a gift. He's ruined enough lives. I don't want him to ruin hers. I'm freeing her from him and what he did. I'm giving her a chance to live.

A dozen letters are started and discarded before I can formulate the words. It takes me nearly a year to answer her.

To finally realize I need to sever her like an infected limb or else risk going insane.

So, I sit down and make the first cut.

CHAPTER FIFTY-NINE

BREE

Someone will go to prison for his murder, one way or the other.

In the week since Bree had spoken to Dylan at Aces, it was becoming more and more apparent how true this was. The chief had started requesting daily updates on her progress. A few days before, he went so far as to hint that maybe they should bring another detective on to the team for "a fresh perspective." Slowly, he was tightening the screw, applying a little more pressure each time. Bree knew she'd let him down. Her days working the Peter Miles case were numbered.

Then, yesterday evening, Dylan called.

"You said you have to close this. One way or another." She was careful to not directly say what she meant, but Bree understood.

"That's right."

"Okay. I'm coming to the station in the morning," Dylan said. "Can you meet me there? I just need time to get some things in order, but it should all be set by tomorrow." After a pause, she added, "I think you know what this is about."

"Just you? Alone?" Bree asked, trying to feel her out, to understand what Dylan had planned.

"Just me. No one else is involved."

Before she even hung up the phone, Bree felt a shift, as if everything was slotting into place. The road before her became painfully clear. She didn't want to ruin a life over *him,* but did she really have a choice?

She phoned Mike next.

"I need you to be at the precinct early tomorrow," she said. "Eight on the dot, okay?"

As she knew he would, Mike agreed without asking why. Bree wanted to reach through the phone and hug him for it.

• • •

The next day, she stood at the bottom of the precinct steps, shivering slightly in the morning chill. Mike was probably already inside waiting but she wasn't ready to join him yet. Instead, Bree lingered a few moments, savoring the juxtaposition between the sting of cold air on her face and the heat of the coffee from her thermos. She pulled her jacket tighter, took a sip, and checked her watch. Two minutes after eight.

Today's the day.

Confession day.

The resolution, as unsatisfactory as it was, brought a strange sort of relief. There would never be a perfect solution to Peter Miles. To his life, his crime, his murder. Bree knew that now. For the first time in a long while, she'd slept well last night. It was like she'd been wandering through a maze for months and suddenly someone had presented her with a map. She just needed to follow the dotted line to its inevitable conclusion.

Bree took one last deep breath, then climbed the steps and entered the station. Her pulse gave a small leap when she spotted Mike standing by reception. He had a coffee in one hand, a brown paper bag in the other.

"Blueberry muffin," he said, holding it out to her.

Bree's heart fluttered. He really was the best of them.

"Thanks, Mike," she said, taking the bag.

"Yep. Interview room two?"

She nodded. "Sure."

Her partner led the way down the hall to the interview room. Bree took the seat opposite him and opened the bag.

"Thanks for coming in early, Mike," she said, flattening the paper and placing the muffin on top. Bree broke off a piece before sliding it within his reach in the center of the table. "I wanted to talk to you."

"Sure." Mike's eyes were trained on the muffin, his hands resting out of sight in his lap. What did he know? Suspect?

"I haven't been completely honest with you, Mike."

There was a web high in one corner of the room, the small black spider in the center barely visible against the gray walls and ceiling.

She stared at the spider, willing it to move, to do something.

"I've been keeping things from you," she continued.

Silence wove a quick, tight net around them as she debated how to say it. How to break his heart. Suddenly, Bree realized she cared an awful lot about what Mike thought of her.

He's going to hate me.

It was painful to think so. But it was the right thing to do. Dylan would be here in forty-five minutes. Bree needed to get this off her chest before then.

A burst of nerves exploded in her brain like bats fleeing a cave. There was no going back after this.

"I have to confess to something," she said.

He nodded, eyes still on the muffin.

"I've been hiding information about the Peter Miles case from you. The simple reason is that I was hoping it would go cold. I didn't want to solve it."

"Why not?" His voice was gruff.

Bree said it fast, before she could lose her nerve. "Because I killed Peter Miles."

His eyes flew up and briefly latched onto hers. For the first time in the years since she'd known him, Bree saw emotion blaze across his features. It was so fast, so intense, it felt like she'd suddenly gazed straight into the sun.

Mike looked like he was going to cry.

Tears sprang into her own eyes. She took a deep breath and pushed on.

"Peter and I met a long time ago." Bree couldn't bear to make eye contact. Instead, she stared at the muffin as she told him about the college party. About what Peter Miles had done.

The story came in fits and starts. The tears surprised her. She rarely let herself cry. It felt almost like a point of pride, as if stoicism meant she was a true survivor. But, as she neared the end of the story, Bree glanced up to find Mike's tears mirroring her own, and she knew that this vulnerability made her strong too.

There was a long moment of silence when she finished.

"Bree. I'm so sorry." Mike half rose from his seat to pull a handkerchief from his back pocket. "I'm so sorry he did that to you." He wiped his eyes and blew his nose—a sharp honk that, under other circumstances, probably would have made her laugh.

"To tell you the truth," he said, folding the handkerchief and placing it on the table in front of him, "I've sensed something was wrong for months."

Of course you did, she thought, remembering the daily pastry gifts, Mike's gentle way of drawing her out of her shell.

"I knew something was off about the case too, just couldn't figure out what."

"I know," Bree said. "You're a good detective. You were bound to get to the bottom of it eventually."

Mike shook his head. "Never imagined it'd be something like this."

The two of them stared in silence at the powder-blue handkerchief. Suddenly, she wished she knew the story behind it. Did Mike go to the mall and choose his own handkerchiefs? Or were they gifts? Was there someone who did it for him? Someone who loved him and made sure he always had a drawer full of clean ones to choose from. Who looked after him the way he'd tried to look after her the past few months.

Mike broke the quiet first. "You've been investigating your own crime." He said it like a fact.

"Yes." Mentally, she steeled herself for what would come next. Bree knew she could do it; lie about killing him and make it believable. From the moment the chief assigned her the case, it was as if she'd been preparing for this without realizing it. Bree wasn't worried. She had motive. Opportunity. And no alibi.

She had wanted to do it anyway. Kill him. Someone just beat her to it.

Her partner pressed a hand to his eyes then lowered it to his lap again. "I wish you'd come to me sooner. I would've stopped you. I'd have talked you out of it."

"You couldn't have stopped me, Mike. For fourteen years I've thought about what he did to me. The first time I saw him here"— she waved her hand in the direction of the door—"I think I already knew what I was going to do. He got away with it, Mike. And he was going to get away with killing Rebecca Grant too. It was the only way."

He nodded, she didn't know if in agreement or because he didn't know how else to react.

"I'm sorry, Mike. I didn't have a choice. Peter Miles he . . . he had to die."

Saying the words felt both damning and cathartic.

CHAPTER
SIXTY

DYLAN

Texas State Penitentiary

The words stamped on the off-white envelope, just below the inmate's name and booking number, stilled Dylan. Despite the pleasant warmth of the day, she shivered. Rolling the gravel beneath the soles of her Doc Martens, she stood for a few moments, squinting at the letter, goosebumps rising on her arms. A car backfired as it drove by, jolting her surroundings back into focus.

Blindly, Dylan dragged the rest of the mail free and slammed the mailbox door shut. Her eyes stayed glued to the envelope as she made her way inside the bar.

Texas State Penitentiary

She laid the letter on the bar top, then stood there and flipped through the rest of the mail. Isabel's latest postcard brought a brief smile to her face. The rest was less interesting; two flyers for the new Chinese restaurant down the street, a Land's End catalog addressed to an Amy Grier, and the monthly electric bill for That Good Night Pub and her small apartment.

She crumpled up the flyers and circled the bar to toss them and the catalog in the trash. For a moment, Dylan lingered in front of the calendar she'd tacked to the wall next to the liquor shelf. October 15,

1994. A year to the day since they'd murdered *him*. Her gaze shifted to the envelope on the bar top, the first line of the address already burned into her brain.

Texas State Penitentiary

It couldn't be a coincidence that this letter, a sudden shout into the void after ten months of silence, had arrived today of all days. Dylan tried not to imagine Bree in a cell, crossing off squares on a calendar of her own, timing it just right to finally reach out. To answer the question Dylan had written in dozens of unanswered letters: *Why?*

Leaving the envelope where it was, she forced herself to focus on her usual pre-opening tasks. This was Dylan's favorite part of the day; when the bar was quiet, and she could take stock of her kingdom. She'd come far in the last four months since she sold the house, then bought and started remodeling this old bar and the overhead apartment.

It still hadn't lost its novelty. The mismatched chairs and tables Dylan sourced from garage and estate sales, the beautiful dark oak bar she spent weeks lovingly restoring, the antique bell she inherited with the building. It was as big as her head and hung above the right corner of the bar. She made it a tradition to ring the bell every night at closing time.

Some of her regulars from Aces had followed her here too. Johnny on Wednesdays, still drinking whiskey, still talking about his cat, Bernard. Darla on Thursdays for her weekly date with Tom Collins. Others who'd grown to like Dylan over the years and preferred her company to whatever new bartender Aces hired after she quit.

That Good Night Pub still had its fair share of problems—the kitchen in the back was a wreck and months away from being in serviceable shape, the men's toilet tended to act up if it was flushed too often, and sections of the floor in the main room would need repairing sometime soon—but it was hers.

Today though, it all felt dimmed. Drab. As if she'd reverted from Technicolor to black-and-white. The envelope lurked in the corner of her vision as Dylan prepped the bar, wiped down the tables and chairs, and unlocked the front door. She was reorganizing the beer fridge, moving the row of Kozel closer to the front, when the door swung open behind her and a voice said, "What does a girl have to do to get a drink in this joint?"

A grin broke across Dylan's face as she swiveled to find Priya standing in the doorway, backlit by the sun. They met halfway across the room and hugged. Echo whined and Dylan crouched to scratch behind his ears.

"I've missed you too, Maneater," she said with a laugh when he licked her cheek.

"Is it okay I brought him along? My parents are weird about taking care of him on their own. He's still jumpy around my dad."

"Of course. Maneater is welcome here anytime." She ruffled his ears again and Echo barked his agreement.

"Why do I suspect I'm breaking some important health code and you're just not telling me?" Priya said as she followed her to the bar.

Dylan shrugged. "I'm the boss, remember? Worst case, you'll get some fur in your drink. And this is a private event anyway, right?" She winked.

Priya slid onto a stool and Echo lowered himself to the floor with a grunt.

"How's Dallas?" Dylan asked.

"Crowded," she said with a laugh.

"I bet you fucking love it." She took the shinbone out of a plastic bag and came back around to give it to the dog.

"I do. It's nice to work somewhere I'm more anonymous. The hospital there is huge; it's a nice change to not have everyone know about my personal life. And there's so much to do in Dallas. I never run out of places to go."

"Make any friends?" Dylan took down three glasses from the shelf behind the bar.

"Yes." Priya smiled and tucked a strand of hair behind her ear. She'd cut it into a short bob that suited her thick, wavy hair. Like she'd stepped out of a 1930s movie.

She looks good, Dylan thought as she poured tequila into each glass. *Happy.*

"I've even been on a few dates," Priya added.

"Ah. So, you are making friends."

She snorted. "Nothing of note. Sometimes I'm not sure . . . I'm not sure romantic relationships are for me, you know?"

"Too many big secrets to keep?"

"Something like that. But I'm not giving up yet. Maybe I'll meet someone with a dark secret of their own."

"You're a hopeless romantic, Pri."

"Emphasis on hopeless." They both laughed.

"Shame you're not a lesbian." She slid the drinks across the counter. "Then you and I could get together."

Priya rolled her eyes. "Yeah, I could picture that relationship turning out well."

There was a beat of silence while Dylan cleaned the counter and put away the bottle.

"You know," she said, wiping her hands on her overalls. "If you ever do decide to come back, we could really move in together."

"Right. Be the weird local ladies that keep everyone guessing about our relationship status," Priya said, waving her hands in the air. "'Are they a couple? Just friends? Related?' No one will ever know."

A smile pulled Dylan's mouth wide. "Confuse the heck out of everybody."

"Sounds great. But not yet."

"Someday?"

"Yeah, someday."

They sat side by side in silence for a few moments—Dylan running her thumb up and down one of the glasses, Priya shuffling her lighter between her fingers.

The crunch of breaking bone spliced the quiet apart, and they both froze. A school of minnows shot through Dylan's gut. From the look on Priya's face, the sound had triggered a similar memory. Of a dark house. Splintering bone. Muffled screams. Then the thoughts faded away again, the minnows receding. They both looked down to where Echo was gnawing on the bone held between his front paws.

"It's weird." Priya leaned over to scratch his ear. "I keep thinking about the connection I have with you and Isa. And how I'll never find that again."

"Fuck, I hope not. I'd be concerned if all your friendships revolved around a murder." She distributed the glasses, one for Priya, one for her, the third she set on top of the postcard.

"Isabel?" Priya motioned to the illustration of pink and yellow buildings shaded by vibrant green palm trees. The words *Saludos de Mérida* were overlaid on top in orange letters.

"Yup. You still getting them?"

She nodded. "Every week. I still can't believe she broke up with Paul, left Octavio Paws with you, and fled to Mexico. That was not on my list of possible outcomes."

"Seemed like the breakup was a long time coming."

"True. I just never thought she'd go through with it. Our little risk-averse Isa."

"Well, we all took some pretty big risks. I'd say it changed her."

Priya sighed, and down on the floor, Echo did the same. "Do you think she remembers today's the day?"

"Yeah." And she really did. Dylan doubted Isabel would ever forget what this day in October meant for all of them.

Most of her postcards from Yucatán were introspective. Short snippets of her temporary life there. How she spent three weeks working in a cousin's restaurant. How one uncle was a rancher, a no-nonsense man of the earth, the other a painter who created charged political pieces about indigenous rights. *How could the two of them be so different, yet so closely related,* Isabel had wondered in one of her postcards. Dylan wasn't sure, but she suspected the contrast comforted Isabel in some way—made her feel that she too could find that balance. That she could make peace between the woman who killed Peter Miles and the woman who couldn't bear to witness any kind of suffering.

"How long do you think she'll be gone?" Priya's question burrowed through her thoughts.

Dylan shrugged. "Until she figures out how to live with it, I guess." Swiveling on her barstool, she lifted her drink. "Speaking of living with it: It's been a year."

Glass held aloft, Priya couldn't resist a quip. "Indeed it has. Glad to hear you have access to a calendar."

She smiled, but neither one of them laughed.

"To Beck," Dylan said.

"To Beck."

They clinked glasses and sipped in silence. Echo snorted in his sleep.

"Is she still refusing your requests to visit?" Priya asked after a while. She didn't have to specify who she meant.

Dylan jerked her chin to the envelope on the counter. "Yeah. But I got that today."

Her gaze followed Dylan's and Priya sat up straighter. "That's from Bree?"

She nodded.

Priya pulled it closer, already opening the envelope as she asked, "Can I read it?"

"Sure." Resting her elbows on the bar, Dylan took another sip. "Read it out loud."

"Okay." She took a long drink of tequila and cleared her throat. She began:

Dear Dylan,

Thank you for reaching out and for the books you sent. They are appreciated. You've sent me a lot of letters the past several months repeating the same question. Since I'd like you to stop writing and to stop requesting visitations, I'm going to try to give you an answer. Please don't respond to this letter. It's not personal, I just don't want to hear from you. It's too hard.

This probably isn't the answer you want, but here goes anyway.

You ask: WHY?

Well, I'm not here because of you. So rid yourselves of that notion. I'm here because I should have stepped in sooner. If I had, your friend would still be alive. Guilt is a funny thing and it's not always logical. You'll have to live with that the best you can and find your own penance.

So, why?

It's simple: I wanted to do it, you just happened to get there first. And isn't that pretty much the same thing? Don't write again.

—Bree.

The last words seemed to dangle in the air, as if Priya had hung them on a clothesline strung between them. She refolded the letter and carefully slid it back into its envelope. Quiet spread over the bar. They sat for a while, sipping their drinks and saying nothing.

Priya was the first to speak. "Do you think she really would have done it if we hadn't?"

Eyes on her drink, Dylan said, "That's the million-dollar question, isn't it."

"I guess." She tapped the side of her glass with her fingernail. "Do you know what Isabel told me when the judge announced the life sentence?"

"What?"

"About the origin of the word 'scapegoat.' I know." Priya held up her hand in a gesture of surrender. "That's Isabel for you; always the word nerd. Anyway, apparently, it's from the Old Testament. It was a custom in Judaism to choose a pair of kid goats and throw one out into the wilderness. The idea was that the banished goat would carry away everyone's sins and impurities with it."

"So, Bree's the scapegoat. Carrying away our sins?" Dylan stared at the smooth wood countertop and willed back the tears pounding against the backs of her eyes. On the other side, just below where her hands rested, her dog-eared *Select Poems* by Dylan Thomas sat in its own cubbyhole.

"It depends on how you look at it," Priya said. "Because the other goat in the pair, the one that didn't get banished, they'd kill it as a sacrifice to God."

"That's fucking bleak, Priya."

"Well, this whole situation is bleak, but that's the reality." Folding her arms on the bar top, she continued, "We're just making the best of it."

"Except for Bree, you mean."

They locked eyes. "Dylan. She knew what she was doing when she turned herself in. She knew what would happen. We keep asking ourselves whether she would have killed him if we hadn't, but I think we know. I think she's given us the answer. You have to find a way to accept it and move on."

For a moment, the ache in Dylan's chest flared. Then the tension, the anger, the grief, began to dull slightly. She would never be free of any of it, but maybe over time it'd start to feel looser. The blade no longer pressed so tightly against her heart. She'd be able breathe a little easier. That was the most she, or any of them, could hope for.

"To Bree," she said, lifting her drink in another salute.

Priya's tone was reverential as she echoed back, "To Bree."

They tapped glasses and drained the tequila to the last drop.

ACKNOWLEDGMENTS

Immense thanks to my agent, Claire Harris at P.S. Literary, for all your guidance and support throughout the years. Thank you for all those reads and re-reads, brainstorming sessions, and pep talks. I love that you think big and never doubted for a second that this book would become a reality. Thank you for sticking with me through the ups and downs of this crazy author life and for making my dreams come true.

I'd like to thank my editor, Jesse Shuman at Ballantine, for approaching this book with such passion and care. You really "got" it and I'm so grateful for your insight. Your ability to see the big picture while lending a keen eye to the small details has truly made this book better.

Thank you to the rest of the Penguin Random House team— Scott Biel, Madeline Hopkins, Ted Allen, Allison Schuster, Vanessa Duque, Kara Welsh, Kim Hovey, Jennifer Hershey, and Kara Cesare— for all your support and hard work on this novel.

To the Dark Scribblers (you know who you are), I'm so grateful to form a part of this dark little writing group. Thank you for being the first to read everything, for your invaluable critiques, and for the occasional virtual workout. I'm the better for having met four such outstanding writers and can't imagine my life without you.

On a more personal note:

Thank you, Jade, for your love and support. Thank you for always being up for a bottle of wine and a good chat about life, love, and art. No matter where you are in the world, we'll always have Willi's.

Mom, thank you for fostering my love of reading (it changed my life), for encouraging me to pursue my passions, and for showing me through example what it means to persevere.

Eric, words cannot describe how lucky I am that you exist. Your unwavering faith that it wasn't a matter of "if" but "when" has always helped me stay the course. Thank you for believing in me. It's a true privilege to have you not only as a brother but as my best friend.

Most of all, thank you to my amazing husband, without whom I wouldn't be able to write a single word. Thank you for providing me with the space and time to write, for propping me up when the ennui inevitably hits, and for listening to me talk endlessly about the fictional people in my head. Thank you for bragging about me to anyone who will listen—even complete strangers. And thank you for keeping me fueled with copious amounts of really great coffee, even though you hate coffee (which I still think is a little weird). You keep me balanced and I'll never get over how insanely lucky I am to have snagged you.

Oh, and Poe, I know you can't read this because you're a cat, but I appreciate your constant company during each early morning writing session.

ABOUT THE AUTHOR

KATIE COLLOM grew up in Mazatlán, Mexico, and is a lifelong expat and world traveler. She spent four years in Texas and has carried a piece of it with her ever since. Currently, she resides in York, England, with her husband and three cats.

Instagram: @strayrhetorist

ABOUT THE TYPE

This book was set in Bembo, a typeface based on an old-style Roman face that was used for Cardinal Pietro Bembo's tract *De Aetna* in 1495. Bembo was cut by Francesco Griffo (1450–1518) in the early sixteenth century for Italian Renaissance printer and publisher Aldus Manutius (1449–1515). The Lanston Monotype Company of Philadelphia brought the well-proportioned letterforms of Bembo to the United States in the 1930s.